Paying

Serena did her very b̲... all, Mr. Macaulay had done what he had been hired to do and done it well. Arabella Lindsay had been found in his arms, with her mouth pressed ardently against his.

But now the infuriatingly self-assured Mr. Macaulay had the effrontery to say, "I know you were not too pleased with me when you saw me kissing Arabella."

"I do not know why you would think that, Mr. Macaulay," Serena declared. "Indeed, I should commend you for your success. I am most grateful to you, and I shall be happy to pay you the one hundred pounds I promised to you. I imagine you found it a very pleasant way to earn such a sum."

To which Mr. Macaulay replied, "Upon my honor, there is another lady I would much rather kiss."

But honor had nothing to do with his evident intent. The meaning of his words was clear as he gazed into Serena's eyes. This libertine from London was not satisfied merely with Serena's cash. He wanted a bonus—that she found herself shockingly willing to give. . . .

Double Masquerade

by

Margaret Summerville

A SIGNET BOOK

SIGNET
Published by the Penguin Group
Penguin Books USA Inc., 375 Hudson Street,
New York, New York 10014, U.S.A.
Penguin Books Ltd, 27 Wrights Lane,
London W8 5TZ, England
Penguin Books Australia Ltd, Ringwood,
Victoria, Australia
Penguin Books Canada Ltd, 10 Alcorn Avenue,
Toronto, Ontario, Canada M4V 3B2
Penguin Books (N.Z.) Ltd, 182–190 Wairau Road,
Auckland 10, New Zealand

Penguin Books Ltd, Registered Offices:
Harmondsworth, Middlesex, England

First published by Signet, an imprint of Dutton Signet,
a division of Penguin Books USA Inc.

First Printing, April, 1995
10 9 8 7 6 5 4 3 2 1

1

Looking down at the sketchbook in her lap, Serena Blake studied her drawing critically. "I fear I am no Leonardo, Muggins," she said finally, addressing the subject of her portrait, a bullterrier, who was sitting patiently on the sofa. "I do not believe I have done justice to you."

The dog did not appear at all concerned by this remark. He yawned, revealing a set of large canine teeth. "Poor Muggins, I know you are frightfully bored," said Serena, smiling. "I shall not be much longer."

The bullterrier stared somberly at his mistress, who returned to her drawing. Muggins was accustomed to posing, since sketching was one of Serena's favorite pastimes and dogs were her favorite subject. Muggins was a squat, powerful animal with a brindled brown coat and the characteristic head of his breed. Serena never tired of trying to capture him on paper although her efforts often met with less success than she would have liked.

As she worked, Serena's brow furrowed in concentration. So intent was she on the drawing that she scarcely noticed when her sister Lucy entered the room. The dog Muggins, however, jumped to his feet and wagged his tail at Lucy.

"Muggins!" cried Serena in frustration. "I am not finished. Sit!" The dog reluctantly complied. Serena turned to her sister. "Lucy, I pray you do not distract Muggins. I am nearly done."

Coming up beside her sister, Lucy looked down at Serena's handiwork. "That is quite good, Serena, although do you not think that the ears are a trifle too large?" Hardly in the mood for artistic criticism, Serena frowned at her sister.

Noting Serena's expression, Lucy thought it prudent to compliment the drawing once again. "But it really is very good."

Serena shrugged. "It is quite dreadful, but I am improving." She continued to draw.

"You are being overly modest, Serena," said Lucy. Sitting down on the sofa beside the dog, Lucy began to stroke Muggins's neck. "I have had a letter from Charles. He wants us to come for luncheon tomorrow at Mainwaring Hall."

"I should like that," said Serena as she added some shading to her portrait. "And I am sure that Muggins will enjoy it as well."

"Serena," said Lucy severely, "you cannot think to bring Muggins. You know that Charles does not like him."

"Really, Lucy, I wonder if it is a mistake for you to marry a man who does not like Muggins. Oh, I am very fond of Charles, but it seems a great fault indeed."

"It is true that Charles is not very fond of dogs, but surely that is his only fault."

Serena laughed. "I must say, Lucy, if you do not change that opinion, I think that you will be very happy together. Indeed, I am so glad for you, Luce."

"I only hope you find someone as good as Charles."

"As good as Charles?" Serena raised her eyebrows in mock astonishment. "Why, you know that is hardly possible. One does not easily find a man as good as your Charles. He is a nonpareil. I shall have to settle for spinsterhood now that my sister is marrying the prize of the county."

"You are ridiculous," said Lucy, smiling. Less than a month ago, she had become engaged to marry Sir Charles Mainwaring, a wealthy young baronet whose estate bordered that of their father. She was very much in love and deliriously happy at the idea of becoming Lady Mainwaring. "I shall be glad to see Charles tomorrow." Lucy took on a more serious expression. "Perhaps he will know what to do about Papa."

Serena frowned at her sister's mention of their father. In the past few weeks, a cloud had appeared over the family residence, Briarly. Mr. Blake, a widower for nearly five years, had suddenly become interested in a most unsuitable woman. The name of this unacceptable female was Arabella Lindsay.

Only three and twenty, Arabella was a widow, who had a rather checkered past. The sisters had known Arabella since childhood when she had often visited her relations in the nearby village of Whitfield. They had never liked her, thinking her vain and mean-spirited.

At seventeen Arabella had married an army officer and had lived abroad with him in various cities. Five years after her marriage, rumors had reached Whitfield that Arabella had had a number of affairs. Tongues had wagged for days in the village when it had been reported that Arabella's husband had fought a duel with a Belgium count over her. While the unhappy officer had come through the duel unscathed, he had been killed in battle a few months later.

Left without any money, Arabella had returned to live with her aunt and uncle, Colonel and Mrs. Osborne. Her reputation had caused most members of Whitfield society to view her askance. Unfortunately, Mr. Blake had been much more tolerant. When Arabella had lavished her attention on him, Serena's father had become infatuated with her.

"I do not think that Charles can help us," said Serena.

"But what are we to do? That odious Arabella is determined to marry Papa."

Serena nodded. "The only one in the county who does not know that is Papa himself."

Lucy nodded glumly. "He will not hear a word against her. I fear he is smitten with her. Oh, Serena, what will we do if they are married?"

"I do not intend to allow that to happen," said Serena resolutely. "Indeed, it should not matter so much to you, since you will marry Charles and live at Mainwaring Hall. It is I who would have to live here at Briarly with that woman. And I assure you that I have no intention of doing so. No, indeed, we cannot permit Father to make such a foolish marriage. Indeed, we will not allow it."

Lucy regarded her sister curiously. Serena sounded so certain, but did she really think that they could prevent such a misalliance? While rather doubtful, Lucy could not discount Serena's abilities. Although she was the younger sister, Serena had always been the one to take charge and get things accomplished.

The two of them were really very different in personality as well as appearance. While keen observers could detect some family resemblance, most people would not have guessed that they were sisters.

Both were exceptionally pretty girls who turned heads wherever they went. Lucy had lovely brown hair that curled naturally about her face. She had striking pale blue eyes and delicate, classical features. Slender and diminutive, she was dainty and doll-like.

Serena, on the other hand, was several inches taller than her elder sister and had a voluptuous figure much admired by masculine observers. Critics might judge that Serena's mouth was a tad too generous and her nose a bit too short for beauty. Yet her remarkable hazel eyes were often praised and her fashionably dark hair was much admired.

The two sisters also differed very much in personality. Lucy was quiet, sweet-tempered, and sensitive to others, while Serena was outspoken and often tactless. A strong-willed young woman, Serena was accustomed to having her own way and it was usually the younger of the Blake sisters who had the last word.

"But, Serena, I do not know how we can prevent Papa from marrying Arabella if he wishes to do so."

Serena tapped her pencil thoughtfully against her lower lip. "Don't worry, Lucy, I shall think of something. We can always have the odious Arabella kidnapped and taken to India."

Lucy laughed. "I do fear that is what we may have to do. Why, poor Papa is in thrall to the creature."

Serena sighed. "I had always thought him such a sensible man. I daresay, I cannot understand why he should take such a fancy to her."

"She is very pretty," said Lucy.

"Pretty? I admit she is not altogether plain," replied Serena grudgingly.

"Not altogether plain?" Lucy laughed. "You know very well she is considered a great beauty by everyone. That is, everyone except Charles. Charles told me that he does not see what all the fuss is about."

"Charles would say that," said Serena with a wry smile. "He is no fool. I only wish Father could be sensible instead of acting like a silly mooncalf."

Lucy nodded even though she thought it rather strong to call their father a silly mooncalf. At that moment they were interrupted by the appearance of their housekeeper, a plump middle-aged lady in a plain gray dress and matronly cap.

"My dear girls," the housekeeper said a trifle breathlessly. "You must come at once. Arabella and her aunt have arrived."

"Not again!" cried Serena, hastily placing her sketchpad and pencil down on the table and leaping to her feet. Noting his mistress's agitation, Muggins the dog jumped off the sofa and raced over to her.

"Oh dear," said Lucy. "Did they just arrive, Mrs. Bishop?"

The older woman nodded. "At this moment the master is taking a turn in the garden with Arabella on his arm. Her aunt is following at a discreet distance."

"Blast!" cried Serena, in a most unladylike fashion. "That treacherous female. We must join them at once! Who knows what might happen if she is alone with Papa!" Serena hurried from the room, followed closely by Lucy, the housekeeper, and Muggins.

As she rushed down the corridor and then made her way downstairs, Serena frowned ominously. So Arabella Lindsay had called again. She could scarcely believe the woman's effrontery in so blatantly throwing herself at her father.

Since Arabella had taken up residence in the village with her aunt and uncle, she had set her cap for Mr. Blake and had pursued him relentlessly. Still a rather handsome man at fifty, Mr. Blake was a pleasant, affable person. Yet Serena knew that her father's attraction for Arabella was his fortune. After all, Augustus Blake was one of the wealthiest men in the west country. He would be a very good catch for a penniless young widow.

There had been other ladies in the area who had set their sights on Mr. Blake, but until recently, Serena's father had seemed uninterested in taking another wife. In Serena's eyes it was most unfortunate that her father now appeared on the brink of asking Arabella Lindsay to be his bride.

It was not that Serena was totally opposed to her father remarrying. Indeed, she had told herself many times that she would be overjoyed if Mr. Blake would find some suitable lady who would make him happy. Yet Serena was totally convinced that marriage to Arabella would make her father miserable.

When they arrived outside the house, Mrs. Bishop took her leave of them. Seeing her father and Arabella in the garden, Serena walked briskly toward them with Lucy and Muggins close behind. The gardens at Briarly were quite spectacular, but Serena did not even glance at the splendid floral borders. She saw only her father smiling fondly at Arabella, who was regarding Mr. Blake with an admiring and flirtatious gaze. Arabella's aunt, Mrs. Osborne, stood some distance from them, appearing to be fully engrossed in examining the snapdragons.

Noting the fond way in which her father was gazing at his visitor, Serena thought that they had arrived just in time. Seeing the Blake sisters approach, Arabella hid her disappointment. She smiled cheerfully at Serena and Lucy. "There are your dear daughters, Mr. Blake."

Serena frowned at the remark. Arabella was fond of treating them as if they were schoolgirls even though she was only three and twenty—barely two years older than Lucy.

While Serena preferred to categorize Arabella as "not altogether plain," less prejudiced observers would pronounce her extremely attractive. Nearly as tall as Serena, Arabella was a striking blonde with a dazzling complexion and aristocratic features. She was wearing a stunning pelisse of primrose satin and a French bonnet trimmed with an ostrich feather.

Serena noted Arabella's modish attire with disapproval. It irritated her that Arabella seemed to have an unending supply of fashionable gowns and pelisses. Despite Arabella's reputed poverty, her clothes were so splendid that Serena always felt dowdy beside her. It was obvious, considered Serena as she surveyed Arabella's fashionable clothes, that Arabella was wildly extravagant.

"Serena and Lucy," said Arabella, nodding regally in their direction, "how lovely to see you both."

"And it is so good to see you, Arabella . . ." Serena paused for effect. "Again," she added. "Why, I daresay it was only yesterday that we saw you last. How nice of you and Mrs. Osborne to call."

"Oh, we cannot stay but a minute," said Arabella. "We were only passing by and we wanted to stop and give Mr. Blake some of my aunt's gooseberry jelly. I was telling him yesterday how marvelous it is."

"Was that not kind of Mrs. Osborne and Mrs. Lindsay?" said Mr. Blake, smiling fondly at Arabella.

"Indeed it was," said Serena.

Arabella's aunt, who had by now turned her attention from the snapdragons, smiled at Serena and Lucy. Mrs. Osborne was a stout, gray-haired lady in her middle fifties. "I fear we must be going, Arabella. Mrs. Claybrook is expecting us and I should not wish to worry her. We must take our leave of you, Mr. Blake, and your dear girls."

"But you have only just arrived," protested Mr. Blake, clearly disappointed.

"But we must go," said Arabella, smiling sweetly at Serena's father. "I do hope you will all call on us in the village."

"Yes, of course," said Mr. Blake. "We will do so very soon."

"We should look forward to it," said Arabella, directing a heartfelt look at Mr. Blake, and extending her hand to him. Mr. Blake took the proffered hand and bowed over it.

Serena found her father's expression particularly worrisome. He was regarding Arabella as if he were a lovesick schoolboy. It was quite unnerving to Serena to see her father behaving in such a fashion. Without question Mr. Blake was enamored of Arabella Lindsay. If something were not done to put an end to the matter, Serena did not doubt that she would soon have a new stepmother.

"If you ladies must leave, I shall show you to your carriage."

Mr. Blake extended one arm to Arabella and the other to Mrs. Osborne. The three of them set off. Lucy and Serena could only follow behind, casting meaningful glances at each other.

The sisters were very much relieved when their father handed the ladies up into their awaiting vehicle and they made their farewells. "Mrs. Lindsay is the most charming creature," said Mr. Blake, watching the carriage make its way down the gravel lane from the house. When neither of his daughters made a reply to this remark, he frowned. "I know very well that neither of you likes Mrs. Lindsay."

Not knowing how to reply to this question, Serena remained silent. After having once ventured the opinion that the newly arrived Arabella was nothing but a fortune huntress, Serena had realized that it was not a good idea to speak against her. To do so only antagonized her father and provoked a stern lecture about making judgments about others.

"I believe that you would like her if you would try," said her father.

Worried that her outspoken sister might say something uncomplimentary about Arabella, Lucy changed the subject. "Papa, Serena has drawn a very good picture of Muggins. I am sure you will wish to see it."

"Yes, I would," returned Mr. Blake, happy to shift the conversation away from the potentially volatile topic of Arabella. "What a handsome fellow you are, Muggins." Muggins, who had been standing there regarding his human companions intently, seemed very pleased at the attention. He wagged his tail and looked up at Mr. Blake. "Let us go in then, my dears," said Serena's father, reaching down to pat the terrier on the head. "I should like some tea. And, Serena, you must fetch this portrait of yours."

"Very well, Papa," said Serena, taking her father's arm. "But it is not in the least good."

"Nonsense, I daresay it is worthy of exhibition in the National Gallery," returned Mr. Blake. They all laughed and very amicably went back into the house.

2

Mainwaring Hall was a country house of grand proportions and recent construction. Built scarcely twenty-five years ago by Sir Charles's late father, it was a Georgian structure with neoclassical lines. Scarcely anyone who saw Mainwaring Hall did not fail to remark on its beauty and elegant design.

As the carriage turned into the long lane that led to the house, Serena had a good view of the impressive residence. She could not help but regard it with admiration.

Mainwaring Hall was very different from Briarly, which was an old house dating back to the time of the Tudors. The Blake ancestral home was a large rambling structure that had been altered numerous times over the years. Its oldest section featured uncomfortable rooms, narrow corridors, and cramped, winding staircases.

Still, for all its modern glory, Mainwaring Hall lacked the charm of Briarly. Serena loved her home dearly and delighted in its quirks and oddities. Always fascinated by history, Serena loved to think of the many generations who had lived at Briarly. Queen Elizabeth had stayed there several times and Serena enjoyed imagining the Virgin Queen passing through the hallways.

"You don't think that Papa will see Arabella while we are gone, do you, Serena?" asked Lucy, casting a serious look at Serena, who was seated across from her in the carriage.

"I hope not," replied Serena, "although I should not be surprised if he calls on her in the village. I do wish we could have persuaded him to accompany us."

"But then how should we discuss the matter with Charles? I know that Charles will know what is to be done."

Serena made no reply. She did not share her sister's confidence in the baronet's abilities. While Serena thought her prospective brother-in-law a charming fellow with many virtues, she had never considered him clever enough to solve the thorny problem of Arabella Lindsay.

When the carriage pulled up in front of the great house, it suddenly began to rain. The morning had been overcast and damp. Now the heavens opened with a downpour.

Footmen with umbrellas rushed out to assist them. Serena and Lucy were quickly ushered into Mainwaring Hall's grand entry hall where they were met by Sir Charles himself.

"Dearest Lucy," he cried, taking his future bride by the hands and planting a kiss on her cheek. "And Serena. Dashed frightful weather. I was worried that you would be soaked."

"Oh, we are fine, Charles," said Lucy, smiling fondly at the baronet. Sir Charles Mainwaring was not considered particularly handsome, although Lucy would have loyally disputed the fact. He was a great bear of a man, very tall and powerfully built, with sandy brown hair. Charles's amiable countenance featured a rather prominent nose and the unfortunate weak chin that plagued so many of the Mainwaring family. But Charles had a splendid smile, which he now directed at his adoring Lucy. "Do come into the drawing room and sit by the fire. There is a chill in the air. Dashed cold for September. Come, my dears."

The baronet escorted the young ladies into the spacious drawing room, which had recently been redecorated with an Egyptian motif. A border of papyrus blossoms adorned the walls and a statue of a sphinx occupied a prominent spot on the mantel. Since Sir Charles's father had been a collector of Egyptian and Greek antiquities, a number of ancient sculptures decorated pedestals and niches throughout the house.

Once they were seated on the sofa, Lucy smiled again at Charles. "Is Lady Mainwaring returned from Bath?"

"Indeed not," replied Charles. "My mother has written me saying she will stay another month. I cannot say what she finds so appealing about Bath. I cannot abide it. That tedious pump room and that ghastly water. But my mother finds Bath the most fascinating place."

"Well, I wish Arabella Lindsay had stayed in Bath," said Serena. "That is where she was living before she came to live with the Osbornes."

"Indeed?" said Charles. "I shall write to Mother and ask if she has heard anything about the lady."

"I daresay she will hear no good of her," said Serena, "but even if Lady Mainwaring reported a dozen new scandals involving

Arabella, it would not signify. Papa will hear nothing bad said of her. He believes all the rumors about her are malicious slander."

"Mr. Blake is quite smitten with her, is he not?" said the baronet.

"I fear so," replied Lucy glumly. "Yesterday we found them standing in the garden. Papa appeared to be entirely under her spell."

Charles nodded. "I think it very sad indeed."

"But there must be something we can do to prevent Papa from asking her to marry him," said Lucy.

"My dear girl," replied the baronet, "Mr. Blake is a grown man who is accustomed to being his own master. I fear there is little that one can do. A man will commit follies, Lucy, and a woman as well."

"Surely, it is not hopeless," said Serena. "I refuse to believe we can do nothing."

"If only she would go back to Bath or the Continent," said Lucy.

"Why would she do so?" said Charles. "Your father is a very good catch, rich and distinguished. I can see why Arabella is eager to get her hook in him."

"Well, I think it quite infamous," said Serena disgustedly.

"Yes," said Lucy. "She does not care one fig for Father. I am sure that if she found another eligible man with a greater fortune, she would transfer her affections in a trice."

This remark caused Serena to regard her sister with a surprised look. "Why, Lucy, I think you have found the solution!"

"I have?" said Lucy.

"Why, of course. I should have thought of it long ago. If Arabella would meet a man with a fortune greater than Papa's, she would abandon our father at once."

"That may be true," said Charles, "but do not forget that your father is a very wealthy man. I can think of no one in the parish who would interest Arabella."

"Nor can I," said Lucy. "The only other man I know who might interest her is you, Charles." She looked over at her fiancé. "In fact, she did try to latch on to you at the Cathcart's ball some weeks ago."

"And I admirably withstood the temptation," said Charles with a grin.

"Were you very much tempted, Charles?" said Lucy.

"Not in the least, my dearest," said the baronet firmly.

"Good," replied Lucy.

"There must be someone," said Serena, a look of intense concentration on her face. "Charles, could you not invite one of your friends to Mainwaring Hall? You know a good many gentlemen of means in London. Some of them must be bachelors. Surely you know someone who might divert Arabella from Papa."

"Good heavens, Serena!" said Charles. "Am I to toss one of my friends to that female shark? What sort of fellow do you think I am?"

"Yes, that would not be right." Serena frowned. "Perhaps we could start a rumor that Papa is not rich at all."

"Yes," said Lucy, warming to the idea. "We could say that he gambled away his fortune and that he is horribly in debt."

Serena nodded. "That may not be a bad idea."

"I daresay Arabella will not believe it," said Charles. "I should not doubt that she has made enough inquiries to know the true state of your father's affairs."

"Yes, I suppose you are right," said Lucy.

"But we might hint that Papa is a terrible lickpenny," said Serena. "Indeed, he is certainly no spendthrift. Perhaps if we could convince Arabella that Papa will never give us any money, she will lose her enthusiasm. We can say that he cannot bear to spend money for our clothes."

"But do not forget that we are having those new gowns made, Serena," said Lucy.

"And at the Cathcart's ball," said Charles, "I seem to remember that both of you were the grandest ladies in attendance. I recall in particular your lovely gown, Lucy. You looked so beautiful."

"Oh, Charles," said Lucy, smiling at him, "how dear of you to remember."

"Well, perhaps we did not look so impoverished," said Serena, "but I still think that the idea of convincing Arabella that Papa is a miserly clutchfist is worth trying."

"There is certainly no harm in it," said Lucy. "We might try."

Serena nodded. "Charles, you often see Colonel Osborne, do you not? You might say something to him to make him think my father is in financial difficulties."

Charles regarded her skeptically. "I shall do my best. Yes, it may be possible to plant a seed of doubt with old Osborne."

"Yes," said Lucy, "and he will tell Arabella, who will want nothing further to do with Papa. It sounds so simple."

"I daresay too simple," said Serena. "Still, we might attempt it."

Having settled on what seemed an admirable plan, the ladies appeared quite pleased. Charles's butler arrived to inform his master that luncheon was ready and the baronet escorted his guests to the dining room.

3

William Arthur Macaulay Savage, Marquess of Trenhaven, rose from his bed at half past noon. Not in the best of moods, his lordship was suffering from the effects of his improvident consumption of alcohol the night before.

As he pulled the bellpull for a servant, Trenhaven winced at the pain in his head. He was paying the price for last night's revels, he told himself. The previous evening he had joined a number of his friends at his club. After dinner, the marquess and his congenial companions had set off for one of the more lively gambling establishments where they had partaken of a great quantity of wine and spirits.

Trenhaven frowned as he tried to recall the evening's events, but he was now a bit hazy on the details. He thought he remembered playing faro. Yes, he had done so, and he had lost very badly.

Fortunately, his lordship was a very wealthy man, who could afford to lose a great deal of money. Trenhaven frowned again. How much had he lost? He was sure it was at least a thousand pounds. The loss was bad enough in itself, but what made matters worse was the knowledge that is father would undoubtedly learn of it.

The thought of his father plunged the marquess into an even fouler mood. His lordship and his father, the Duke of Haverford, did not get along very well. Trenhaven thought his father was a cold, unfeeling tyrant, while the duke considered his son a foolish wastrel, who would bring disrepute to the family name. He was always lecturing the marquess on behaving in a manner better suited to his illustrious station.

Whenever Trenhaven and his father got together, they quarreled. Therefore, the two men endeavored to keep apart as much as possible. Since the marquess had his own establishment in town, it was not too difficult to avoid seeing the duke. When they met at social occasions, they usually behaved with cold formality.

"You rang, my lord?"

The marquess noted the arrival of his valet, a burly young man with a serious demeanor, with another frown. "I've got the most damnable headache, Judd, so I warn you to be very quiet."

The valet nodded solemnly. "There is a note for you, my lord, hand delivered a few moments ago. It is from His Grace."

"His Grace? Good God! Take it away, Judd."

"The servant who brought the note said that it was very important, my lord."

"Damn and blast," muttered the marquess, taking the note from the silver salver on which it was extended to him. After reading the short missive, he cursed under his breath. "My father commands me to call at Haverford House this afternoon."

"Indeed, my lord?"

"Deuced bad luck this is, Judd. Well I must face the old lion in his den. You'd better make me look respectable." Glancing over at a gilt mirror that hung on the wall, the marquess noted his disheveled appearance. His dark brown hair looked wild and his eyes were bloodshot. Trenhaven rubbed the stubble on his unshaven chin. "You'll have a bit of work to do, Judd."

"A bath and a shave and your lordship will be good as new," said the servant.

"I hope so," returned the marquess glumly.

Some time later, Trenhaven was dressed in his fine clothes and restored to his usual splendor. The marquess was a very handsome man, who cut a fine figure in his perfectly fitted coat and pantaloons.

Tall and broad-shouldered, Trenhaven was well suited to the fashionable coat of dove-gray superfine he was wearing. Known as one of the leading tulips of fashion, the marquess always took particular care with his appearance. His linen was a brilliant white and his elaborately tied cravat was a thing of beauty.

Trenhaven's dark locks were now carefully combed. Cut in the fashionable Corinthian style, the marquess' hair had just the right amount of curl to look suitably Byronic.

His lordship eyed his appearance once again in the mirror. "Thank God I am fit to go out in public. You have outdone yourself, Judd."

"Will your lordship be having breakfast?"

"Indeed not, Judd. I feel altogether ill. I'll not risk eating anything. No, have Wiley bring my carriage round. It had best be the old one, mind you. I shall go at once to my father's."

"Yes, my lord," said Judd, bowing and retreating from the room.

"And Judd . . ."

"Yes, my lord?" said the servant, stopping in his tracks.

"Ask Cook to prepare a draught for my headache."

"Very good, my lord."

Trenhaven made his way from his bedchamber to his drawing room. There he stood looking out the window until a footman appeared with a glass on a tray. The marquess took the glass with some revulsion, knowing that it contained his cook's famous potion for relief of hangover.

The marquess had never asked the cook what was in the drink, for he was rather afraid to find out. Yet the dreadful-tasting liquid seemed to have a most beneficial effect, so he gulped it down manfully.

"Give Cook my deepest thanks, Tom," said the marquess, placing the glass back on the tray.

"Indeed, my lord," returned the footman, trying very hard to refrain from smiling.

"Your carriage is ready, my lord." Trenhaven's butler appeared in the drawing room.

Trenhaven acknowledged the servant with a nod. The butler handed him his hat and walking stick and hurried to open the door for him.

Climbing into the awaiting phaeton, the marquess had a sinking feeling, something akin to what a doomed man must feel like before his sentencing. Trenhaven knew very well that his father intended to give him a dressing down.

Sitting back in his carriage seat, the marquess sighed. The duke must have already heard about his disastrous night at cards, he thought. Trenhaven shook his head. His father had a good many spies about town eager to inform him of his errant son's misdeeds.

Resentment welled up inside his lordship. His father was only too happy to find fault with him. There was no pleasing him. No, all the duke could ever do was criticize his only son and heir.

Trenhaven stared out at the passing scenery, but took little note of it. Intent on his impending meeting with his father, he folded his arms across his chest and frowned grimly.

It did not take long to arrive at Haverford House. The ducal residence was one of the grandest private buildings in all of London. An imposing structure of gray granite, it was a well-known landmark.

The marquess detested Haverford House. He had spent many unhappy days there in his youth, and it held few pleasant memories for him.

The butler who admitted his lordship made a grave bow. "His Grace is expecting you, my lord."

"Is Her Grace at home as well, Preston?" said the marquess, handing his hat and walking stick to a footman who stood near the door.

"Yes, my lord. The duchess is in the drawing room with His Grace. Follow me, my lord."

Trenhaven was pleased to hear that the duchess was there. A doting mother, Her Grace was always ready to take his side. She spent a good deal of time trying to patch things up between her son and her husband.

Opening the large oak doors to the drawing room, the butler entered the room. "Lord Trenhaven, Your Grace," he intoned solemnly.

Following the servant into the room, the marquess found his father sitting in his favorite armchair. Trenhaven noted that the duke's foot was bandaged and propped on a footstool. It was not a good sign. The duke suffered from gout, a condition that oftentimes caused him considerable pain. The marquess knew that if his father's foot was bothering him, the duke would be even more bad tempered than usual.

The duchess sat nearby on an elegant French sofa. Her Grace was an attractive lady who looked younger than her fifty-one years. A renowned lady of fashion, the duchess had been one of the great beauties of her day. Age had been very kind to her and the duchess was still considered to be a very fine looking woman.

Trenhaven approached his parents. "Mother, you look beautiful as ever," he said, taking her hand and bringing it to his lips.

"Trenhaven," said the duchess, directing an icy look at her son.

The marquess was surprised at the coolness of his mother's reception. It was clear he was in her black books as well as the duke's.

Turning to his father, Trenhaven bowed respectfully. "Sir," he said.

"Trenhaven," said the duke.

"I do hope that your foot is not troubling you badly, sir."

"It is troubling me very much, sir," returned the duke testily. "But it is not troubling me as much as you are."

The marquess stood before his father, steeling himself for his father's wrath. "I am very sorry if I have displeased you, Father."

"Displeased me? By God, you have displeased me. But it is your mother whom you have most offended. You must apologize to her."

Trenhaven regarded the duke blankly. Receiving no further explanation, he turned to his mother. "I am sorry, Mother, but, indeed, I do not know what I have done to offend you."

"You do not know?" said the duchess, eyeing him in disbelief.

"No, I do not."

"Then you are a great blockhead," said the duke. "You know very well you were to have dinner here last evening. Where were you?"

"Last evening?" A glimmer of recognition came to his lordship. Of course, he had promised to attend a dinner at Haverford House, but it could not have been last night. No, he was sure it was next week some time. "The dinner was last night? I do apologize. I quite forgot."

"Forgot?" said the duke disgustedly. "I daresay you remembered well enough. No, you preferred to spend your time with your dissolute friends rather than attend your mother and myself."

"I assure you, sir, it was an oversight."

"I wish I could believe that," said the duchess, dabbing her eyes with a lace handkerchief. "I was so embarrassed. You cannot know how you humiliated me."

Trenhaven viewed his mother in some alarm, fearing she would burst into tears. "What do you mean, Mother?"

"I had told Lord and Lady Esterbrook that you would attend. They were there with their daughter Charlotte. Lady Charlotte was so disappointed when you did not appear."

"And I felt like an idiot, Trenhaven," said the duke. "I had been telling Esterbrook how much you like Charlotte and how you were so looking forward to seeing her. We had discussed the marriage settlement, you know. She will bring a rich dowry."

"Good God, sir," said the marquess, "You were discussing the marriage settlement? I daresay that was premature. I care nothing for Lady Charlotte. I have never said that I was in any way interested in her."

"You have never been interested in any respectable girl," said the duchess accusingly. "Charlotte Cavendish is a fine young lady. She is very pretty and she is from one of the best families in London. She has all manner of beaux dangling after her. I cannot imagine why you would not find her a most attractive prospect for your bride."

"Mother, you know I have said many times that I intend to choose my own wife in my own time," said the marquess.

"And when is that to be?" exclaimed the duke. "You are five and twenty years of age. It is time you married. We have been over this matter many times before."

"Indeed, we have, sir," said the marquess.

"You told me that you would find a bride this season," said the duke. "The season is at an end and you are no closer to being wed."

"I have found no one I wished to marry," said Trenhaven, who was rapidly losing his temper.

"If you would spend less time carousing with your friends and more time in respectable drawing rooms, perhaps you would find a wife," said the duke angrily.

"Trenhaven, you know very well it is your duty to marry," said the duchess. "You are your father's only heir. You must marry and have sons. Both your sister Elizabeth and I have spent considerable time this season trying to select the right girl for you. You have not considered even one young lady whom we have suggested for you. And you promised us both that you would marry this year."

"I did not promise that, Mother," said the marquess. "I simply said that I would give the matter serious consideration."

"And have you done so?" demanded the duke.

Trenhaven shrugged. "I believe I have. I do not feel I shirked my duty. I attended all manner of boring affairs. I danced with an unending number of empty-headed females. Can I be blamed if I did not meet anyone whom I had any wish to marry?"

"You can indeed be blamed," said the duke, getting rather red in the face. "You are surrounded by pretty girls, all of them eager to marry you. Refusing to consider any of them is sheer perversity. You do it to plague me. Do not think that I don't know it!"

"Upon my honor, sir, you are very much mistaken!" said the marquess growing very hot under the collar.

"If I am mistaken, you will prove me wrong by offering for Lady Charlotte Cavendish."

Trenhaven regarded his father in astonishment. "You cannot be serious, sir. I scarcely know her well enough to consider marriage." The marquess might have added that he found Lady Charlotte insipid and her mother an overbearing shrew.

"How well do you have to know her?" said the duke. "Your mother and your sister Elizabeth have decided she is perfect for you."

"She is a lovely girl, Trenhaven," said the duchess. "One must choose very carefully. After all, your wife will one day be Duchess of Haverford. It is a daunting responsibility."

"So you expect me to ask for this lady's hand?"

"Yes," said the duke. "Unless you can find another young woman as well suited. There are certainly others whom we would approve. But I grow sick of waiting. I warn you, Trenhaven, if you continue to disappoint your mother and me, you will regret it. Now leave us. I do not wish to discuss this any further."

The marquess stared indignantly at his father. "Very well, sir," he said. "I shall go. Good day, Mother." He bowed stiffly first to the duchess and then his father. "Sir," he said, turning and stalking from the drawing room.

As he walked out of the house, the marquess shook his head. Would his father never stop treating him like a child? He was his own man and he would do as he pleased. He had no wish to marry, and he certainly had no wish to marry some bird-witted creature selected for him by his mother and sister. Did they think he was some hound in the kennel ready to be mated to any female with the proper bloodlines?

The marquess seethed with righteous indignation as he climbed into his phaeton and ordered his driver to return home. By the time he arrived at his town house, he was in a vile temper.

Trenhaven went to his drawing room where he stood by the window, looking out at the park in the square across from his residence. Rain had begun to fall, which did nothing to improve his lordship's mood.

Frowning, the marquess watched the traffic passing on the cobblestoned street. Remembering his interview with his parents, he grew thoughtful. The duke and duchess had been urging him to marry ever since he had reached his majority. Throughout the past year there had been a good many quarrels about Trenhaven's lack of cooperation.

The marquess turned away from the window. He was heartily sick of the idea of matrimony. Indeed, he was heartily sick of everything.

Trenhaven's butler entered the room. "I beg your pardon, my lord, but the post has arrived."

"Put it down on the table, Baker."

"Yes, my lord," replied the butler, doing as his master requested, and then quietly exiting the room.

Life in town had become a dead bore, reflected Trenhaven as he walked to the table and picked up the pile of letters. Sitting down on the sofa, he began sifting through them, stopping at one envelope. Recognizing his sister's handwriting, he frowned again as he opened it. His sister Elizabeth was writing to invite him to a dinner party she was having. "Several exceedingly pretty girls will be in attendance including Charlotte Cavendish," his sister's letter said. The name Charlotte Cavendish had been underlined for emphasis. "Should you refuse to come, I shall be quite vexed with you."

Trenhaven tossed the letter down. His sister could be as tiresome as his father, he told himself. While he was very fond of his only sibling, he was losing patience with her attempts at matchmaking.

The marquess glanced through his other mail, which mostly consisted of tradesmen's bills and invitations. One letter, however, caught his attention, and he opened it eagerly, knowing that it was a communication from his oldest friend, Sir Charles Mainwaring.

As Trenhaven began to read the letter, his mood improved. He always enjoyed hearing from Charles. Although he had not seen his friend in several years, the marquess corresponded with him regularly.

Not long ago, Charles had written to inform Trenhaven that he was engaged to be married. While his own matrimonial prospects were a sore subject, the marquess had been happy to hear that his friend would soon be relinquishing his bachelor status. After all, for more than a year Charles's letters had been filled with the praises of a certain Miss Lucy Blake, who, according to Charles, was the sweetest, prettiest, and most wonderful girl in all of England.

Charles's present letter rambled on about the weather and the corn crop. There were also several paragraphs about an exceptionally fine bull that the baronet had purchased. It ended with Charles's usual request that Trenhaven come to Somerset to visit him. "I do wish you would come, William," the letter stated, "although I daresay you might be frightfully bored out here in the provinces. But we are not so very dull, really. And you would adore my Lucy. Do come sometime."

The marquess put down the letter. Usually he only smiled indulgently at his friend's invitation to visit him. After all, the Marquess of Trenhaven could hardly be expected to spend time in some provincial backwater.

Taking up Charles's letter again, his lordship studied it thoughtfully. Perhaps he should visit Charles. He had a great desire to see his old friend once again, and, in his present mood, the idea of leaving London seemed very appealing. The more Trenhaven considered the matter, the better the idea seemed to him. It would be good to be away from his parents and his sister and the young ladies of good family who were so eager to marry him.

Rising from his seat, the marquess left the drawing room. Calling for his valet, Trenhaven informed a very surprised Judd that they would be leaving at once for the country.

4

Tying the ribbons of her bonnet, Serena stopped at the doorway of her sister's bedchamber. "Lucy, are you ready?"

Lucy stood in front of the mirror in her dressing room. She called out to Serena. "No, I am not. Serena, I cannot wear this dress to go anywhere."

Serena strode impatiently into the dressing room. "What is the matter?"

"This dress," said Lucy, eying her reflection in the mirror with horror. She was attired in a drab, brown walking dress. "It is so dreadfully plain."

"It is exactly right," said Serena. "But look at me. Don't you agree that I look stunning?"

"Serena!" said Lucy, turning for the first time from the mirror to regard her sister in surprise. Serena was wearing a faded plum-colored creation. Several sizes too big, it hung like a shapeless sack. "Where did you find that?" cried Lucy.

Serena burst into laughter at her sister's expression. "In an old trunk in the attic. It is rather funny."

"Serena," said Lucy severely, "you said that we should dress in our oldest, plainest clothes. But you are ridiculous."

"We must look as if we have no money for clothes."

"But it is utterly absurd," protested Lucy. "I should think everyone will be more apt to regard us as addlepated than impoverished."

Serena laughed again. "In any case it may give Arabella pause to see us dressed like this. But come along, Lucy. I am in need of a walk. And Muggins is growing restless."

The terrier looked up at his mistress at the mention of his name. He wagged his tail expectantly.

"Very well," said Lucy, taking up her bonnet from the bed and placing it on her head. "But I am quite ashamed to be seen with you, Serena. Could you not wear your pelisse over that monstrous garment?"

"Indeed not. It is quite warm outside, but I shall take my shawl."

"Good," returned Lucy, glad to see her sister take up her fringed shawl and wrap it around her shoulders. At least it hid some of the dreadful frock, thought the elder of the Blake sisters.

Lucy and Serena left the room and proceeded out of the house. It was a lovely September day. The weather was particularly fine, sunny and pleasant. Serena smiled at the warmth of the sun on her face. "Is it not a splendid day?" said Serena as they set out, walking briskly down the lane. The dog Muggins, ecstatic at being out, ran ahead of them.

"Yes, it is beautiful," said Lucy. "I do hate to think that summer is ending."

Serena nodded, but made no reply. The two sisters walked on in silence. The village of Whitfield was nearly three miles distant, but Serena and Lucy did not consider that a very great distance. Accustomed to walking, they often went to the village on foot. Most days when the weather was good, they thought of some excuse to go there.

That afternoon Serena had declared she needed some ribbon to trim a hat. Lucy had been only too glad to accompany her. As they walked along, the elder of the Blake sisters grew pensive. In a few months she would be married and living at Mainwaring Hall. Their walks to the village would be ending shortly.

"Is something the matter, Lucy?" said Serena, noting that her sister seemed unusually solemn.

"Oh, I was only thinking that when I am married, we will not have our walks together."

"No," said Serena, "but it is not as if we won't be seeing each other. Why, Mainwaring Hall is scarcely four miles from Briarly."

"Yes," said Lucy. "I do not know what I would do if I had to move very far away and could not see you or Papa. I do hope you will not live far away when you are married."

"Good heavens," said Serena, "I daresay I shan't marry at all."

"Of course you will," said Lucy.

"I truly believe I will not," said Serena matter-of-factly. "But I am content to remain unmarried. Indeed, I daresay I should prefer it. It is different for you. You and Charles have fallen in love."

"But do you not think you will fall in love, Serena?"

Serena smiled. "It would greatly surprise me if I did so. I have met a good many gentlemen, and not one has ever made me even think of love. No, I believe I shall remain a spinster, Luce. The role of maiden aunt will suit me quite well."

Lucy was about to reply that her sister was very much mistaken, when she noted the approach of a vehicle some distance ahead. "Serena, is that not Freddy Osborne in his curricle?"

Looking ahead, Serena caught sight of the vehicle approaching. "Oh dear, it is Freddy Osborne! Is it too late to hide behind a tree and hope he did not see us?"

"Oh, Serena!" said Lucy with a smile. "He has surely already seen us."

"I fear you are right," replied Serena. "What dashed bad luck. We shall have to face him, but I cannot promise that I shall be civil."

"Serena, you must not be rude to him!"

"And why not? He is quite detestable. Why must one be polite to such persons?"

"I know he is horrid, Serena, but one must be polite to everyone. And he does appear to be fond of you."

"Fond of me? That is utter nonsense, Lucy. He may be fond of my fortune, but that is a very different matter."

"Why must you always believe every young man who pays attention to you is interested only in your fortune?"

"Because I know it to be true," said Serena firmly.

"That is nonsense," said Lucy, regarding her sister in frustration. "But do try to be civil to Freddy, Serena."

"I shall be charm itself," said Serena, casting an ironical glance at her sister. Then looking toward the approaching vehicle, Serena appeared more interested. "Why, I do believe Freddy has a new horse. And a fine one at that."

Lucy found herself wishing that her sister could show as much interest in young men as she did in horses. Serena was passionately fond of horses.

As the curricle grew closer, Serena regarded the horse closely. She barely looked at the driver of the vehicle, who was smiling broadly at her.

Mr. Frederick Osborne was one of a number of young men who thought of themselves as Serena's suitors. Serena, however, could not abide him, thinking him vain, foolish, and filled with his own self-importance. The fact that he was Arabella's cousin made him even more objectionable.

Osborne, however, had not given up hope that he might still win Serena's hand. A tenacious gentleman, he was determined to try. After all, Serena Blake might be a strong-minded, difficult female, but she would have a very large marriage settlement. A confident young man, Osborne was certain he could control Serena once she was his wife.

Having spotted the young ladies on the road ahead of him, Osborne smiled. He was very happy at the idea of meeting Serena in an informal setting.

Pulling up the mare beside the young ladies, Osborne tipped his hat politely. "Good day, Lucy and Serena. Why, I was just on my way to call at Briarly."

"Good day, Freddy," said Lucy.

Serena, however, did not immediately acknowledge Osborne. Calling to Muggins and commanding him to stay, she took a closer look at the horse. Patting the animal's sleek neck, she finally glanced up at its owner. "What a fine mare, Freddy," she said.

"Yes, yes, indeed she is. You have a good eye for horses, Serena. I bought her just yesterday. Irish blood. You'll not find another like her in all the county."

"She is a beauty," said Serena, stroking the horse's withers.

Osborne was encouraged by Serena's interest in his horse. He wished that she would pay some attention to him, however. He had dressed with great care, having worn his fine new coat and his splendid striped waistcoat. Osborne considered himself something of a dandy. He was very conscious of his appearance, and considered himself a veritable sprig of fashion.

Osborne was a rather handsome young man. Not very tall, he was shorter than Serena, a fact that irritated him. A good many ladies in the vicinity thought Osborne quite dashing, but Serena did not share that opinion.

"And are you ladies walking to the village?"

"We are, sir," said Serena. "But I fear we must not detain you since you are on the way to visit our father. He is at home and is receiving visitors."

"But I was hoping—"

Serena cut Osborne off abruptly. "I fear we are rather in a hurry, Freddy. Good day to you. Come, Muggins." Serena started to stride quickly past Osborne's vehicle. Lucy, who was a bit dismayed at her sister's incivility, could only nod to Osborne and hurry after Serena.

"Serena," whispered Lucy. "That was quite rude. You might have spoken with him for a few moments."

"I do not wish to encourage him," said Serena.

Osborne sighed as he watched the two young ladies and the ter-

rier continue on toward the village. Serena Blake was a difficult
creature, he told himself. After pausing a while to watch them, he
continued on down the road. He would still call at Briarly, he decided. All would not be lost if Mr. Blake would receive him.
After all, it would not hurt to ingratiate himself with Serena's father.

Tapping his horse smartly with his whip, Osborne started off.
Serena glanced back at him. "Good, he is going on. I do not doubt
he intends to call on Father. He is wasting his time. He must
know that I have no intention of marrying him. I have never liked
him and Muggins cannot abide him."

Lucy smiled. "Muggins's opinion does hold great weight."

"Indeed it does," said Serena. "Muggins is an excellent judge
of character."

"But Muggins does not like Charles," protested Lucy.

"Well, Muggs can be wrong sometimes," said Serena. "But he
is quite right about Freddy. He cares only for my fortune. That is
very clear. Now, I pray you, Lucy, do not speak any more of
Freddy or any of my tedious suitors. I shall be very vexed with
you if you say another word."

"Very well," said Lucy, feeling it best to say nothing further.

They continued on, talking of other matters. In what seemed
like a very short time they arrived at the village. Serena fastened a
leather lead on Muggins's collar and cautioned him to be on his
best behavior.

Whitfield was a small village of neat thatched cottages and
well-kept shops. Serena and Lucy strolled leisurely past the store
windows, pausing now and again to look inside. "Oh, look at that
hat, Luce," cried Serena, catching sight of a stylish French bonnet
on display in the window of the milliner's shop. "That would look
splendid on me. I must try it on."

Lucy eyed the hat for a moment. "Perhaps, but must I remind
you that you have no money for new hats? If you want everyone
in the village to think Papa is a lickpenny, you cannot go about
buying new hats."

"You are right," said Serena. "Oh well, I did not need a new
hat anyway. But look!" Serena's voice grew excited. "Look who
is inside. It is Mrs. Claybrook! This is dashed good luck, Luce!
We are going inside."

"What do you mean, Serena? Why would you wish to see Mrs.
Claybrook? She is horrible and the worst gossip in the village."

"That is precisely why I am so glad to see her. Come on,

Lucy!" Grasping her sister by the arm, Serena propelled a rather bewildered Lucy into the milliner's shop.

The proprietress of the shop, Mrs. Westcott, smiled brightly at the young ladies. "Good afternoon, Miss Blake and Miss Serena."

"Good afternoon, Mrs. Westcott. Good afternoon, Mrs. Claybrook."

Mrs. Claybrook nodded to Serena and Lucy. Serena was certain that she was staring at their dresses. Pleased, Serena pretended to be interested in the hats.

"I shall be with you in a moment," said the proprietress.

"Oh, there is no hurry, Mrs. Westcott," said Serena, taking the shawl from around her shoulders and folding it over her arm. "You are busy with Mrs. Claybrook. Do take your time."

Lucy and Serena walked around the shop, examining the milliner's creations. Serena then turned her attention once again to the bonnet on display in the window. Taking it from the stand, she placed it on her head. "What do you think, Lucy?"

"It is very nice, Serena, but"—Lucy paused and then continued in a whisper—"you know what I said. You cannot buy a hat."

Serena snatched the bonnet from her head. "I know I cannot afford a new hat," she said loudly. "It was only wishful thinking, Lucy." Placing the hat back on the stand, Serena sighed rather dramatically. "I know that Papa would be furious if I bought anything new. No, Lucy, I should not face his wrath for anything."

Both Mrs. Claybrook and Mrs. Westcott, the milliner, heard Serena's words with keen interest. Mrs. Claybrook's eyebrows arched slightly as she regarded her reflection in the mirror. Atop her head was a broad-brimmed leghorn hat decorated with silk flowers. She took the hat off and handed it to Mrs. Westcott. "I fancy that I would like to try the straw bonnet once more."

"Here it is, Mrs. Claybrook."

Mrs. Claybrook took the other hat and put it on. She could see Serena and Lucy reflected in the mirror. Mrs. Claybrook could not fail to note the drab, unattractive clothes that the Blake sisters were wearing. It was very odd considering the fact that Lucy and Serena Blake were among the best dressed young ladies in the county.

Mrs. Claybrook wondered at Serena's words. Could the girl actually be fearful of her father's wrath? Why, everyone knew that Augustus Blake was the most mild-mannered of men who spoiled his younger daughter dreadfully. Of course, Mrs. Claybrook considered, perhaps Mr. Blake was exerting some long overdue parental authority.

"I shall take this bonnet," said Mrs. Claybrook finally. "I shall wear it. Please box my other hat, Mrs. Westcott."

"Yes, Mrs. Claybrook," replied the milliner, happy at the sale.

"That is a lovely hat, ma'am," said Lucy, addressing Mrs. Claybrook.

"How good of you to say so, my dear," replied Mrs. Claybrook. "I do hope you find something you like as well, Lucy."

"Oh, I am not going to buy a hat today, Mrs. Claybrook."

"Nor am I," said Serena, "but I do enjoy looking."

"I hope your father is well," said Mrs. Claybrook.

"Very well, thank you," replied Serena.

"But how are you, Mrs. Claybrook?" said Lucy.

This seemingly innocuous question dismayed Serena, who knew that it was an invitation for Mrs. Claybrook to discourse on her numerous medical conditions. "I fear my back has been troubling me," began Mrs. Claybrook. "And I must tell you about my toothache."

Serena silently cursed Lucy for her blunder. It was well known that one did not ask the garrulous Mrs. Claybrook about her health unless one was prepared to listen for hours. Serena stood there, trying to be polite. She knew she was far too impatient with others. It was a defect of her character that she knew she ought to correct.

Fortunately for Serena, Mrs. Claybrook did not rattle on for very long. She had another appointment, she informed them, and regretfully, must be off. Taking the hat box from Mrs. Westcott, she took her leave.

"How may I help you ladies?" said Mrs. Westcott.

"Oh, I fear we are only here looking, Mrs. Westcott," said Serena. "I do think that hat, the one in the window, is simply wonderful. However, I shall not be able to buy it. Indeed, Mrs. Westcott, I have really come to tell you that we may not be able to pay our account for some time." Lucy regarded her sister in some surprise. Ignoring her, Serena continued, "I cannot explain, Mrs. Westcott, but we shall pay as soon as we can."

"My dear Miss Serena," said the milliner, "do not trouble yourself. Why, your father paid me but two weeks ago. There is very little to be paid at this time."

"Oh," said Serena, feeling rather foolish. Having hoped to make the milliner think they were suddenly impoverished, she had not counted on the fact that her father might have already paid the bills. "That is good news. I daresay we must be going. Good day to you, Mrs. Westcott."

Once outside the shop, Lucy eyed her sister with disapproval. "Oh, Serena, I felt as if I might die of embarrassment. To tell Mrs. Westcott that we cannot pay our account!"

"We want everyone to think we are poor, don't we? It will be all over the village by tomorrow."

"It will be all over the village that Serena Blake is quite out of her wits."

Serena laughed. "Well, at least I was not the one to ask Mrs. Claybrook about her health." Lucy grinned and the two sisters continued on down the village street.

5

As Trenhaven drove his phaeton down the narrow road through the Somerset countryside, he found himself surveying the landscape with approval. He was glad to be out of the grime and congestion of London.

With every mile he had traveled away from the great city, his lordship's mood had improved. This fact was happily noted by Trenhaven's valet, Judd, who sat beside him in the driver's seat of the modish high-perch phaeton.

The marquess enjoyed driving himself. After having made the decision to leave London, Trenhaven had determined to leave his driver and groom at home, taking only Judd, his valet.

While Judd was well aware of his master's reputation as a splendid hand at the ribbons, the valet would have preferred to have had his lordship's driver at the reins. That would have allowed Judd to sit back in the comfortable passenger seat rather than roosting precariously on the high driver's seat with his master.

Judd had not understood why Trenhaven had taken the new phaeton in any case. It was a sporting vehicle ill suited to long journeys. As he clung to the seat, Judd thought of the comfortable chaise that his lordship might have taken.

At least, thought Judd, as the phaeton traveled along, they were not so far from their destination, having traveled more than one hundred miles from London. The trip had gone very well. The weather had been good and the roads passable. Highwaymen and footpads had been fortunately absent and the inns they had stayed at on the road were tolerable.

Judd would have preferred to stay in town. Having lived his entire life in the city, he had little regard for rural England. The pastoral scenery with its green pastures and groves of trees held little attraction for Judd.

His master, however, found himself in better spirits than he had been for many weeks. He was eager to see his old friend, Charles

Mainwaring. What a surprise it would be for Charles, considered the marquess. He had not had time to write. Although he knew it was very bad form to descend on someone in such a way, Trenhaven knew that Charles would forgive him.

They continued on for a time, following the directions they had received at a village a few miles back. Then suddenly Mainwaring Hall came into view.

"There it is, Judd," said Trenhaven.

"Aye, m'lord," said Judd, very glad to be finally arriving.

The marquess directed his horses toward the front door of the mansion. "And Judd . . ."

"M'lord?"

"I have been thinking. During my visit here I shall be incognito."

"Incognito, m'lord?" said Judd with a puzzled look.

"That means that I do not want anyone to know who I am. I shall go by the name of Mr. Macaulay. You must not call me 'my lord.' Remember. I shall be Mr. Macaulay."

"As you wish, m'lord," returned Judd. "I should say, Mr. Macaulay."

"Good," said Trenhaven, pulling up his horses at the front entrance to Mainwaring Hall.

Judd tried not to show his disapproval. He did not like the idea of his master going by some other name. It seemed very strange. And, indeed, what was the use of being a lord if no one knew it? Still, there was nothing he could do if his master had a strange whim from time to time. Aristocratic young gentlemen did have their whims, Judd reflected.

A liveried footman hurried out to meet the stylish phaeton. Trenhaven jumped down agilely from the driver's seat, leaving Judd to climb down with the footman's assistance. Charles's butler admitted the marquess. The servant regarded the visitor with some interest. It was not often that strangers visited at Mainwaring Hall, especially gentlemen of such obvious quality as the man who now stood before him.

"I should like to see Sir Charles," said his lordship, handing his hat to the butler.

"And who may I say is calling, sir?"

"Say it is his old friend William. That is quite sufficient."

"Very good, sir," said the servant. "Do follow me, sir."

The butler escorted his lordship to the drawing room and then left him to wait. Trenhaven walked about the room, noting its Egyptian motif with some amusement. It appeared that his old friend had taken up the mania for things Egyptian that had seized many fashionable Londoners.

"I cannot believe it!" A masculine voice made the marquess turn to see his old friend enter the room. "When Davis said that 'my old friend William' was here, I thought it was impossible, but here you are!" The baronet opened his arms to receive his friend in a bearlike embrace.

"By God, it is good to see you, Charlie," said the marquess, hugging Charles enthusiastically.

"Do sit down, my dear William," said the baronet once he had finally released his former school chum. "This is so wonderful. I can still scarcely believe that you are here!"

Trenhaven sat down in an elegant armchair of exotic design. "You look very well, Charlie. And very prosperous. By heaven, how long has it been since we have seen each other? Five years at least."

"Six I should think," replied Charles. "I have so wanted you to visit."

"And I have invited you to town each year."

Charles grinned. "And I detest London and you detest the country. So there we are! But you are here now! Do say you will stay for a good visit. A month at least!"

"My dear fellow, I cannot say how long I shall stay. I must beg your pardon for coming unannounced. I should have written."

"Bosh," said Charles. "You are welcome anytime. My mother will be so disappointed that she was not here to see you. She is in Bath, you know."

"Indeed, you had written that, Charlie. I hope she is well."

"Excellent well, I am glad to say. But really, this is famous that you are here. You will meet my dearest Lucy. I know you will adore her. She is the sweetest, kindest young lady!"

"You had written that as well, Charlie," said the marquess with an indulgent smile.

"It is so splendid having you here," said Charles. "You will cause a sensation, William. Our local society will scarcely know what to do when it is known that the Marquess of Trenhaven is here."

"Good God, Charlie," exclaimed his lordship. "I have come here to avoid society. While I have truly wished to visit you many times before, I must confess that I have another reason for appearing at your door." Charles regarded his guest with keen attention as the marquess continued. "I have quarreled with my father. I wished to leave town so that I would not see him for a while. I thought of you, Charlie. I did not think you would mind my coming."

"Mind your coming? My dear friend, I could not be happier that you are here. But this quarrel with the duke? Was it serious?"

Trenhaven nodded. "I believe it was. And I daresay my father will be very unhappy when he finds that I have left London. I did not leave word where I was going. I have come here because I am in need of a friend and also of some peace and quiet."

"You have both here, William," said Charles.

"Thank you, Charlie," said the marquess. "But I must ask a favor of you."

"Ask away, old lad."

"I should prefer that no one knew that I am the Marquess of Trenhaven while I am here. Nothing creates more feverish activity among matchmaking mamas than knowing that an unmarried duke's son is in the vicinity. I have had enough willing virgins paraded before me to last a lifetime. I need see no more of them here in the country."

Charles laughed. "My poor friend. I shall try hard to keep the ladies at bay. But marquess or not, you are a fine-looking fellow. When the ladies get wind of an unmarried man staying at Mainwaring Hall, they will not leave you alone for long."

"Well, you must see to it that I am considered an unmarriageable man."

"My dear William, around here the only unmarriageable men are married already. Shall we invent a wife for you?"

"God no," muttered Trenhaven. "I have no interest in a wife even if she is only an invention."

"You cannot mean you intend to remain a bachelor forever?"

"I should prefer to remain so for as long as possible. And I'm damned if I'll have anyone force a bride on me. No, indeed. I shall avoid society of any kind while I am here."

"But you cannot do that," said Charles. "I have a great many engagements here at Mainwaring Hall. You cannot hide in your rooms. I shall not permit it."

"I have no wish for any society other than yours, Charlie. And I am very serious when I say that I have no desire to be pursued by predatory females in search of a rich, titled husband. That is why I should prefer to be known as Mr. Macaulay when I am here."

"Mr. Macaulay? Oh, yes. William Arthur Macaulay Savage. I suppose that is a good idea. Everyone will think you an ordinary, common sort of man."

"And you must tell anyone who inquires that I have no money. Indeed, that I am penniless."

"You don't look penniless," said the baronet, regarding his friend with amusement. The marquess was dressed in his trademark sartorial splendor. "Of course, it might be put about that you are an extravagant wastrel."

"Yes, that should be completely believable," said the marquess with a wry smile.

Charles grinned broadly, warming to the idea. "Yes, I shall tell a few persons in the strictest confidence that you have squandered your fortune and that you are horribly in debt." Charles seemed to have another idea. "I have it! I shall say that you are a gambler and a drunkard! Even the most desperate of matrons would not wish her daughter to be shackled to such a fellow."

Trenhaven laughed. "An excellent idea, Charlie. Yes, you must give me a monstrous reputation, even worse than the one I have."

"My dear fellow, I was not aware that your reputation was anything but sterling."

"I fear it may be a bit tarnished in some circles. Indeed, my father thinks me quite dissolute. I confess I have of late been spending a good deal of time at the gaming tables. But here under your good influences, Charlie, I shall doubtless mend my ways."

"I do hope so," said Charles with a broad grin. "There is little gaming hereabouts in any case, although there is a public house in Whitfield where money changes hands."

"Indeed?" said Trenhaven, quite interested. "Shall we go there tonight?"

Charles burst into laughter. "It sounds as if you are an incorrigible fellow, William. We will steer well clear of the place, my friend. Lucy is very much opposed to gambling."

"Good God, Charlie, you are not even wed to the girl. That is why any sensible man wishes to avoid the shackles of matrimony."

"Shackles? When you meet my Lucy you will see that any sensible man would love being shackled to her. She is an angel. You will meet her tomorrow, William. She lives scarcely four miles distant with her father and sister."

"Her sister?" said Trenhaven. "I suppose she is a single lady in search of a husband?"

"My dear William, it appears you have an unnatural aversion to single ladies. But you have nothing to fear from Serena Blake. I assure you she is not interested in finding a husband. She has told me so herself."

"Then you are easily gulled, Charlie. I do not think that there is an unmarried woman on earth who is not seeking a husband."

"You are quite wrong there, my friend. Why, Lucy quite despairs of her sister's disinterest in marriage. Serena Blake has had many suitors, but she has been totally disinterested in any of them. Serena is not an ordinary girl. And she is so unlike Lucy, who is so sweet and docile. Serena is very headstrong and opinionated. She is well accustomed to having her own way." Charles smiled. "Most gentlemen who have attempted to court Serena Blake have been happy to abandon the venture even though Serena will have a very substantial marriage settlement."

"Good God," said the marquess, "this Serena sounds like a veritable termagant."

"No, indeed, she is very charming. And very pretty as well. Oh, I daresay she is not as pretty as Lucy, but then Lucy is the most beautiful girl in all of England."

"I can see you are making a great cake of yourself over your Lucy, Charlie," said Trenhaven, grinning at his friend. "Well, I shall be happy to meet her, but I fancy I should prefer to avoid this sister of hers."

"I fear I have done Serena a great disservice in my description of her. Truly, she is a delightful young lady."

His lordship's eyebrows arched slightly. "Well, I shall soon make my own determination. But I abhor nothing more than a strong-minded female."

"Well, you will like Serena, I am sure of it," said Charles stoutly, although he was really not so confident. "But you must be very tired. My servant said that you have come with but one servant. Did you drive from town yourself?"

"Yes, but I do not advise taking such a vehicle as that phaeton on such a journey. My man Judd was so rattled about that I daresay he was ready to give notice any number of times."

"Well, you must be very tired and hungry. A servant will show you to your room and then we will have luncheon."

"Splendid," replied the marquess, rising from his chair. As he followed Charles's servant from the drawing room, Trenhaven reflected that he was very glad to have come to visit his old friend. He looked forward to a peaceful and rather dull stay in the country.

When Trenhaven had gone, Charles went to the library where he sat down at his desk and took a piece of writing paper from the drawer. Very excited at the visit of his old friend, he could hardly wait to inform Lucy.

Dipping his pen into the ink, Charles hesitated as he looked down at the blank sheet of paper. He knew that Trenhaven did not want his true identity known, but it was hard to keep such information from Lucy.

Charles debated with himself for a short time before deciding to do as his friend wished. He began to write to Lucy with the wonderful news that his dearest old school chum had arrived unexpectedly.

When Lucy and Serena returned from the village, they were in exceedingly good spirits. Serena thought the outing had been a great success. They had had great good fortune in seeing Mrs. Claybrook since she was the worst tattlemonger in the village. Serena knew very well that Mrs. Claybrook would lose no time in visiting the Osbornes.

It gave Serena a great deal of satisfaction to think of Mrs. Claybrook reporting their meeting at the milliner's shop to Arabella. Serena hoped that Arabella would be wondering about them. Maybe if they spread enough rumors about, Arabella would begin to have doubts about the state of the Blake family fortune. Serena was quite certain that if she did, she would abandon her pursuit of Mr. Blake very quickly.

Once back at Briarly, Serena and Lucy changed their clothes before meeting for tea in the drawing room. Now attired in a fashionable silk dress with purple and ivory stripes, Lucy felt much better.

Serena had likewise returned to her usual stylish attire. She wore a pale blue creation of jaconet muslin with a small ruff at the collar and long, loose sleeves. Serena walked across the room followed closely by Muggins. When she sat down on the sofa near the fireplace, the terrier lay down at her feet and promptly fell asleep.

"Poor Muggins," said Serena, looking down at the dog. "He is quite exhausted."

"I am exhausted as well," said Lucy, sitting down across from her sister. "Mrs. Bishop said that Papa will not join us for tea. He is at the vicarage playing chess."

"That appears to be safe enough," said Serena. "I doubt Arabella will call there. After all, her aunt, Mrs. Osborne, is still feuding with the vicar's wife."

"That is lucky," said Lucy.

"I am quite famished," said Serena, looking toward the door in hopes of seeing the servants enter with the tea things. Instead, a servant entered the room carrying a letter on a silver salver.

"Miss Blake, a messenger from Mainwaring Hall brought a letter for you." Taking the missive, Lucy eagerly opened it. "Thank you, George," she said. The footman nodded and left them.

"Another billet-doux, Luce?" said Serena. "I must say Charles is a reliable correspondent."

Lucy scarcely heard her sister's remark. "Oh, this is most interesting. An old school friend of Charles' has come to visit quite unexpectedly. Charles is so glad to see him. He says that we will like him very much. His name is William Macaulay." Lucy glanced up from the letter and directed a meaningful look at her sister. "He is a bachelor."

"How fortunate for him."

Lucy ignored this remark. "Charles says that Mr. Macaulay is one of his dearest friends. Perhaps you will like him. Perhaps you will fall in love."

"What a goosecap you are, Lucy," said Serena, very much amused. "Yes, I am sure I shall fall madly in love with Mr. Macaulay and he with me."

"It is not impossible," said Lucy absently as she continued reading to herself. "Oh dear."

"What is the matter, Lucy?"

"I fear that Mr. Macaulay is hardly for you, Serena."

Serena burst into laughter. "Now I am devastated. How could you raise my hopes only to dash them? Pray, what is wrong with Mr. Macaulay?"

"It appears he has a good many faults," said Lucy, looking up from the letter. "I shall read what Charles says. 'Although I love William very much, I am not blind to his imperfections. I regret to say that he is addicted to gaming and drink.' "

"Oh dear," said Serena, quite intrigued.

" 'He has squandered his fortune and has gone heavily into debt. And I fear it is my duty to say that his reputation as far as the fair sex is concerned is quite lamentable.' " Lucy frowned at her sister. "I find it very odd that Charles would have such a friend. He never mentioned him before."

"I daresay he did not wish to mention such a debauched fellow." Serena smiled. "I shall be eager to meet this Macaulay."

"Charles says that I should not hesitate to warn the other ladies that we know of Mr. Macaulay's unsuitability. He fears that Mr. Macaulay may be something of a fortune hunter."

"Indeed?" said Serena, a thoughtful expression on her face. "That has given me an idea."

"What sort of idea?" said Lucy, a bit worried at her sister's expression. She had not been very pleased with Serena's last idea about wearing old clothes and pretending to be poor. Lucy was afraid that her sister would come up with some other idea equally as bad.

"What if no one knows the truth about Macaulay? What if we say he is very rich? Perhaps Arabella Lindsay might divert her attentions from Papa to him?"

"But he is not rich."

"That does not signify. What if Arabella thinks him rich? Oh, I do hope he is handsome. That would help. Lucy, you must write to Charles at once." She rose abruptly. "I must fetch George," she said, hurrying from the room.

Lucy could only regard her in surprise. Then with a confused shrug, Lucy began to reread her letter. Serena returned to the room quite excited. "I had George go see if he could stop the messenger from Mainwaring Hall. We are in luck because he had not even started back yet. He is having a cup of tea in the servant's hall. It is Jem Walker, Cook's nephew. Anyway, he will wait until you have written to Charles."

"But what shall I write?"

"You must tell Charles that he is to say nothing further about Mr. Macaulay. He is to tell no one about him until we see him. Tell him it is vitally important! Tell him we will call at Mainwaring Hall tomorrow."

"But Charles had planned to call upon us here tomorrow."

"That would not do at all," said Serena. "Papa may be here when he calls. No, we will go to Mainwaring Hall. I have a plan. I believe we will be able to convince this Mr. Macaulay to help us."

Lucy was skeptical, but she made no protest. Instead, she rose from her chair to go and write the letter to Charles.

6

Trenhaven awakened early in the morning, much earlier than was his custom in town. Taking his pocket watch from the table beside the bed, he eyed the time. Noting that it was six-thirty, the marquess wondered when he had last wakened at such an outlandish hour.

His lordship looked around the bedchamber. It was a large room, well furnished and comfortable. The sun was streaming in through a wide gap in the draperies.

Rising from bed, Trenhaven went to the window to peer out at the grounds of Mainwaring Hall. It was a picturesque sight, rolling hills dotted with groves of trees. It had rained heavily throughout the night. Now the sky had cleared and the only evidence of the evening's storm were numerous puddles on the gravel lane and the wet and glistening grass. All was quiet save for the chirping of birds.

The marquess stared out at the pastoral scenery for a time, debating about returning to bed. Feeling rather restless, he decided to dress.

Leaving his room and going down the grand staircase, Trenhaven saw that the servants of Mainwaring Hall were hard at work. A number of footmen and parlor maids hurried about, going from one task to another.

One of the footmen noted the marquess as he reached the entry hall. "Good morning, sir."

"Good morning," returned his lordship.

The footman, a gangly youth of seventeen, made an awkward little bow. He had seen his master's friend arrive and had been very impressed. Mr. Macaulay was obviously a man of consequence. One could tell by the cut of his coat and the bang-up phaeton he had been driving. "Sir Charles has not yet risen, sir," said the youth. "Would you be needing anything? Shall I fetch Mr. Judd for you, sir?"

"That is not necessary. No, I am in need of nothing save my hat. I am going for a walk."

"I'll fetch your hat then, sir," said the footman, hastening off. He returned in a few moments with his lordship's fine beaver hat. "There are fine walks hereabouts, sir," he said, handing Trenhaven the hat. " 'Tis quite a pretty walk along the lane there toward Briarly. Very nice views, sir. Turn left at the road there and you'll have a fine walk indeed."

Trenhaven thanked the young man for his advice and started off. Walking down the gravel lane in front of the house, the marquess found himself thinking that it was a pleasant day. The air was cool and the sun was breaking out from behind the clouds.

His lordship did not spend much time in the country. He resided most of the year in London where he had his own town house. Even during the times when most of society left town for their country estates, Trenhaven lingered on until he was finally forced to travel to Haverford Castle for Christmas.

As he walked along that morning, however, the marquess wondered why he hated the country. After all, he had to admit that it was very pleasant there on the grounds of Mainwaring Hall. Continuing his walk, Trenhaven found himself reevaluating his well-known aversion to rural life. He thought that an estate like Mainwaring Hall would not be a bad thing in the least.

The marquess had no country home of his own and no desire to have one. He also avoided stays at Haverford Castle or any of the duke's homes when his father was in residence since they invariably quarreled.

Trenhaven strolled briskly along. When he came to the road, he turned left as the footman had suggested. Finding himself in unusually good spirits, the marquess proceeded in the direction of Briarly.

Serena rose from bed early in the morning, eager to greet the new day. The terrier Muggins, who slept on a rug at the side of her bed, jumped up and looked expectantly at his mistress. "Good morning, Muggs," she said, walking over to the window and peering out. "It appears to be a fine day. Don't you think it would be a splendid idea if we took Juno for a run this morning?"

Muggins cocked his head and regarded Serena with keen attention. She went over to the massive mahogany wardrobe that stood in her bedchamber. Opening the doors, she pulled out her riding habit. A splendid garment fashioned from crimson velvet, the habit was new and very fashionable. "I daresay I do not look very impoverished wearing this," said Serena, taking the dress from the wardrobe. "But I doubt anyone will see us, will they, Muggins?"

Muggins wagged his tail in reply as Serena's lady's maid entered the room. "You've risen early, miss."

"Good morning, Betty," said Serena, handing the riding habit to her servant. "I am going riding. It appears to be a fine day."

"Oh, yes, indeed, Miss Serena," replied the maid, setting about her duties.

Serena hummed cheerfully as she dressed. She had given a good deal of thought to her plan to enlist Charles and his friend Macaulay in helping them thwart Arabella Lindsay. The more she had thought about it, the better the idea seemed to her.

If only Macaulay were a dashing sort of fellow who might appeal to Arabella, Serena considered, it might be easy. From what she knew of Arabella, she was the sort of silly female who lost her head in the presence of a handsome man.

When she had finished dressing, Serena eyed herself in the mirror. "You look beautiful, Miss Serena," said Betty.

"Thank you, Betty," returned Serena with a smile. "Although you are a prejudiced observer. But I confess this color suits me well enough." She adjusted her hat slightly. It was a high-crowned creation with a short brim. "There, that will do."

"It is quite perfect, miss," said Betty, handing Serena her gloves.

Serena smiled again at the maid, and then she and Muggins left the room. Making her way downstairs, Serena went outside and across the grounds to the stables. There she was greeted by the servants at work grooming horses and cleaning tack.

"Good morning, Miss Serena," said one of the grooms, tipping his cap respectfully. "I'll fetch Juno for you, miss."

"Thank you, Roberts."

Serena walked through the stables, looking at the horses and addressing a few words to each of the servants. Since she adored horses, Serena loved nothing better than to linger about the stables. An accomplished horsewoman who knew as much about horses as most of the grooms, Serena was a favorite of the stablemen. Roberts, the head groom, was quite devoted to her. Having taught her to ride when she was a child, Roberts was very proud of his former pupil.

"Here she is, miss," said Roberts, leading a dappled gray mare to her.

"Good morning, dear Juno," said Serena, stroking the horse's forehead and then placing a kiss above her nose. "You appear in fine fettle, my girl." The horse murmured as if in reply. "I shall not be gone long, Roberts," said Serena as the groom assisted her up into the sidesaddle.

"Shall I accompany you, Miss Serena?"

"Oh, that is not necessary, Roberts. I shall not go far."

"Very good, miss."

Serena smiled at the groom. Then tapping the mare lightly with her riding crop, she was off with Muggins close at the heels of the spirited little mare.

Having walked some distance from Mainwaring Hall, Trenhaven found to his surprise that he was enjoying himself. The quiet country road afforded excellent views of the picturesque landscape. The weather was exceedingly good and the bright sun felt warm on his lordship's face.

The marquess was well aware that there was some irony in his enjoying a country walk. He had always thought such an occupation was frightfully dull. Indeed, in town, it seemed he was always in search of more and more stimulating diversions. Now, however, he was quite content to stroll down the peaceful road.

Continuing on, Trenhaven followed the road as it curved past a wooded area. Going past the trees, he espied a two-wheeled cart and horse on the road. As he neared it, it became clear to the marquess that the vehicle was in great difficulty. Leaning at a precarious angle, the cart was stuck in a hole, one of its wheels buried to the axel in mud. Its owner stood beside it, regarding the cart with a forlorn look.

"Good day," said the marquess as he approached the man, an elderly fellow in a farm laborer's smock and wide-brimmed hat. He was a small man, with a tanned wrinkled countenance and white hair.

"Oh, good day to you, sir," said the man, directing an inquiring gaze at his lordship. A local farmer, he was not accustomed to meeting strangers on the road, especially strangers dressed like Trenhaven.

"It looks like you have run into some trouble," said his lordship, looking at the cart.

" 'Tis my own fault, sir," said the man. "My eyes are not what they once were. I didn't see that hole, till I was in it. I was toppled clear off. I thank Providence I did not break my foolish neck. This part of the road was never so bad afore, sir. Now I'm stuck tight as you please."

Trenhaven nodded and then drew closer to assess the situation.

The wheel of the cart was so deep in the hole that the horse could not pull it free. "It will have to be lifted out," said the marquess.

"Aye, sir. I see that. I'll have to get some help."

"I daresay that I could do it with your assistance."

"Oh, nay, sir," said the farmer. " 'Tis hardly work for a gentleman."

"Nonsense," returned the marquess. "If you see to the horse, I shall lift up the wheel. When it is high enough, your horse will be able to move it."

"Nay, sir," returned the other man. "I could not ask you to do any such thing. Why, you'd ruin your fine coat."

"That is hardly an insurmountable problem," said the marquess, taking his coat off and tossing it into the cart. He took off his hat as well and placed it on top of the coat.

"Wait, a moment, sir," said the man as Trenhaven stepped toward the wheel. "I've a smock in the cart. I was just bringing it from Whitfield. My sister made it for me, sir. Why don't you put it on? Then you'll not dirty your fine shirt and waistcoat." He hurried to the back of the cart and pulled out a neatly folded garment.

"I assure you that is not necessary," said the marquess a trifle impatiently. "Do see to the horse and I shall lift the wheel."

"Do put on the smock, sir," said the farmer. "I should not forgive myself if you ruined your clothes on my account. 'Tis new, just made for me by my sister Meg."

"Oh, very well," said Trenhaven, taking the garment. As he slipped it over his head, a slight smile came to his lips. His friends in town would think it very amusing to see the Marquess of Trenhaven attired like a peasant in a farmer's smock. Now wearing the loose-fitting shirt, he looked at the old man. "All right now . . ."

"My name is Jenkins, sir."

"All right, Jenkins. At my signal, pull hard."

"Aye, sir."

Trenhaven reached down and grabbed hold of the wheel at the axel. He lifted up slowly. "Now, Jenkins!"

The horse lurched ahead, pulling the cart from the hole. Trenhaven, in his haste to stay clear of the wheel, jumped back. Losing his balance, he fell into the mud. "Damnation," he muttered.

"I am sorry, sir!" cried Jenkins. "Are you hurt?"

Rising to his feet, Trenhaven shook his head. "No, not in the least. A bit muddy perhaps, but otherwise unscathed."

"I cannot thank you enough, Mr. . . ."

"Macaulay," replied Trenhaven, rubbing his hands together to get the mud off them.

" 'Twas very good of you, Mr. Macaulay," said Jenkins. "I'll be bound that there are not many gentlemen who would have helped me like you did, sir."

"Nonsense," said Trenhaven.

"Oh, look, someone is coming," said Jenkins, gesturing in the direction Trenhaven had come. A curricle pulled by a bay horse was approaching. Jenkins frowned. " 'Tis Mr. Osborne."

The marquess noted from his frown that the elderly man did not much like the newcomer. He regarded Osborne and his curricle with some interest, noting with approval the good-looking bay mare that was pulling the vehicle.

Freddy Osborne pulled his vehicle to a stop in front of them. He looked from Jenkins to Trenhaven and then back at the elderly man. "What is going on, Jenkins? Why are you and your blasted cart blocking the road? Do get out of my way." Osborne pointed a finger at Trenhaven. "Move out of the way, fellow. I am in a hurry."

The marquess stared at Osborne in some surprise. It occurred to him that he had never been addressed in such a manner in all of his twenty-five years.

"Mr. Osborne," said Jenkins, "this gentleman helped me with my cart."

"Gentleman indeed?" said Osborne, eyeing Trenhaven's muddy farm laborer's smock. "Get out of my way at once!"

"I'll not move until you ask me to do so in a civil manner," said Trenhaven, directing a dark gaze at Osborne.

Osborne was somewhat taken aback by Trenhaven's belligerent tone and his speech, which had no trace of west country accent in it. He looked at Jenkins. "Who is this man?"

"It does not matter who I am," said his lordship testily. "You would do well to address anyone with courtesy if you claim to be a gentleman."

Osborne frowned at Trenhaven, but was suddenly diverted. Looking beyond Jenkins and the marquess, he appeared to forget them.

Turning to see what had so completely taken his adversary's attention, Trenhaven saw a gray horse and its rider approaching. " 'Tis Miss Serena," said Jenkins.

The marquess scarcely heard him, so intent was he upon Serena. Trenhaven had never been one to be unduly affected by feminine beauty. It was not that the marquess did not appreciate a pretty face, but he had always prided himself in being level-headed where women were concerned. When his friends and acquaintances had become enraptured over the charms of one lady or another, the marquess had always thought them ridiculous.

Now as he stood watching Serena come toward them, he could only stare at her, thinking that she was without a doubt the most striking woman he had ever seen. Riding with effortless grace, Serena sat regally in the saddle, her crimson riding habit molded to her excellent figure. Trenhaven took in Serena's lovely face, noting with approval her hazel eyes and the dark ringlets that peeked out from beneath her fashionable hat. There was a trace of a smile on her full, red lips and vibrant color in her cheeks.

Coming alongside Trenhaven, Serena pulled up Juno. She viewed the marquess with keen interest, wondering who he was. She knew virtually everyone in the surrounding area, all of the villagers and all of her father's tenants. Her eyes met his with a questioning look. What a handsome man, she said to herself, then chided herself for the thought. She was not some empty-headed schoolgirl who daydreamed about handsome strangers. Still, the man who stood there looking up at her with intense gray eyes oddly discomfitted her.

"Whatever is going on?" said Serena, directing a cool look at Osborne.

"Good morning, Serena," said Osborne, tipping his hat and smiling brightly. "It is nothing. These men were blocking my way. I asked them to move aside. And I must say that these two men were quite uncooperative. That fellow there"—he pointed at Trenhaven—"why, I've never met a more insolent person. I shall be certain to speak to your father about the manners of his tenants."

Serena looked at the marquess, with an expression that was a mixture of curiosity and amusement. Directing her attention once again to Osborne, she smiled. "Freddy, I fear this . . . gentleman is not one of my father's tenants so there is no point in bothering him about it. And, indeed, it appears to me that a driver of your skill could maneuver a curricle around Jenkins's cart with no difficulty at all." These words were spoken with obvious sarcasm. Serena continued. "I know you are in a hurry and I could not possibly wish to delay you even one moment longer. Do go on, Freddy. Good day to you."

Very much affronted by Serena's words and obvious disdain, Osborne nodded. "Good day to you, Serena." Striking his horse sharply with his whip, he pulled his curricle around them and drove on down the road at a fast trot.

"That is a fine horse," said Serena, frowning at Osborne's vehicle. "What a pity she is owned by him. I have never seen such an utterly hopeless hand at the ribbons. He'll ruin her within weeks."

"I don't doubt it," said Trenhaven. "The man is a fool."

Serena directed a curious look at the marquess. She was unaccustomed to men dressed in farmers' smocks speaking in such a way about their betters, but it was clear from the man's speech and demeanor that he was no simple farmer.

Muggins, who was normally very wary where strangers were concerned, seemed particularly interested in his lordship. Serena looked down at her dog in some surprise as he went directly up to Trenhaven. "There's a good fellow," said the marquess, reaching down to rub Muggins behind the ears. Muggins's tail wagged furiously. "Good lad," said Trenhaven. He looked up at Serena. "He is a fine dog."

"It seems you have a way with dogs, sir," said Serena, quite amazed at Muggins's uncharacteristic reaction. "I have never seen Muggins take to someone so quickly." Watching Trenhaven and the dog, Serena suddenly noticed his boots. He was wearing a pair of fine Hessians, which were not at all standard footwear among the rural populous.

"Mr. Macaulay is a very kind gentleman, Miss Serena," said Jenkins, entering the conversation. "He was walking along the road and stopped to help me."

"Your name is Macaulay?" said Serena, her eyes widening in surprise. So this was Charles's friend, the dissolute drunkard?

Trenhaven nodded. "Your servant, ma'am."

"I am Serena Blake."

"I am pleased to make your acquaintance," returned the marquess with a slight bow. So this lady was the sister of Charles's betrothed, he asked himself, the strong-willed lady Charles had described to him?

While Trenhaven and Serena regarded each other curiously, Jenkins stepped into the conversation. "Mr. Macaulay helped me, Miss Serena. My cart was stuck in that hole. He lifted it out. He is a kind gentleman and very strong." Jenkins reached into his cart and pulled out his lordship's coat. "Here is your coat, sir," he said. Looking up at Serena, he continued. "I had Mr. Macaulay put on the smock Meg made for me so his clothes would not get dirty."

Serena burst into laughter. "I fear, Mr. Macaulay, that Osborne took you for someone else. It is really quite funny." The marquess grinned, noting that Serena Blake had a delightful laugh. She continued. "My sister Lucy and I will be calling at Mainwaring Hall this afternoon."

"I shall look forward to that with great pleasure, Miss Serena," said Trenhaven, fastening his gray eyes on hers once again.

"I must be returning home," said Serena, strangely agitated by his lordship's gaze. "It was so good to meet you, sir. And, Mr. Jenkins, do be careful."

"Aye, miss," replied Jenkins.

"Good day," said Serena. Calling to Muggins, who seemed to be a bit reluctant to leave the marquess, she turned her horse and rode off.

"Miss Serena is a fine lady," said Jenkins. "As is Miss Lucy, her sister."

Trenhaven nodded absently as he watched Serena ease her horse into a canter and finally vanish beyond a grove of trees at the bend in the road. Pulling the farmer's smock over his head, he handed it to Jenkins, who exchanged it for his coat.

"I must thank you again for you help, sir," said Jenkins, fetching his lordship's hat.

"It was nothing, Jenkins," said Trenhaven.

The old man climbed up into his cart. After thanking the marquess once again, he set off down the road at a slow pace.

His lordship continued on toward Briarly for a time. As he walked along, he found himself thinking about Serena Blake. He realized very clearly that he had never met a woman before who had so affected him upon first meeting. There was something about her that seemed quite extraordinary. After a time, Trenhaven stopped and turned back to return to Mainwaring Hall, but he continued to think about Serena all the way there.

7

When she returned home, Serena was very eager to tell her sister that she had met Charles's friend. Still attired in her riding habit, Serena hurried to Lucy's sitting room where she found Lucy intent upon her embroidery.

"Lucy! You will never guess whom I met on my ride."

Lucy looked up from her needlework. "I cannot imagine, Serena. Whom did you meet at such an early hour?"

Serena sat down in a chair near Lucy. "I met Charles's friend Macaulay!"

"Wherever did you meet him?" said Lucy, very much surprised.

"I was riding Juno on the road to Mainwaring Hall. As I came around the curve by the big oak tree, I saw a cart and horse and Freddy Osborne's curricle. Old Mr. Jenkins was standing there with another man.

"Freddy was all red in the face. It seems the man beside Jenkins had been rude to him. It was Charles's friend Macaulay! What was so amusing was that Mr. Macaulay was wearing a smock exactly like Jenkins. One might have thought him a farmer, although upon closer inspection, it was clear he was a gentleman. Mr. Macaulay was wearing a very fine pair of boots, you see."

"That is very odd," said Lucy. "Why would Mr. Macaulay dress in such a manner?"

"He was helping poor old Jenkins with his cart. It was stuck in the mud. Jenkins did not wish him to ruin his clothes."

"What was Mr. Macaulay like?" said Lucy. "Charles made him sound quite dreadful."

"I hardly spoke to him long enough to know very much about him," returned Serena, "but one would never guess he had such serious defects of character. There is nothing in the least dissolute looking about him." She paused, a thoughtful expression on her face. "Muggins was very much taken with him."

"Muggins?"

"Indeed, it was very curious. You know that Muggins does not like strangers overmuch, but he acted as if this Macaulay was an old and dear friend."

"You always say that Muggins is a good judge of character."

Serena smiled. "Yes, I have always thought so. From Muggins's reaction, I might have concluded that Mr. Macaulay is a paragon, but Charles has said he is a drunkard and debauchee."

Lucy shook her head. "One can never know about a person from outward appearances. What did he look like?"

"Oh, I suppose one must describe him as handsome," said Serena with feigned indifference. "He is quite tall and he has dark hair."

"Then Arabella might be interested in him?"

"My dear Lucy, there is not a woman in all of Somerset who would not be interested in such a man, especially if he had a fortune."

Lucy regarded her sister with a shrewd look. "Perhaps Muggins was not the only one taken with Mr. Macaulay."

"Don't be ridiculous," said Serena.

Lucy laughed. "I was only quizzing you. I know that you are quite impervious to masculine charm." She smiled. "Or that is what you always claim. But I am very glad that Charles informed us of Mr. Macaulay's failings. What a dreadful thing it would be if you lost your heart to such a man."

"Yes," said Serena, thinking of Trenhaven's eyes fastened upon hers.

Lucy put her embroidery down. "I fancy that we should go down to breakfast. Papa is doubtlessly wondering where we are. You must hurry and change."

"Yes, you go on down. I shall be there in a short while. And Lucy . . ."

"Yes, Serena?"

"Do not say anything to Papa about my meeting Macaulay. I think it best we wait until after we see him at Mainwaring Hall today."

"Very well," said Lucy. "I shall say nothing about it."

Serena rose from her chair and made her way to her bedchamber where her maid Betty was waiting for her. When she had changed into a morning dress of pale green muslin, she hurried down to the dining room. Mr. Blake and Lucy were seated at the table with plates of food in front of them. "Good morning, my dear," said her father.

"Good morning, Father," said Serena, going to Mr. Blake and kissing him on the cheek. "I hope you slept well."

"Very well indeed," replied Mr. Blake. "Did you have a good ride?"

"Excellent. The weather is quite splendid. Juno was in fine form as always." Serena smiled brightly and then went to the sideboard to get some breakfast. She sat down next to her father and across from Lucy. "We are going to call at Mainwaring Hall this afternoon, Papa. Would you like to accompany us?" Serena looked expectantly at her father, knowing very well that he would decline.

"No, I have other plans for this afternoon," said Mr. Blake. "Do give Charles my best wishes."

"We will do so, Papa," said Lucy.

Mr. Blake took a forkful of kippers. "You must invite Charles to dinner on Wednesday."

"That would be wonderful, Papa," said Lucy. "I know he will be happy to come. He did say in a letter that he was having a houseguest, a friend from school."

"We would be happy to have any friend of Charles'," said Mr. Blake. "It will be a small party. I have taken care of the invitations save for Charles of course."

"You have, Papa?" said Serena in surprise. It was not her father's custom to invite people to dinner without consulting them. Serena knew at once why he had not done so. "Do tell us whom you have invited, Papa."

"The Claybrooks and Lady Desmond," said Mr. Blake, taking another bite of his food. "And Colonel and Mrs. Osborne and Freddy. And Mrs. Lindsay." Mr. Blake spoke Arabella's name with admirable aplomb.

Lucy directed a worried look at Serena, fearful that her younger sister would express the irritation she was undoubtedly feeling at this announcement. To her relief, Serena only smiled. "That sounds like a very pleasant evening, Papa. Lucy and I will discuss the menu with Cook."

"Yes, thank you, my dear," said Mr. Blake, very much relieved to have avoided a scene. He had expected Serena to make a fuss, knowing how she felt about Arabella. "We have not had many dinner parties here at Briarly lately."

"That is true," said Serena. "We must have many more. I so enjoy dinner parties especially with such dear friends."

Mr. Blake could not fail to detect the irony in his daughter's voice. "There will be twelve at table with Charles and his guest. Yes, that will be a good number."

"Indeed, yes," said Serena, not wanting to argue. "I am glad that you have issued the invitations. You must feel that you are free to invite whomever you wish. After all, you are master of Briarly."

Mr. Blake smiled. "I am gratified to see that you finally realize that, Serena."

Serena laughed. "Papa, you are quite horrid to say such a thing. You know that I defer to you in everything."

"Indeed, miss?" said Mr. Blake. "I was not aware of that, but I am very glad to be informed of it." They all laughed.

Mr. Blake looked fondly at Serena, happy to have such a pleasant breakfast with his daughters. It was a welcome change from recent mealtimes when Serena made no secret of her disapproval of Arabella. Mr. Blake found himself growing hopeful that perhaps Serena and Lucy were becoming more accepting of Arabella Lindsay.

The conversation turned to other topics and proceeded quite pleasantly. After breakfast, Mr. Blake retreated to the library while Serena and Lucy went to the drawing room.

"I am very proud of you, Serena," said Lucy, as they entered the room. "You did not argue with Papa about inviting Arabella."

"I have decided to cease arguing with him," said Serena. "It does no good. And why should I oppose Arabella coming to dinner? Indeed, her coming will further my plans."

"Your plans?"

"Why, to make her fasten her tentacles on another prey. Don't you see, Lucy? Mr. Macaulay will be there and all we have to do is allow her to think him very rich."

"It would be wonderful if it would work," said Lucy skeptically. "But what if she truly loves Papa?"

"Then I shall withdraw all objection to her," said Serena. "I am not averse to changing my opinion. If I am wrong about Arabella, I shall be very glad." She smiled. "And I shall also be very, very surprised."

Nodding, Lucy expressed a similar opinion.

When Trenhaven returned to Mainwaring Hall, he was greeted in the drawing room by a very surprised Charles. "I say, William, I was quite astonished to hear that you had gone out so early. Did you have a pleasant walk?"

"Very pleasant. It seems the country agrees with me."

"I am very glad to hear it. You must be devilish hungry. Will you have breakfast?"

"There is nothing I should like better, Charlie," said his lordship. The two friends walked to the dining room where the sideboard was laden with all manner of food.

"You have an excellent cook," said Trenhaven, piling his plate with a variety of dishes.

"Oh, yes, I am very fortunate," said Charles, spooning some deviled kidneys onto his plate.

After seating themselves at Charles's enormous dining room table, the two friends began to eat with relish. "I had a most interesting walk," said the marquess, cutting off the top of the boiled egg sitting in its fine china cup. "I met some interesting people."

Charles appeared surprised. "My dear fellow, whom would you meet at such an hour?"

"A Mr. Jenkins."

"Jenkins? Ah, yes, a good old man. He is one of Blake's tenants."

"And a Mr. Osborne."

"Freddy Osborne? What was he doing about so early in the morning?"

"Driving a very good-looking bay mare in a very inept fashion."

"That would be Freddy," said Charles. "I must confess that I never liked him much. Indeed, he is a detestable fellow. He wants to marry Serena Blake."

"He wants to marry her?" repeated Trenhaven.

"Oh, yes, but she thinks him odious."

"It did appear that way," said the marquess, digging his spoon into the egg.

"What do you mean, it appeared that way?"

"Why, I met Miss Serena Blake. She was riding a bang-up gray. She came upon me when I was engaged in discussion with Osborne and Jenkins. She has a very good dog."

"Muggins?" said Charles. "Good heavens! What a monstrous, vicious animal. He threatened to take my hand off one day. I should advise staying away from that brute if I were you."

Trenhaven smiled. Since childhood he had had a special way with dogs. He was very fond of them. "What utter nonsense, Charlie. Muggins behaved like a gentleman. I see you are not a good judge of dogs. Indeed, I do not know if you are a very good judge of women either."

"Whatever do you mean, William?"

"Why, from your description of Serena Blake, I expected her to be quite dreadful. She was charming. Why, had I met any girls like her in town, I might reconsider my aversion to marriage."

"Good God," said Charles, "you cannot be serious."

"I am perfectly serious. Indeed, Charlie, I have never felt such keen interest in a lady. I shall be glad of meeting her again. Fortunately, she and her sister will be calling here this afternoon."

"I know that," said Charles, regarding his friend with a perplexed expression. It was very unlike Trenhaven to express such great interest in a female. It seemed that Serena had affected him to a surprising degree. Charles thought suddenly of the letter he had written to Lucy the day before. "If you are serious about your interest in Serena, I fear I might have done you a great disservice, William."

"What do you mean?"

"Why, after you arrived, I wrote to Lucy, telling her my dear friend 'Macaulay' was here."

"And what is wrong with that?" said Trenhaven.

Charles grinned. "You see I described you to her in such a way that no reasonable female would ever be interested in you. You told me you wanted to be left alone while here at Mainwaring Hall. I told Lucy that you were a hopeless drunkard."

"Thank you very much, Charles."

The baronet laughed. "It was at your bequest I did so, William. And that is not the worst of it. I wrote that you were a gamester, hopelessly in debt. And that you were in search of a rich wife and that you had a deplorable reputation with the ladies. I daresay that if you wish to attract Miss Serena Blake, such a description as I gave you may seriously impair your ability to impress the lady."

"What a mutton-headed thing to do, Charlie," said the marquess, rather irked with his friend.

"My dear fellow, how was I to know that you might lose your head over someone you would meet here?"

"I have not lost my head in the least," returned Trenhaven.

"And to lose your head over Serena is not a good idea. You must accept my word on that. She is too strong-minded a female to give a man any peace at all. Indeed, I would not be your friend if I did not warn you against her."

"You are quite preposterous, Charlie."

"Indeed I am not," said Charles, laughing again. "Well, you will have ample opportunity to see that Lucy's sister is far too troublesome a female for any sensible man to wish to marry."

"It is not as though I am ready to make an offer for the lady," said Trenhaven, "but I am not certain I wish her to think me an unredeemable blackguard."

"But my dear William, I daresay women never think any man unredeemable. It is part of their nature. Indeed, I should not be surprised if a reputation such as the one I was giving you will make you irresistible." Smiling, Charles paused and took another bite of his breakfast. "Yes, if you are truly interested in Serena, I may have done you a service.

"And you cannot expect me to now inform Lucy and Serena that I was only joking about you," continued Charles, "and that you are in reality a wealthy, virtuous fellow, heir to a dukedom. What would Lucy think of me, playing such a prank on you?"

"Oh, I will not insist you change your story in the least. I shall remain a debt-ridden drunkard."

"Good," said Charles, taking up a piece of buttered toast. "After all, I daresay you will soon lost interest in Serena when you know her better. And you do wish to keep all the other predatory females in the county at bay."

Trenhaven nodded absently, but he found himself thinking that Charles was quite wrong. There was something about his brief meeting with Serena Blake that made him feel he would not lose interest very quickly. The marquess returned to his breakfast as Charles began to talk of other things.

8

When the carriage in which she and Lucy were riding pulled up in front of Mainwaring Hall, Serena was filled with a sense of eager anticipation. She had given a good deal of thought to the matter of Mr. Macaulay assisting them in her scheme to rescue her father from Arabella's clutches. If she could convince him to agree to her plan, Serena was certain that Macaulay would quickly cause Arabella to leave Mr. Blake in peace.

Lucy looked forward to meeting her fiancé's friend. Charles's description of Macaulay had certainly piqued her interest. There was something very exciting about the prospect of meeting such a disreputable person. Of course, what had been even more interesting to Lucy had been Serena's reaction to the man.

After being accustomed to her sister's indifference to every suitor who had called at Briarly, Lucy found it fascinating that Serena had apparently been so affected by a gentleman she had just met. It was a very great pity, considered Lucy, that Charles's friend was so totally unsuitable.

Lucy and Serena were greeted at the door by Charles's butler. "Sir Charles is expecting you, Miss Blake. He and Mr. Macaulay are in the drawing room. Do follow me."

"Thank you, Davis," replied Lucy. The two young ladies followed the servant to the drawing room where they found Charles and his houseguest.

"Miss Blake and Miss Serena Blake," announced Davis.

"Lucy!" cried Charles, leaping to his feet and hurrying to place a kiss on Lucy's cheek. "My darling!"

Trenhaven, who had risen hastily to his feet, looked at Lucy and Serena. Despite his interest in the future Lady Mainwaring, it was Serena who caught his lordship's attention.

Attired in a rose-colored pelisse trimmed with ivory satin ribbons, Serena looked splendid. The marquess found himself thinking she was even more attractive than he remembered. While some of the beauties of the London *ton* came closer to achieving

classical perfection, Trenhaven thought Serena had a vivacity that
outshone anyone he had ever met.

Serena smiled at Trenhaven, who looked very dashing standing
there in his magnificent coat, buff-colored pantaloons, and gleam-
ing Hessian boots. If Arabella did not fall immediately in love
with him, Serena found herself thinking, she was a great ninny.

"Lucy, I must introduce you to my dear friend, William. Miss
Lucy Blake, I have the honor to present . . . Mr. Macaulay.
William, this charming lady will soon make me the happiest fel-
low in the kingdom."

"Your servant, Miss Blake," returned the marquess, bowing
over Lucy's hand. "Charles has not been exaggerating in describing you as one of the loveliest ladies in England. He is a lucky
man."

Lucy blushed prettily. "You are too kind, sir," she said.

"Yes, I am a lucky fellow, aren't I," said Charles, very pleased
with his friend's reaction. He turned to Serena. "And I have been
told you have already made my friend's acquaintance."

"I have indeed," said Serena, offering her hand to Trenhaven,
who took it and bowed gravely.

"Let us all sit down," said Charles, ushering the ladies to the
sofa. He quickly seated himself next to Lucy while the marquess
sat down in an armchair across from them. "It is a splendid day. I
have arranged for tea in the garden later."

"Oh, Charles," said Lucy, placing her hand on his arm, "that
would be wonderful. It is such a fine day." She smiled across at
Trenhaven. "Have you ever seen such fine weather, Mr.
Macaulay?"

"Not in a very long time, Miss Blake," replied the marquess
pleasantly.

"Are you enjoying your stay at Mainwaring Hall, sir?" asked
Lucy.

"Very much so," replied Trenhaven. "It has been far too long
since I last saw Charles."

"Indeed," said the baronet. "For years I have begged him to
come, but he prefers town."

"You do not like the country, Mr. Macaulay?" said Serena.

"I did not think I did," said his lordship, fastening his gray eyes
upon Serena's extraordinary hazel ones, "although I suspect that
my visit here will change my feelings about the country, Miss
Serena."

"I do hope so," said Serena. "I adore the country. I am sure that town is all very well in its way. I confess I can hardly judge, having been in London so little."

"Yes," said Charles. "Mr. Blake thinks London a horrible place. He would allow neither Lucy nor Serena to have a London season." He paused to smile fondly at his betrothed. "I am very glad of that, for doubtlessly some London buck would have swept Lucy off her feet and I should be miserable."

"I would not have met anyone as wonderful as you, Charles," said Lucy, gazing sweetly at him. "I am so lucky."

"Now, now," said Serena, "If you two are going to sit billing and cooing like turtledoves, Mr. Macaulay and I will think you both empty-headed."

Charles laughed. "I fear Serena thinks me empty-headed at the best of times, William."

"That is not true, Mr. Macaulay," said Serena with a smile. "Charles can be altogether sensible upon rare occasions."

Everyone laughed. "You cannot expect a man in love to be sensible," said Charles.

"No, I suppose not," said Serena, thinking of her father. Certainly Mr. Blake was not acting sensibly where Arabella was concerned. Did he fancy himself in love? wondered Serena.

"Do tell us about London, Mr. Macaulay," said Lucy. "Charles said that you spend most of the year there. I expect that London society is very exciting."

Trenhaven shrugged. "I should not call society exciting, Miss Blake, although I warrant there are many who find it so."

"Well, if you do not find London society exciting, Mr. Macaulay," said Serena with a smile, "I fear you will find our society exceedingly dull."

"I don't believe I shall find anything of the kind, Miss Serena, if you ladies are examples of the sort of society one finds here in the country."

Serena raised one dark eyebrow slightly, while Lucy smiled delightedly. The elder of the Blake sisters thought Charles's friend was a very charming man. He was also undeniably handsome. It was very easy to see why Serena had been so impressed with him. "How kind you are, Mr. Macaulay," said Lucy. She turned to Charles. "Mr. Macaulay will have the opportunity to sample our local society. We are having a dinner party at Briarly on Wednesday."

"That is splendid," said Charles. "You will very much enjoy that, William."

"I know I shall," said Trenhaven, looking at Serena and thinking that her eyes were very lovely. He was very pleased at the prospect of dining at the home of such an intriguing lady.

"It will not be a very large party," said Serena. "It was Papa's idea. He invited Arabella, you see."

"Oh," said Charles, turning to Lucy.

"Yes, it is most unfortunate," replied Lucy.

Noting the somber expressions of the others, Trenhaven concluded that Arabella was a most unpopular person. "But who is this Arabella?" he asked.

"She is a fortune huntress," replied Serena matter-of-factly. "And she is intent upon marrying my father."

"Indeed?" said his lordship.

Serena nodded. "And she is scarcely older than Lucy and I. We are afraid that Papa wishes to marry her. I know that he will be miserable if he does so."

"The ladies are determined to save Mr. Blake from the fate of marrying Arabella," said Charles.

"Yes, we are," said Serena. "I am confident that we will succeed." She smiled at the marquess, who found himself thinking how splendid she looked.

"Well, why don't we go to the garden?" said Charles. "The day is too fine to stay indoors. We will have tea soon."

"I have not seen the garden for some time," said Serena, rising from the sofa. Lucy and the gentlemen rose as well. She smiled again at Trenhaven. "You know, Mr. Macaulay, the garden at Mainwaring Hall is quite exceptional."

"I am gratified to hear you say that," said Charles. He turned to the marquess. "Serena is really quite convinced that our garden is decidedly inferior to Briarly's. Whenever she visits, I find her giving advice to my gardener."

"Wheeler appreciates my suggestions," said Serena with a mischievous grin. "And I am glad to say that he has the good sense to implement them."

Charles laughed. "How could he not do as you say, Serena?" He looked at Trenhaven. "She bullies the poor fellow unmercifully whenever she is here."

"That is utter nonsense," said Serena with mock indignation. "I hardly think saying one should thin one's daylilies can be construed as bullying. Do not take what he says seriously, Mr. Macaulay. He is quite absurd."

Charles burst into laughter once again. "William never takes what I say seriously, Serena. Have no fear of that."

"That is very wise of you, Mr. Macaulay," said Serena, smiling at the marquess once again.

Trenhaven could only smile in return. Serena and Lucy made their way out to the garden, followed by the gentlemen. The gardens of Mainwaring Hall occupied several acres of land adjoining the house. They were dominated by a grand Italian fountain decorated with baroque sculptures of mermaids and King Neptune.

"What a splendid day," said Charles as they came out into the bright sunlight. A number of servants were busily setting up a table and chairs in the shade near the house.

"It is such a good idea to have tea outside," said Lucy, taking Charles's arm. "And the garden looks magnificent."

"Thank you, my dear," replied Charles, regarding her fondly. Wanting very badly to have some time alone with his fiancée, Charles looked over at Lucy's sister. "Tea will be ready soon, Serena. Why don't you show William the garden?"

"I should be more than happy to do that," said Serena.

The marquess could scarcely believe his good fortune at the idea of walking about the garden with Serena. "That would be very good of you," he said, offering her his arm.

"Mainwaring Hall's gardens are wonderful," said Serena as they walked along the path toward the fountain. "And I adore the fountain even though I do think King Neptune looks a trifle silly. See how he glowers at us. I fear he must have heard me."

Trenhaven eyed the fountain in some amusement. The sea god stood there, his trident raised in a fearsome pose. The expression on his face could most properly be described as a grimace. "I admit he does look a bit silly."

Serena looked up at the marquess, who was smiling at her. She felt a strange flutter of excitement pass through her. Cautioning herself to be sensible, Serena reminded herself that Mr. Macaulay, for all his obvious charm, was a drunkard and a scoundrel. It would not do for her to lose her heart to such a man. Yet Serena was very much aware that it was ironic that the first gentleman to truly interest her was so entirely unsuitable.

Serena felt it wise to return to the serious business of her father and Arabella. "Mr. Macaulay, there is something that I must discuss with you. It is a rather serious matter."

"A serious matter, Miss Serena?" replied the marquess, regarding her with a questioning gaze.

"You see, Mr. Macaulay, I have been very much occupied with how I might prevent my father from marrying Arabella Lindsay. I believe you can help me."

"I? I cannot imagine how I could be of any help, but I should be glad to offer my assistance."

"That is very good of you, Mr. Macaulay," said Serena. "I really think that you are the answer to my prayers."

"Indeed?" said his lordship, raising one eyebrow.

Serena smiled in some embarrassment. "You see, Arabella Lindsay is a very mercenary person. I have it on good authority that she is seeking a rich husband." While the marquess might have remarked that, in his experience, this was not in the least unusual, he wisely kept silent. Serena continued. "I am convinced that if another wealthy man were to come into Whitfield society, and if that man were to be younger and richer than my father, Arabella would abandon Papa very quickly."

Trenhaven listened to these words with keen interest, but he did not at once grasp Serena's intent. "That may be so, Miss Serena," he said.

"Oh, I know it would be the case," said Serena firmly. "That is why your coming to Mainwaring Hall is so fortuitous."

"My coming here?"

Serena nodded. "Why, yes. You see, I have in mind that you are the gentleman who can turn Arabella's attentions away from my father." She paused and then continued. "That is, if she is convinced that you are rich as Croesus."

"Indeed?" said the marquess, highly amused at what he considered a most unflattering remark. "So you believe I might appeal to this lady . . . if she thinks me rich enough?"

Realizing for the first time how her remark had sounded, Serena laughed. "I suppose that did not come out quite right. It is only that Arabella cares only for a man's fortune. I daresay a gentleman's other positive attributes would carry little weight with her."

"Then you do think I might have other positive attributes?" said the marquess with a hopeful smile.

Serena's eyes met his and she felt her pulse quicken. Why did he have to be so attractive? she asked herself. Admonishing herself to remember Mr. Macaulay's unfortunate defects of character, Serena replied seriously. "I fear, Mr. Macaulay, that I know the truth about you."

"The truth about me?" repeated the marquess.

Serena nodded. "Charles wrote to Lucy, explaining your circumstances. I know that you are hopelessly in debt, sir. I also know of your addictions to gaming and drink, Mr. Macaulay."

Serena regarded him with such solemnity that Trenhaven nearly burst into laughter.

"That blackguard, Charles," said his lordship with mock indignation. "How care he carry tales about me?"

"You cannot fault Charles for informing Lucy about you. A man should have no secrets from the lady he is to marry."

"I should hope a man might keep a few secrets from his intended bride," said the marquess. "What woman would marry him if he did not?"

"That may be true in some cases," replied Serena, directing a meaningful look at Trenhaven.

"It is clear that you think me a rogue, Miss Serena," said the marquess with a serious expression despite the fact that he was finding the conversation highly entertaining.

"Perhaps," returned Serena with a smile, "and that is why I believe you might be willing to assist us with Arabella Lindsay. If you will do so, I am prepared to pay you well."

"Indeed?" said his lordship. "So you will pay me to court this fortune huntress of your father's?"

Serena nodded. "It should not be difficult for you, Mr. Macaulay. Charles has said that you"—she paused—"that you have a good deal of experience with the ladies."

"Will Charles spare me no calumny?" cried Trenhaven, trying hard to keep a straight face. "So he has said I am a philanderer? You must think me a monster."

"It does not signify in the least what I think of you, Mr. Macaulay," said Serena sternly. "Now will you help me? Will you agree to pay your attentions to Arabella Lindsay?"

"I do not know," replied the marquess, using all his self-control to refrain from bursting into laughter. "She is not horse-faced or too skinny?"

Serena shook her head disgustedly. "I do not know why it should matter what she looks like. But Arabella is considered by many to be a great beauty."

"Ah, good," said Trenhaven, enjoying himself immensely. "I imagine I might be able to help you. But if I am not being too indelicate, may I inquire how much did you intend to pay me?"

Serena frowned, thinking Mr. Macaulay a bold fellow indeed. "I had not quite decided. I must discuss it with Lucy."

"And you do have this money? That is, you have money of your own?"

"Yes, I do," said Serena, regarding him with an exasperated look. "You need have no fear that you would not be paid."

"It is just that paying court to a lady is a very serious and difficult business. A man must exert himself a good deal. And, getting a woman to abandon your father, who is doubtless a charming and personable gentleman, may require a fair amount of work on my part. But, if we can come to an equitable arrangement regarding the price of my services, I shall do my very best, Miss Serena."

Serena regarded Trenhaven with disfavor. His voice had a bantering tone that seemed to indicate he regarded the matter in a rather flippant way. Still, if he would cooperate, Serena was sure that the problem of Arabella Lindsay would be quickly solved. "Good," said Serena. "I shall discuss the matter of financial remuneration with my sister and with Charles. But I daresay that charming Arabella will not be difficult. When she has heard the rumors about you that I shall set loose upon the parish, she will pursue you like a pack of hounds."

Trenhaven grinned, but before he could reply, he heard Charles calling to them that tea was being served. The marquess escorted Serena back to her sister and the baronet.

"Did you see the asters, Serena?" said Charles. "They are in full bloom."

"Indeed, I did not," said Serena, taking a seat beside her sister at the table. "Mr. Macaulay and I were speaking of other things. I fear we did not pay much attention to the garden."

"Yes," said Trenhaven, smiling at his friend. "Miss Serena and I had a very interesting conversation." The marquess sat down opposite Serena. "She has offered me employment."

"The devil, you say!" said Charles.

"Yes, and a dashed good job it is, Charlie. I am to pay court to the fair Arabella."

"What?" said the baronet, regarding his friend in some surprise.

"You see, Charles," said Serena, "I thought that Mr. Macaulay could charm Arabella and she would forget all about Papa. Of course, we would put the word about that he is very wealthy."

"Yes," said Trenhaven, grinning at his friend. "Miss Serena is sure that I would appeal to Arabella if she believes me to be as rich as a nabob."

"Then you will do it, Mr. Macaulay?" said Lucy.

"I believe I shall," said Trenhaven, "as a favor to you ladies."

Serena turned to her sister. "He will assist us, Lucy," said Serena, "if we can come to a decision regarding his fee."

"Oh," replied Lucy. "We did not discuss a fee. How much would be appropriate, Charles?"

"I have no idea," said the baronet eyeing his friend with an odd look. "Perhaps you might ask Mr. Macaulay what he thinks is fair."

"Very well," said Serena. "What do you think, Mr. Macaulay?"

Trenhaven looked thoughtful. "It is hard to say." Thoroughly enjoying himself, he suppressed a smile. "Perhaps five hundred pounds?"

"You must be joking," said Serena, regarding the marquess incredulously. "Five hundred pounds! That is utterly ridiculous! I should think fifty more to the mark."

"Fifty?" said Trenhaven. "Truly, madam, for fifty pounds I might be moderately civil to the lady. But I could hardly be irresistibly charming for less than two hundred and fifty."

"I am not certain that you could be irresistibly charming for a thousand," said Serena in considerable irritation. "Two hundred and fifty pounds is out of the question."

"Perhaps it is not a good idea anyway," said Lucy, who was quite uncomfortable with the conversation and found it disconcerting to hear her sister haggling like a fishwife.

Serena ignored her sister's remark. "I shall offer one hundred pounds," said Serena. "That is my final offer."

Trenhaven glanced over at Charles who was eyeing him with an amused look. "Very well, Miss Serena. I shall accept."

"Really, Serena," said Charles, his eyes sparkling with amusement, "are you certain this is a good idea?" He looked over at his friend. "After all, Arabella may not take a liking to William. Then you would have spent one hundred pounds without result. I recommend that you pay him only after he secures Arabella's affections."

"By heaven, Charlie," cried his lordship, "that is hardly fair. A gentleman might do his best and still have a lady reject him. Why, women are monstrously unreliable. They do not always act in a sensible fashion. Despite my best efforts, this Arabella might spurn my attentions.

"Really, Mr. Macaulay," said Serena, "I find that most unlikely."

"You do?" said the marquess, pleased at the implied compliment.

"Indeed," replied Serena. "I told you that we will inform Arabella that you are far richer than my father."

Charles burst into laughter, and Trenhaven directed an annoyed look at him. "Truly, Miss Serena, if I am to go to considerable effort on your behalf, I should think that I deserve to be paid in advance."

"I could not think of paying you until the job is done," said Serena firmly. "I feel that is fair."

"Very well. I see I must agree. Shall we shake hands on the bargain, Miss Serena?" said Trenhaven, extending his hand.

Serena offered her own with seeming reluctance. As her hand touched his, she experienced a peculiar feeling. Her hazel eyes met his gray ones for a moment and then, pulling her hand away, she looked down in momentary confusion.

"I think you will have a most interesting visit, William," said Charles, smiling at his lordship.

"Yes," said Trenhaven, smiling at Serena. "I believe I shall."

Lucy did not fail to note the way her fiancé's friend was regarding her sister. Picking up the teapot, she began to pour the tea.

9

Arabella Lindsay sat in the parlor of her aunt and uncle's home, listlessly thumbing through the pages of a fashion magazine. After a few moments, she tossed the periodical aside and gazed out the window.

Arabella was bored. Life in Whitfield was very tedious to someone who had lived in far more interesting places. Having resided in London, Brussels, and Antwerp, she considered herself a very cosmopolitan young lady. Whitfield was, in Arabella's view, a place of stultifying dullness.

As she stared out at the neat brick houses of the Osborne's neighbors, Arabella wondered how long she would be required to endure life in Whitfield. At least, she reflected, she had almost reached her goal. Soon she would be married to Augustus Blake and mistress of Briarly.

Not that she would spend much time at Briarly, Arabella told herself. The country house was charming in its old-fashioned way, but it was hardly a place where anyone would wish to live for very long. No, once she was married, Arabella would insist on living in town most of the year. She would tolerate Briarly for a few months, but London was where she really wanted to be.

Of course, Arabella knew very well that Mr. Blake abhorred the city. He had told her that often enough and she had always assured him that she adored Somerset and had no wish to go anywhere else. A faint smile crossed Arabella's lips. Mr. Blake was a very naive man, she considered. It would not be difficult to bend him to her will once she was married. After all, a young wife had many ways to influence a doting husband.

"Arabella, there you are."

Arabella tuned toward the doorway to see her cousin, Frederick. "Good afternoon, Freddy," she said with a smile. She was fond of her cousin. They had quickly become friends and allies when Arabella had come to stay with the Osbornes for they had much in common. Both shared an aversion to Whitfield and each was determined to find a wealthy spouse. Arabella, of course, was having considerably more success than her cousin.

Osborne sat gingerly down on the sofa for his tight-fitting pantaloons made sitting down a decidedly uncomfortable business. Manfully ignoring his discomfort, Osborne took out a silver snuff box, opened it, and took a pinch of snuff. Placing the tobacco into his nostril, he took a long sniff. "An excellent blend," he said, placing the snuff box in his pocket. "My friend Bellamy sent it from town. Good old Bellamy. He'd like me to come to London and stay with him."

"Why don't you?" said Arabella. "It is so wretchedly dull here. I would give anything for a fortnight in town."

"My dear girl," said Osborne, "Bellamy is as poor as a churchmouse. He already owes me twenty pounds and doubtless would put the touch on me for more. I can ill afford to visit him. And besides, I must stay and plan my assault upon the citadel of Miss Serena Blake. You must help me. Now that you have captured her dear papa, you can assist me in winning Serena."

"Good God, Freddy," said Arabella, "I cannot imagine why you want to marry that girl. I quite detest her."

"I have it on excellent authority that her settlement will be at least thirty thousand pounds," said Osborne languidly. "I cannot think how I could be anything but happy with money like that."

Coming over to sit down in a chair near him, Arabella nodded. "Still, I don't see how you will manage it. Serena is not in the least interested in marriage. And I believe that she likes you only slightly more than she likes me."

Osborne nodded gravely. "She is dashed difficult. I do admit that, but I shall not give up. After all, at the risk of sounding immodest, I must say that there are a good many ladies of my acquaintance who think me not unappealing. And Serena has no other suitors since she has driven them away. If I am patient I may have success with her."

Arabella did not look altogether convinced of this, but she only shrugged. "Well, I do wish you luck, Freddy. But do keep in mind that once I am married, I shall convince Blake to take a house in town. You will stay with us and doubtless meet all manner of heiresses. So it is certainly not the end of the world if Serena Blake refuses you. Indeed, I should think you better off without her.

"And was it not odd how she was acting at Mrs. Westcott's? I was very much surprised when Mrs. Claybrook told me that peculiar story. Imagine Serena saying she could not afford a hat!

Everyone knows that her father spoils both of them dreadfully. I daresay he can refuse them nothing."

Osborne nodded. Mrs. Claybrook had lost no time in informing the Osbornes and Arabella of her meeting with Serena and Lucy in the milliner's shop. That Serena had acted as if she could not afford a hat had seemed quite ludicrous. "Serena is a vexatious creature," said Osborne. "Perhaps I am a blockhead to pursue her. She was quite rude to me when I saw her this morning."

"Indeed? Do tell me what happened."

"I was driving down the road and I came upon some idiot farmer whose cart was blocking my way. This fellow, Jenkins is his name, is one of Blake's tenants. He was with another man, an impudent rascal whom Jenkins claimed was a gentleman. He was no gentleman, of that you can be sure. Serena appeared riding that gray horse of hers. She took Jenkins's part and virtually ordered me to be off. I was really quite offended."

"But not offended enough to abandon pursuit of her."

"Indeed not," said Osborne. "Why, she has been much ruder to me than that. One must not be thin-skinned in these matters."

Arabella laughed and her cousin smiled broadly.

After escorting Serena and Lucy to their carriage and bidding them farewell, Charles and Trenhaven stood watching the vehicle travel down the gravel drive. When the carriage was out of sight, the gentlemen remained for a time standing outside the house.

"I must say, William," said Charles, "that was a very interesting afternoon."

"Yes," said Trenhaven, smiling.

"Well, I'm not certain that I much like this masquerade of yours. When Lucy finds out who you really are, she'll be furious with me. I cannot even contemplate what Serena will do when she learns the truth."

Trenhaven laughed. "Did you see her face when I said I expected five hundred pounds to court this Arabella? It was really too funny."

"Yes, yes, it was all very amusing," said Charles, "but do you really intend to pay court to Arabella Lindsay?"

"Why not?" said his lordship. "I said I would do so. Miss Serena and I have made a bargain."

"But it is utterly ridiculous. Really, William, I think it would be best to tell the ladies the truth."

"Indeed not, Charles. I am enjoying myself far too much. I should like to remain William Macaulay, unprincipled rogue for the time being. And I should very much like to see a good deal more of Serena Blake."

"Surely you cannot be interested in Serena."

"I think her the most fascinating lady I have ever met."

"Good God!" said Charles, noting the expression on his friend's face.

"And is she not beautiful? Those eyes of hers are quite exquisite."

"You sound as if you had fallen in love with her," said Charles, regarding his friend with incredulity.

"Is that how I sound?" said the marquess.

"Indeed so," said Charles. "I find this extraordinary."

"So do I, Charlie," said Trenhaven, smiling again.

Charles directed a perplexed look at his friend and the two friends went into the house.

10

Mr. Blake happily approached the breakfast table where Serena was waiting with Muggins on the floor beside her. It was Tuesday, the day before the dinner party, and he was looking forward to the event and the prospect of seeing Arabella. Pleased that his daughters had seemed unusually cooperative about the upcoming dinner, he was in a cheerful mood.

Neither Lucy nor Serena had made the slightest fuss about the upcoming dinner party. In fact, both Serena and Lucy had worked with the cook, planning the menu. Mr. Blake had even overheard Serena discussing the table settings with the butler and she had sounded quite eager. He was now hopeful that his daughters were becoming more accepting of Arabella.

"Good morning, Papa." Serena, rising to greet her father with a kiss on the cheek.

"Good morning, my dear," said Mr. Blake. Noting the presence of Muggins the dog, he nodded at the creature. "Muggins appears in fine fettle."

"Oh, yes," said Serena, "he is quite chipper this morning. I promised him a long walk."

"You'll enjoy that, won't you, Muggins?" said Mr. Blake. Muggins only cocked his head and regarded his mistress's father with an inquiring look. "Be a good lad and I'll have a bit of sausage for you." Muggins licked his chops, causing Mr. Blake to grin delightedly.

"Good morning, Papa. Good morning, Serena." Lucy entered the dining room. Like her sister, she greeted their father with a kiss. "It is a fine day, is it not?"

"Yes, it is indeed, Lucy," said Mr. Blake, smiling fondly at both his daughters. The three of them made their way to the sideboard.

Once they were seated at the table, Mr. Blake smiled again as he cut into a fat sausage with his knife. Taking a piece, he tossed it to the terrier, who caught it neatly in his mouth and devoured it instantly. "That is a clever dog," said Mr. Blake. He then turned to Serena. "I must say I am very glad to see that you are both being so understanding about the dinner party."

"Understanding?" said Serena. "I am sure I do not know what you mean, Papa."

"I mean that I appreciate your not creating a fuss about Mrs. Lindsay coming."

"Why ever would we do that?" said Serena.

"Why, because I know that neither of you likes her."

"Oh, I would not say that," said Serena, hoping she sounded convincing. "Lucy and I have decided that we may have judged Arabella too hastily. If you are fond of her, we must not close our minds against her. Is that not so, Lucy?"

"Yes," said Lucy, nodding in agreement.

Mr. Blake smiled. "I must say that this pleases me very much. That you disliked Arabella was most distressing to me."

"You must forgive me, Papa, for being so horrid," said Serena, warming to the occasion and feeling as though she were an actress in a play. "I fear that I have behaved like a spoiled child. It is not the place of a daughter to prevent her father from achieving happiness. I realize that now."

"You cannot know how happy I am to hear you say that, Serena," said Mr. Blake, his voice filled with emotion.

"I am glad, Papa. And we will have a splendid dinner." She looked over at Lucy. "I know the guests will enjoy meeting Charles's friend, Mr. Macaulay."

"Yes," said Lucy, "he is a very charming gentleman."

"I shall be glad to meet him," said Mr. Blake. "He is an old school friend of Charles?"

"Yes," replied Lucy.

"And he is a bachelor?"

"Yes, Papa," said Lucy.

Mr. Blake looked at Serena. "And what did you think of him, Serena?"

"Good heavens, Papa, what does it signify what I think of Mr. Macaulay? Every time you hear about some bachelor passing through the county, you think him a prospective husband for me. Mr. Macaulay is not a disagreeable man. And he is not unattractive."

Mr. Blake found these remarks promising. "What are his circumstances? Is he a man of independent means?"

"Oh, he is quite wealthy," said Serena. "Charles says that he has at least ten thousand a year."

"Indeed?" said Mr. Blake, quite interested. "And he comes from a good family?"

"Oh, an ancient, well-respected family . . . in the north," said Serena, pleased at her ability to improvise. "I believe his family is from Northumberland and Mr. Macaulay will inherit a great estate one day from his father."

"A great estate?" said Mr. Blake. "Is his father a peer?"

"Oh, yes," said Serena, thinking it a very good idea for Mr. Macaulay to be the scion of a noble house. "He is the son of Lord"—she paused, searching for an appropriate name—"Lord Ravenswood. That was the name, was it not, Lucy?"

"Yes," said Lucy uncertainly. "Lord Ravenswood. I believe that is what Charles said."

"Yes, I think I am right. Baron Ravenswood. Yes, I'm sure that is correct."

"This Mr. Macaulay sounds like a very good catch indeed," said Mr. Blake. "I hope you were civil to him."

"Really, Papa, when am I not civil to anyone?" Mr. Blake raised his eyebrows at this comment but wisely chose to remain silent. Serena continued. "But I am not interested in a husband. And, Papa, you would not wish me to go off to Northumberland? Why I should never see you or Lucy."

"No, I would not like that," said Mr. Blake. "But I shall be most eager to meet this friend of Charles'."

"Oh, you will like him," said Lucy. "Everyone will."

"Well, it will be a most enjoyable evening I am sure," said Mr. Blake, returning to his sausages.

Serena smiled knowingly at her sister and began to eat her breakfast. She could not help but feel a little guilty at the idea of deceiving their father. He had looked so happy at the idea that his daughters might be accepting Arabella.

Taking a bite of a scone, Serena pondered the matter. If Arabella did abandon their father for Mr. Macaulay, Mr. Blake would probably be devastated. Still, thought Serena, it was better to be hurt now than humiliated later.

When they had finished breakfast, Lucy and Serena took their leave of Mr. Blake and retreated from the dining room with Muggins at their heels. Serena had decided that a walking expedition to Whitfield was in order. She was eager to go to the village so that she could tell everyone she met about Mr. Macaulay. She was particularly interested in preparing Arabella to meet this great prize of a bachelor.

"I shall be glad to walk to the village," said Lucy as they made their way upstairs to their rooms, "but first I must write a letter to Aunt Agatha. I could post it in the village."

"Very well. Let us leave here in an hour."

Lucy nodded. "Serena, I refuse to be seen in that old dress again. And I do hope you do not plan to wear that dreadful purple thing."

Serena laughed. "No, I promise I won't. But it would be best if you did not wear your new pelisse. Your green one will suffice. And I shall wear my saffron spencer. It is old but serviceable. We should not appear overly fashionable if there is a chance of meeting Arabella."

Although she thought her sister's idea rather silly, Lucy made no comment. She only nodded and vanished into her room.

Serena made her way to her own bedchamber where she rang for her maid. Muggins, who had followed her into the room, sat down on the rug beside the bed. "We will be going to the village, Muggins," she said. Muggins pricked up his ears and regarded her intently. "We must have Arabella learn all about Mr. Macaulay. You remember Mr. Macaulay, do you not? You fawned all over him in a most undignified fashion. Let us hope that Arabella will share your opinion of the gentleman."

Muggins only cocked his head. Serena frowned slightly. She was really not altogether pleased at the picture of Arabella throwing herself at Macaulay. She wondered what Charles's friend would think of Arabella. Certainly a good many men found her irresistible. It was not unlikely that Macaulay would find her very attractive. Serena frowned at the idea although she hastened to reassure herself that she did not care one fig what Macaulay thought of anyone.

Scarcely more than an hour later, Lucy and Serena, accompanied by a very excited Muggins, set off for Whitfield. It was another exceptionally fine day with bright sunshine and mild temperatures. "What glorious weather," said Serena, looking up at the fluffy white clouds that dotted the sky.

"Yes, it is," agreed Lucy. "I am glad we are going on a walk. I should hate to stay inside on such a day."

Serena nodded. "I do hope we meet Arabella in the village. I cannot wait to tell her about Macaulay."

Lucy glanced over at her sister as they walked along. "Did you not think it sufficient to say that Mr. Macaulay is a wealthy bachelor without having him inherit a peerage?"

"But it is a good idea, isn't it?" said Serena with a smile.

"Don't you think Arabella will like the idea of becoming a baroness?"

"Yes, but what will Mr. Macaulay say?"

"Oh, why would he care, Luce? He will have his one hundred pounds. That is all he is concerned with."

Lucy nodded. "He did seem rather unscrupulous. I must say I am surprised that he is a friend of Charles'. But he did not really look so dissolute, did he? I mean, he did not look like a drunkard."

"No," acknowledged Serena, "but appearances can be very misleading. I am very glad that Charles warned us about Macaulay. I would never had guessed the truth about him."

"And you might have fallen in love with him?" said Lucy, very much interested.

"I do hope I would have had more sense." Serena spoke these words with more confidence than she felt, for she was very much aware of the effect Macaulay had had on her when they had been together at Mainwaring Hall. Falling in love with such a man would be a very great folly indeed.

They continued on for a time, talking of Arabella and Macaulay and then of Charles. Lucy was always happy to talk about her fiancé and the impending wedding. She chattered on for a good distance, allowing Serena to interject a word now and again.

When they had gone halfway to the village, the sound of a man's voice calling to them made Lucy and Serena turn around. Two horsemen were coming rapidly toward them. "It is Charles and Mr. Macaulay!" cried Lucy, overjoyed at the idea of seeing her beloved once again.

Not expecting to see them, Serena regarded them in surprise. As the two men came closer, Serena noted with approval the expert way Trenhaven handled his horse. He looked exceptionally handsome seated atop one of Charles's best saddle horses, a fine coal-black gelding.

Pulling their horses up next to the ladies, both men dismounted. "My dear Lucy!" cried Charles, taking Lucy's hands in his.

"Oh, Charles!" said Lucy. Her adoring expression emboldened Charles enough to place a quick kiss on her lips.

The dog Muggins rushed up to Trenhaven, wagging his tail furiously. "Muggins, old fellow," said the marquess, reaching down to pat the eager terrier.

"Good God," said Charles, looking down at Muggins and his lordship. "Do take care, William. The brute may bite you."

"Don't be absurd," said the marquess, rubbing Muggins's ears.

"I'm dashed if I can understand it," said Charles. "Why, Serena, your dog appears to adore William."

"I had thought him a good judge of character," said Serena, meeting Trenhaven's gaze.

The marquess grinned. "He is a very intelligent animal to be sure."

"Well, he never liked me," said Charles, "and I shall be happy to stay away from him." Turning to Lucy, he smiled. "Your father said we would find you on the road to the village."

"You saw my father?" said Serena.

"Yes, we called at Briarly," said Charles. "Oh, I know it is not a fit time for paying calls, but we were out on a ride and where could we go but to Briarly? And I could hardly ride by without stopping. Your father seemed very pleased to see us. In fact it was he who insisted we go off to find you."

"Yes," said Trenhaven, speaking for the first time, "Mr. Blake urged us to join you and escort you to the village."

Lucy smiled. "I daresay my father was very pleased to hear about you, Mr. Macaulay. Serena sang your praises in such a fashion that I fear Papa thinks you an ideal suitor for my sister."

"Lucy!" cried Serena. "Don't speak nonsense."

"It is really very funny. This morning Serena was telling Papa all about you, Mr. Macaulay."

Trenhaven directed an amused look at Serena. "So you were singing my praises, Miss Serena? How kind of you."

"It was not actually you, Mr. Macaulay," said Serena. "Not the real you in any case. I was speaking of that fictional Mr. Macaulay, the exceedingly wealthy one."

"Yes," said Lucy, "and Serena said you were the son of a peer, and that you will inherit a great estate—in Northumbria."

Charles restrained himself from bursting into laughter. He raised his eyebrows at his friend and then grinned at Lucy. "That is very amusing, is it not, William? What an idea! That you are the son of a peer!"

"I do not find it so fanciful an idea," said his lordship with mock indignation. "Obviously Miss Serena thinks I have the look of a fellow who will inherit a great estate."

"I would not say that," said Serena severely, "but I thought it a good idea to say you will inherit a title. It will make you more appealing to Arabella."

"And you did not think I would be appealing enough to her?" said the marquess, casting an amused look at Serena.

"I cannot say," said Serena. "But there are few ladies who can resist the idea of marrying a lord. You must not forget that your father's name is Lord Ravenswood—Baron Ravenswood."

"Baron?" said Trenhaven. "You might have made him a viscount. Egad, if I am to be the heir of a peer, I should like a higher rank."

"Baron will do for you, Mr. Macaulay," said Serena, eyeing him with disfavor. "I apologize for not making you the heir to a dukedom." Charles could not contain himself but let out a whoop of laughter. "What is the matter, Charles?" said Serena.

"Nothing, Serena. It was just that the idea was quite ridiculous. William the heir to a dukedom!" Charles looked at his friend once again and started laughing again.

"I do not see what is so funny," said Serena. "Mr. Macaulay, you *will* remember that your father is Lord Ravenswood?"

"I shall endeavor to do so, madam," said Trenhaven. "However, I do hope that no one will be acquainted with the actual Lord Ravenswood."

"Oh, there is no such person," said Serena. "It was a name from a novel. It came into my mind."

"A novel?" said the marquess.

"Oh, it was an obscure work that I found in our library. I daresay no one has read it. Lord Ravenswood was a minor character"—she paused—"and a villain."

"No wonder the name came to mind," said Trenhaven, smiling at her. Serena smiled in return and his lordship found himself thinking what a dazzling smile she had. He thought she looked very pretty standing there in her bright yellow spencer worn over an ivory-colored dress. He did not fail to note that the tight-fitting short-waisted jacket accentuated her excellent bustline.

Meeting Trenhaven's amused gaze, Serena directed a mischievous grin at him. "Oh, I don't think you are nearly as villainous as Lord Ravenswood, Mr. Macaulay."

"I am relieved," returned the marquess.

"Well, I fear you are making a mistake, Serena," said Charles, "making up things about William to impress that woman. When Arabella finds out the truth, she'll be furious."

"By the time she learns the truth about Mr. Macaulay—if, indeed, she ever finds out about him—she will have long abandoned Papa," replied Serena. "Really, Charles, there is nothing at all to worry about." She glanced over at Trenhaven. "Except, of course, that Mr. Macaulay will be sufficiently charming to interest Arabella."

"In that case, madam," said the marquess with a broad smile, "you have no worries whatsoever."

Raising her eyebrows slightly at this remark, Serena smiled in return. "I do hope you are right, sir. Now, I do think we should be going. We intend to call on Arabella in the village. Since you gentlemen are accompanying us, it will be a good opportunity for Mr. Macaulay to meet her."

"I shall look forward to that with great pleasure," said Trenhaven. "Let us proceed to the village. My quarry awaits!"

Charles and Lucy seemed very amused by this remark, but Serena only raised her eyebrows once again at Trenhaven. She thought he was exhibiting a rather frivolous attitude about his assignment.

The four of them began walking along the road with the gentlemen leading the horses behind them. Muggins the dog appeared happy at the resumption of his exercise. He trotted ahead, pausing now and again to stop and look back as his human companions.

Serena found herself walking beside the marquess. Charles had offered his arm to Lucy and Serena's sister was leaning heavily on it. The two of them began talking together, seemingly oblivious to Serena and Trenhaven.

His lordship glanced over at his friend. "I daresay Charles and your sister have forgotten we exist. I am very happy for them. I wonder what it is like being so much in love?" Trenhaven looked over at Serena, who was rather taken aback by the question.

"I would think you would know more about that than I, Mr. Macaulay," she said.

"Then you have never been in love, Miss Serena?"

"Most assuredly not," replied Serena.

Trenhaven laughed. "Then you are a remarkable lady. I thought girls fell in love all the time. My sister Elizabeth is always falling in and out of love."

"Perhaps she will soon find the right man to marry."

"My dear Miss Serena," said Trenhaven with an amused look, "my sister has been married for years."

Serena regarded the marquess with a shocked look. "She is married?"

Trenhaven nodded. "Oh, yes, but then she does live in London."

"I imagine things are very different in town," said Serena.

The marquess laughed again. "I expect they are."

"And you have always lived in London, Mr. Macaulay?"

"Yes, most of the time."

"I see," said Serena thoughtfully. "But you have never been in love yourself?"

He shook his head although the thought occurred to him as he looked into Serena's hazel eyes that perhaps he was not quite telling the truth.

"But you never loved any of them?" said Serena, eyeing Trenhaven with keen interest.

"Any of them?" returned his lordship with a puzzled look.

"Any of the ladies." Serena paused awkwardly. "Charles led us to believe that you had had a good many . . . amours."

"Good God," muttered Trenhaven, "I daresay that is a topic that I am unaccustomed to discussing with young ladies such as yourself. I shall have to speak to Charles. One does not appreciate his friend saying he is some sort of debauchee. I assure you Charles was exaggerating. I am not one of the town's greatest rakehells."

"Then you are one of the minor rakehells, Mr. Macaulay?" said Serena with a smile.

"I shall pretend I did not hear that question, Miss Serena," said Trenhaven, smiling in return. "I think we had best change the subject."

"I fancy you are right, sir," said Serena. "Indeed, perhaps I should take this opportunity to tell you about Arabella. I do hope we will see her in Whitfield."

"So do I," said Trenhaven.

Serena frowned slightly, thinking he seemed overly eager. "It might help you to know what she is like."

"She is very beautiful, I am told," said Trenhaven, knowing very well the remark would irritate Serena. He tried not to laugh at her disgusted look.

"I suppose she is not ill-favored," said Serena. "And I do wish men would look beyond superficial beauty once in a while. My father is so blinded by Arabella's blue eyes and blond hair that he cannot think sensibly."

"While they are not the fashion in town, you know, I do think blue-eyed blondes very attractive," said Trenhaven, trying hard to appear solemn as Serena frowned at him. "But do tell me more about her."

Suspecting that he was trying to vex her, Serena frowned again. "Arabella Lindsay is a vain, selfish person whose only thought is ensnaring a rich husband. You will do well to flatter her outrageously."

"Then she is like every other woman I have met," said Trenhaven. "Flattery never fails. It should be the motto of every gentleman seeking a lady's heart."

"Not every lady," said Serena severely.

"You mean you do not enjoy being flattered, Miss Serena?"

"I know flummery when I hear it, sir."

"Then you do not like hearing that you have the most beautiful hazel eyes I have ever seen and that your smile is utterly devastating?"

"Really, Mr. Macaulay."

"I mean it," said Trenhaven, fixing his eyes on hers. "It is not mere flummery to say that you are as beautiful a girl as I have ever seen at any London ball."

Serena looked at him startled. Then turning away, she laughed. "I can see that you will do well with Arabella Lindsay. But there is no need to practice on me, Mr. Macaulay. It appears you are well versed in flattery."

The marquess was about to protest that he had very sincerely meant what he had said, but Charles chose that moment to finally recognize their existence. "What are you two talking about?" he said.

"I thought you had forgotten us, Charlie," said Trenhaven.

"I confess I nearly did so," said Charles, directing a fond gaze at Lucy, who blushed prettily. "But we are nearly at Whitfield. There, you see the houses ahead."

"Yes," said the marquess. He realized that he was a little disappointed that his walk with Serena was coming to a close.

"I wonder if we will see Mrs. Lindsay," said Lucy.

"Oh, I imagine she will see us and come out to investigate," said Serena as they continued to walk along. "If we do not see her, we will call at the Osborne's."

"Do you think it a proper time to call?" said Lucy dubiously.

"This is not the time to quibble over formalities," replied Serena. "And I am sure she will be most happy to meet Mr. Macaulay. I had best put Muggs on his lead. Come, Muggins."

Muggins obediently returned to his mistress. As Serena fastened the leash onto his collar, she noted that Muggins was looking up adoringly at the marquess.

When they arrived at the village, the gentlemen tied their horses to a hitching post and proceeded to escort the ladies along the row of shops that graced Whitfield's main street. "What do you think of the village, Mr. Macaulay?" said Lucy. "I daresay you must think it dreadfully small."

"I think it quite charming, Miss Blake," said Trenhaven amiably. He was in an exceedingly good mood and he was surprised that he did find the little settlement oddly appealing. It was a neat, prosperous village with pleasant houses and well-tended gardens.

"I am certain Mr. Macaulay finds Whitfield utterly provincial and dull after London," said Serena.

"Not in the least," returned his lordship. "Indeed, I can see why Charles finds it quite unnecessary to come to town."

"Do you, old fellow?" said Charles. He grinned at the ladies. "I daresay he has thought me crack-brained all these years for never venturing away from here. Why, William, you are a country man at heart."

"I'm not sure whether one might go quite that far," said Trenhaven. He cast a look at Serena. "But I must say that I find my visit here a good deal more interesting than staying in town."

"Good," said Charles. "Now what shall we do? Parade William in front of the Osborne house so that Arabella can see him?"

Lucy laughed. "Oh, Charles, you are quite ridiculous."

Serena came to a halt in front of one of the shops. "I promised Mrs. Bishop"—Serena turned to Trenhaven in explanation—"our housekeeper, that I would buy her some lavender water here at Mr. Cooper's. We should do that first."

Without waiting for comments, Serena walked into the shop with Muggins. The others followed. Cooper's shop was a very important establishment in Whitfield since it sold a wide assortment of items from toiletries to kitchenware. Small and cluttered, it was a great favorite of the ladies of the area.

Trenhaven looked about the shop with interest while Serena instructed a very solicitous Mr. Cooper to supply her with a bottle of lavender water. Quickly fetching the required item, Cooper smiled brightly at Serena, who was a great favorite of his.

"Fine day, Miss Serena."

"Indeed it is, Mr. Cooper," said Serena, opening her reticule to produce a coin to pay the shopkeeper. "We had a lovely walk from Briarly. Oh, I daresay you would like to meet Mr. Macaulay, who is staying with Sir Charles. Mr. Macaulay, may I present Mr. Cooper?"

Trenhaven nodded amiably. "Good day to you, Cooper," he said. While his lordship was not accustomed to being introduced to shopkeepers, he thought the idea pleasingly democratic.

"Very honored to meet you, sir," said the proprietor. It was very clear to Cooper from Trenhaven's dress and manner that he was a fine gentleman. He seemed a very amiable man as well, thought Cooper. Oftentimes gentlemen of quality were haughty and patronizing, but Mr. Macaulay seemed pleasant and affable.

Cooper eyed the marquess hopefully, wondering if he might be a man to interest Serena. Like most everyone in the village, Cooper took a keen interest in Serena's matrimonial prospects. Having known her since she was a little girl, the shopkeeper was very fond of Serena and hoped to see her marry well.

"Serena!" Lucy's voice made her sister turn around. Lucy, who was standing beside Charles looking out the window, gestured toward the street. "Why, there are Arabella and Freddy. What good luck!"

"Indeed!" said Serena, taking the bottle of lavender water and stuffing it into her reticule. "We must hurry off, Mr. Cooper. We are eager to see Mrs. Lindsay. Good day to you. Come, Muggins."

As Cooper watched his customers leave the shop, he wondered why Serena was eager to see Arabella Lindsay. Everyone knew that the two ladies detested each other. Since Arabella had come to live in Whitfield, she and her plan to win Mr. Blake had been the main topic of conversation in the village. It was common knowledge that Serena and her sister were adamantly opposed to the idea of having Arabella Lindsay for a stepmother. Going to the window, Cooper was very eager to watch the meeting.

Unaware of the interest she had generated in the shopkeeper, Serena hurried toward the retreating forms of Arabella and her cousin. Lucy and the gentlemen followed closely after her. "Arabella!" called Serena. Arabella and Osborne stopped and turned around. Serena waved as she walked briskly toward them. "Good morning," she said as she caught up with them.

"Good morning, Serena," said Arabella, regarding her in some surprise. It was certainly not unexpected to meet Serena and her sister in the village, but most times, Serena seemed to go out of her way to avoid speaking with her. Arabella noted Charles's presence with indifference, but she could not help but be interested in the handsome stranger who stood beside the baronet.

Freddy Osborne tried to hide his dismay at seeing Trenhaven, whom he immediately recognized as the man who had stood with Jenkins blocking his carriage. Osborne eyed his lordship's splendid coat, shiny Hessian boots, and the fashionable beaver hat he was wearing. He frowned.

"We saw you walk by while we were in Mr. Cooper's shop. I thought that we should endeavor to stop you since I was certain that you would be most eager to meet Mr. Macaulay." Serena nodded in Trenhaven's direction. "He is a dear friend of Sir Charles, who is visiting from London. Arabella, may I present Mr. William Macaulay? Mr. Macaulay, this is Mrs. Lindsay. And this gentleman is Mr. Frederick Osborne, Mrs. Lindsay's cousin."

"How do you do, Mr. Macaulay?" said Arabella, extending her hand.

"Your servant, ma'am," said the marquess, tipping his hat and bowing over Arabella's hand. He smiled at her. "I am so very pleased to meet you, Mrs. Lindsay." Trenhaven acknowledged Osborne with a cursory nod. "Sir."

Osborne nodded stiffly. "Mr. Macaulay."

"We will not delay you long," said Serena, shortening Muggins's leash so that he would not get too close to Osborne. Muggins clearly loathed Serena's would-be suitor, and Serena always worried that he would one day bite him. "I thought that it would be good to introduce you since we will all be at dinner tomorrow evening."

"I am so looking forward to it," said Arabella, batting her long eyelashes at Trenhaven. He was a fine-looking man, she thought, clearly a man of fashion and sophistication.

"And I look forward to the dinner at Briarly even more now that I have met you, Mrs. Lindsay," said his lordship.

Arabella smiled in reply and directed what Serena thought was a flirtatious look at Trenhaven. Although one might have thought Serena would be pleased at the obvious effect Mr. Macaulay was having on Arabella, she felt strangely annoyed. Glancing over at his lordship, Serena noted that he appeared very clearly impressed with Arabella's charms.

"Is this your first visit to the area, Mr. Macaulay?" said Arabella.

"Yes, it is."

"I imagine you find Whitfield dreadfully provincial."

"Well, one must make allowances," said Trenhaven. "After all, a small village cannot be like London." Casting a condescending look toward the shops, he shrugged. "I imagine it does have its charms."

Serena looked over at the marquess, irritated by his comments. Arabella appeared delighted. "Perhaps you are right, sir, but Whitfield's charms have thus far eluded me. I have only recently come to live here. After living in Brussels and London, it is a very great change, I assure you."

"I daresay Whitfield society has been greatly improved by your arrival, ma'am," said his lordship.

"You are too kind, Mr. Macaulay," returned Arabella.

Serena found herself even more annoyed by this exchange. "Well, you must excuse us, Arabella and Freddy. We must be getting back to Briarly. We do look forward to seeing you tomorrow. Good day."

Taking Trenhaven's arm, she led him away with Lucy and Charles following closely behind. When they had put sufficient distance between them and Arabella and Osborne, Lucy was eager to speak. "I believe Arabella likes Mr. Macaulay already. Perhaps this idea will work."

"And she is not yet aware of my impressive fortune and the barony I shall inherit," said Trenhaven, glancing over at Serena. "I daresay the one hundred pounds is as good as mine already."

Serena frowned up at him. "Did you not think you were doing it a bit too brown, Mr. Macaulay? 'Whitfield society has been greatly improved by your arrival' indeed."

"You said I was to flatter her, Miss Serena. I thought I was very good. I must say I did not know I had such a talent for play-acting."

"Playacting?" said Serena. "Is that what you were doing?"

"Yes, of course. But I must say I found Mrs. Lindsay very charming."

"Did you?" said Serena, frowning at him.

"Why yes. Oh, I know you dislike her and Charles has called her a female shark, but I was most favorably impressed with the lady." He smiled at Serena. "And she is very attractive." This remark elicited a scowl from Serena much to Trenhaven's amusement. "Is something wrong? I thought you would be pleased."

"I am pleased," said Serena, hoping she sounded convincing. Indeed, she should have been very happy to see how easy it was going to be for Mr. Macaulay to divert Arabella's attentions from her father.

"Well, I think Mr. Macaulay has made an excellent start," said Lucy.

"Yes," said Charles, regarding his friend with an amused look.

Serena made no further comment as they continued on to retrieve the gentlemen's horses. As they walked down the street, Arabella and Osborne stood watching them. "What an extraordinarily handsome man," said Arabella.

"That fellow Macaulay?" said Osborne. "I see nothing out of the ordinary about him."

"Then you are blind, my dear cousin," returned Arabella. She looked thoughtful. "He was very well dressed. I should like to know more about him."

"I'm not even certain he is a gentleman," said Osborne. "That was the man who was with Jenkins on the road, the one who was so insolent to me."

"Not a gentleman? Don't be ridiculous. He is a friend of Sir Charles Mainwaring. What else would he be?"

"I cannot say. I never liked Mainwaring and I most assuredly do not like his friend. Dashed bad luck his coming to dinner at Briarly. I shall hardly have a chance to speak to Serena."

"She seemed very taken with him, don't you think?"

"What?" said Osborne, regarding Arabella in surprise. "Taken with Macaulay?"

"It appeared so to me. Did you see how unhappy she looked when he complimented me? My dear, she was jealous."

"You are imagining things, Arabella."

"Oh, I don't think so."

"Damnation," muttered Osborne. "Why did the blasted fellow have to come here?"

"Well, I find this all very interesting. I can scarcely wait until the dinner party tomorrow evening. I shall be very glad to see Mr. Macaulay again. And if I am not mistaken, the gentleman has a similar opinion about seeing me."

"Good heavens, Arabella. You had best take care. I shall advise you to keep your distance from Macaulay. I doubt Blake will enjoy seeing you flirt with him."

"That is all the more reason that I should. Blake is very slow in making an offer for me. Perhaps making him jealous would be a good idea. But do not worry about me. I'll not lose Blake." Arabella paused and smiled. "Unless I want to lose him. Come, let us go call on Mrs. Claybrook. Perhaps she has heard something about Macaulay."

Although Osborne thought his cousin's interest in Macaulay most unfortunate, he could only nod and accompany Arabella to Mrs. Claybrook's home.

11

Dressed and ready for the dinner party, Serena sat at her dressing table contemplating her reflection. She had to admit that she was pleased with her maid Betty's efforts. That worthy servant had done an admirable job of arranging Serena's raven hair into ringlets that framed her face with her back hair pulled into a knot atop her head. Dainty white flowers and tiny satin bows ornamented her elegant coiffure.

As she studied her face absently in the glass, Serena thought of Trenhaven. On the way home from Whitfield, he had walked beside her. Although she had first been a bit put out with him for his overly enthusiastic response to Arabella, Serena had not remained annoyed for long.

While Lucy and Charles had held their own conversation, Serena and the marquess had talked of many things. She had been interested to find that he had met the Prince Regent on many occasions and that he loved the theater. He had discovered that she adored books and horses and rode to the hounds even though her father disapproved. They spent a good deal of time discussing Muggins's many talents as well as other remarkable dogs of their acquaintance. In short, the distance from Whitfield to Briarly had seemed very short indeed.

Fearing that she was growing dangerously fond of Mr. Macaulay, Serena rested her head on her hands and sighed. She knew that she was acting like a silly schoolgirl for, after all, he was completely unsuitable. Indeed, Serena reminded herself, according to Charles's letter, she could scarcely choose a more unacceptable man.

"Serena?" Serena turned away from the mirror to see her sister enter the dressing room. "Is something the matter?" said Lucy.

"No, Lucy. I was just waiting for you. My, you look lovely." Lucy was wearing a stunning gown of pale blue satin trimmed with lace.

"Do you think so?" said Lucy uncertainly. "I have worn this

dress a good many times. I know you wanted us to wear gowns that Arabella had seen before, but I do wish I could have worn the new pink crepe."

"You will have plenty of opportunity to wear it, Luce. I think it best that we continue to try to show Arabella that Papa does not squander his money on the fripperies of fashion." She stood up from the dressing table. "You see what I am wearing, my old Italian silk. Arabella has seen it several times. She'll think I own nothing else."

"But it is beautiful, Serena," said Lucy. "I have always loved that dress."

Serena smiled. She loved the gown as well. It was a splendid creation of white silk with a very low-cut bodice and dainty puff sleeves. The skirt of the dress was festooned with tiny silk roses. "Yes, it is a favorite of mine, I must admit."

"And Mr. Macaulay has not seen it."

Serena frowned at her sister. "What does that signify? I am not concerned what Mr. Macaulay thinks of me in the least."

"But I thought you liked him, Serena. Indeed, Charles commented that you and Mr. Macaulay seemed to find each other's company very agreeable."

"Did he indeed?" said Serena. "Well, Charles should know better than anyone why I must not find Mr. Macaulay so agreeable."

"I know," replied Lucy. "But it is such a great pity. He is so charming and so handsome. But he would not do for your husband. As Mrs. Bishop says, excessive drink is the ruination of a man. And the fact that he has no money is a very great problem. Of course, that might be overlooked if Mr. Macaulay were a respectable gentleman not addicted to gambling and drink. Yes, it is a very great pity."

Serena nodded. "Yes, it is."

"I do hope you have not fallen in love with him already, Serena."

"Don't be a ninnyhammer, Lucy. Of course, I haven't fallen in love with him. What a ridiculous idea." Serena hoped that she said these words convincingly for, in truth, she suspected that she had indeed fallen in love. She would, of course, have to overcome such an unacceptable attachment. After all, one could never think of marrying such a man.

"I imagine we should think of going downstairs. The guests should be arriving soon." Lucy frowned. "Papa is so excited. I cannot help but feel a bit guilty about what we are doing. He does seem to be very fond of Arabella."

"He has lost his senses, Lucy," said Serena firmly. "That horrible woman has him in thrall. Yes, he will be hurt, but we are only thinking of him. Do not forget how much worse it will be when she breaks his heart when they are married."

Lucy nodded, hoping her sister was right. Serena took up her gloves and fan and the two young ladies left the dressing room.

A good deal of care had gone into the arrangements for the dinner party that evening. The servants had worked tirelessly, cleaning every inch of the house, polishing silver, and making the dining room ready. The house was filled with flowers gathered from Briarly's famed gardens and arranged by Serena, Lucy, and Mrs. Bishop.

The young ladies had scarcely joined their father in the drawing room when the first of the guests arrived. The Rev. Mr. Woodbury and his wife were warmly greeted by Serena and Lucy. They were accompanied by Lady Desmond, a diminutive, elderly lady who was the widow of an impoverished knight. Lady Desmond lived simply in a small house in the village, but she was unfailingly cheerful and good-natured.

Next to arrive were the Osbornes. Serena did not fail to note her father's obvious excitement as Arabella entered the drawing room on her cousin Freddy's arm. Even Serena could not deny that Arabella looked stunning dressed in her gown of apricot satin. Her splendid blond hair was elegantly coiffed and adorned with apricot silk flowers.

Serena looked over at her father who was regarding Arabella with a worshipful expression. While he greeted Osborne and Colonel and Mrs. Osborne, Mr. Blake could scarcely keep his eyes off Arabella. "You look very beautiful, Mrs. Lindsay," said Mr. Blake, affixing a look of lovesick adoration upon Arabella.

"You are too kind, Mr. Blake," said Arabella, smiling warmly at the master of Briarly. She extended her gloved hand and Serena's father took it eagerly. "It is such a great pleasure to see you again, sir," she said in a throaty whisper.

While one might have expected that Serena would have been disgusted with Arabella's greeting, she regarded her adversary with admirable equanimity. After all, if things went well, it would not be long until Arabella abandoned Mr. Blake, thought Serena.

At that moment the butler announced two additional guests, Mr. and Mrs. Claybrook. Mr. Claybrook was a well-to-do man of property. An exceedingly gregarious person, Mr. Claybrook looked very pleased to be at Briarly. He greeted his host and hostesses enthusiastically. Mrs. Claybrook, who was looking forward to the evening with eager anticipation, smiled and nodded to everyone.

Serena addressed polite words of welcome to the Claybrooks. She did not like Mrs. Claybrook very much since that lady was, in Serena's view, too fond of gossip. Also, Serena considered Mrs. Claybrook an ally of Arabella's since she was such an intimate friend of Arabella's aunt, Mrs. Osborne.

"Sir Charles Mainwaring and Mr. Macaulay," intoned the butler, interrupting the small talk Serena was exchanging with Mrs. Claybrook.

Serena turned toward the door. There was Trenhaven standing beside Charles. It took considerable self-control on Serena's part to appear indifferent to the new arrival. The marquess looked very handsome, dressed in his fine evening clothes. His claret-colored coat fit his tall, broad-shouldered frame to perfection. He wore champagne-colored knee breeches and silk stockings that revealed his muscular calves. His lordship's cravat was tied with admirable skill in the modish oriental style. In short, Trenhaven was a vision of sartorial splendor as grand as Beau Brummell himself.

This fact was not lost upon the assembled guests who eyed Trenhaven with fascination. One did not expect to find pinks of the *ton* appearing in country drawing rooms, at least not in country drawing rooms that the Briarly guests usually frequented.

Arabella smiled at Trenhaven. She had thought him an extraordinarily handsome man when she had met him in the village, but he seemed even more attractive standing there in his finery. Arabella was dying to know more about him. She had been very disappointed to find that Mrs. Claybrook hadn't heard anything except that Macaulay was staying at Mainwaring Hall. He certainly appeared to be a gentleman of means, thought Arabella, studying the marquess with unabashed interest.

Trenhaven and Charles came forward to greet their host and his daughters. "Good evening to you, Mr. Blake," said Charles. He looked at Lucy. "My dear Lucy, you look as lovely as a princess."

"Oh, Charles," said Lucy, blushing charmingly.

"Good evening, Charles," said Serena. She looked up at the marquess. "Good evening, Mr. Macaulay."

"Good evening, Miss Serena." Trenhaven smiled at her, thinking she looked beautiful in her white evening gown. The marquess's eyes traveled from Serena's hazel eyes and rosy lips down her elegant neck until they rested on the admirable cleavage revealed by her low-cut bodice.

Reddening under his scrutiny, Serena thought Mr. Macaulay a very bold fellow indeed. "Do allow you me to introduce you to the other guests, Mr. Macaulay," she said.

"That is very kind of you, Miss Serena," said Trenhaven, somewhat reluctantly taking his eyes from Serena's breasts to once again focus on her remarkable hazel eyes.

Serena ushered the marquess toward the other guests. Everyone in attendance was very pleased at meeting such an impressive looking young man. Even the vicar's wife, who normally a very dour, humorless woman, smiled brightly when Trenhaven bowed over her hand and commented that he had not expected to find so many charming ladies assembled under one roof.

Arabella watched Trenhaven travel about the room, talking to all the guests. Since Mr. Blake was monopolizing her attention, she had no opportunity to speak with the fascinating newcomer.

Glancing from Mr. Blake to Mr. Macaulay, Arabella was suddenly discontented. Mr. Blake was a bore, she found herself thinking. She scarcely listened as Serena's father talked in an animated fashion. Smiling with a fixed, frozen expression, she nodded occasionally whenever there was a pause in the conversation.

Watching Trenhaven as he walked about the room with Serena, Arabella determined that her prospective daughter-in-law had clearly set her cap for Mr. Macaulay. The idea of Serena capturing such an obvious prize did not please Arabella in the least. She wondered about his fortune. He certainly looked wealthy enough although Arabella knew as well as anyone how appearances could be deceiving. After all, she had been deceiving people about her own circumstances for a good many years.

When dinner was announced, the assembled guests and the Blakes made their way to the dining room where they eagerly took their seats. Arabella could scarcely believe her good fortune in finding that Trenhaven was seated beside her. On her right was Mr. Blake, who sat at the head of the table, beaming at his guests like a benevolent monarch.

Serena, who had carefully worked out the seating arrangements, noted that Arabella smiled brightly at Trenhaven as the footman assisted her with her chair. It seemed, thought Serena, that Arabella was already growing quite interested in Mr. Macaulay.

Seated diagonally across the table from the marquess, Serena had a good view of his lordship and Arabella. She had placed

Freddy Osborne safely on the other side of the table a good distance away so that he would have no opportunity to spoil her dinner.

Serena had positioned herself between the Rev. Mr. Woodbury and Colonel Osborne, amiable gentlemen who never lacked for conversation. Of course, the colonel's discourse oftentimes turned to relating his experiences in the Peninsular War, a topic that little interested Serena. Despite that, Serena was glad to be sitting beside Arabella's uncle as it would allow her to speak to him about Macaulay. The colonel would certainly relate anything she said to Arabella and later to the entire community.

While dinner parties at Briarly were not frequent, most of the guests were well aware that no one kept a better table than Augustus Blake. Briarly's cook was reknowned in Somerset for her talents. From the time that the footmen served the first course, it was apparent that her reputation was well deserved.

The fortunate guests would proceed from pea soup to veal and pigeon pie. They would then sample pork cutlets, roasted turkey, and leg of lamb. Also on the menu were casserole of rice, turnips, stewed carrots, calf's-foot jelly, a trifle, almond pudding, cherry tarts, and Cook's famous apple cake. In short, there was very little chance of anyone going home hungry.

Most appreciative of the fine dinner they were eating, the guests appeared in the best of moods, all save Osborne. Positioned near the foot of the table between Lucy and Mrs. Woodbury, he scowled into his plate. He was too far from Serena to exchange a word with her. Mrs. Woodbury preferred her own company, only deigning to speak when asked a direct question. Since such questions usually elicited only a word or two in response, Osborne felt it hardly worth the effort to attempt conversation.

Lucy, who sat on Osborne's other side, was so immersed in conversation with Charles that she quite forgot her duties as hostess and ignored Freddy. Very much put out by Lucy's lapse of good manners, Osborne could only eat his food in grim silence while watching Serena enjoy herself.

While putting on an admirable appearance of having a wonderful time, Serena was, in actuality, not altogether happy with the evening. Trenhaven was apparently relishing his job of charming Arabella. Serena watched him smile and laugh and even lean over and whisper something in her ear. Arabella seemed to think Trenhaven the wittiest, most fascinating man she had ever met.

Fortunately for Mr. Blake, his attention was taken by Lady

Desmond. Seated at his right, that lady discoursed on a wide variety of subjects, keeping Mr. Blake from having the chance to talk to Arabella. Serena noted that her father was not completely unaware of his beloved Arabella's interest in Mr. Macaulay. She caught Mr. Blake directing a somewhat disapproving glance in his direction as Arabella erupted in gales of laughter.

"I must say, Mr. Macaulay appears to be a charming gentleman," said Colonel Osborne, turning to Serena.

"Oh, yes, he is very charming," said Serena, taking a forkful of pigeon pie.

"I am told he is a good friend of Sir Charles'."

"Yes," replied Serena, happy that Colonel Osborne had brought up the subject. Knowing very well that whatever she told the colonel would be quickly repeated to his wife and niece, she smiled. "They were at Eton together."

"And I believe that Mr. Macaulay is an unmarried gentleman?" said Colonel Claybrook.

"Yes," returned Serena. "He is a bachelor."

Hearing that exchange, the vicar entered the conversation. "He appears to be a very pleasant young man. From his appearance one might surmise that he has a respectable income."

"Oh, indeed," replied Serena. "Sir Charles told us that Mr. Macaulay is a very fortunate gentleman. He will inherit a barony and an enormous fortune for he is the only son of Lord Ravenswood."

"Lord Ravenswood?" said the colonel. "I have not heard the name before."

"They say Lord Ravenswood is as rich as Croesus," said Serena, noting Colonel Osborne's fascinated expression. "His estates are in Northumberland. Of course, Mr. Macaulay has his own fortune inherited from a great-uncle."

"It appears that Providence has been very kind to Mr. Macaulay," said the vicar. He smiled at Serena. "Perhaps you should set your cap for him, Serena. You could do far worse."

"Oh, Vicar," said Serena with a smile. "Mr. Macaulay is not in the least interested in me. I'm certain he finds me too countrified. He is accustomed to the great ladies of society, you see. He is one of the Prince Regent's circle."

"That does not recommend him to me," said the Rev. Mr. Woodbury, who had a rather low opinion of the royal personage. "But I must say Mr. Macaulay is exhibiting admirable condescension. He was very pleasant to me."

"He appears very much taken with my niece," said the colonel, looking down the table at Arabella and Trenhaven.

Serena glanced in that direction. Arabella was smiling merrily and Trenhaven appeared quite delighted with her. "Indeed," said Serena, frowning a bit even though she knew she ought to be glad of Macaulay's apparent success in charming Arabella.

"Mr. Macaulay looks very much like a young lieutenant under my command in the Peninsula," said the colonel.

While such a remark would have ordinarily caused Serena to seize the conversation and divert it to a more interesting topic, she allowed the colonel to launch into his military reminiscences. While she appeared to listen, Serena's attention was riveted upon Trenhaven and Arabella. Very curious about what they were saying, she was rather frustrated that she could only catch snippets of their conversation.

Casting a glance at her father, Serena noted that Mr. Blake had taken on a somewhat gloomy expression. He was nodding absently to Lady Desmond, who was chattering away happily. Every so often Serena saw him look over at Arabella, apparently hoping to divert her away from his handsome young guest. He was not having much success since Arabella seldom looked in his direction.

Dinner continued on with Colonel Osborne dominating most of the conversation with his military anecdotes. Serena was glad when the meal was finished and the ladies retired to the drawing room, leaving the gentlemen to their port.

"What a lovely dinner," said Lady Desmond as she entered the drawing room. "Truly, Serena, your cook is quite marvelous."

"Yes, she is," said Serena. "We are very lucky to have her."

"Indeed you are," said Mrs. Osborne. "We have such ill luck with cooks. It is so hard to find a good one."

"That is so true," said Mrs. Claybrook, sitting down on the sofa. She was joined by Lady Desmond and Mrs. Osborne. Mrs. Woodbury situated herself in an armchair at some distance from the others. Taking her knitting out of a bag she was carrying, she began to industriously work her needles.

Arabella stood for a time talking to Lucy and then the two of them joined the others. Serena sat down in a chair next to Arabella. "I do hope you are enjoying the evening, Arabella."

"Oh, very much," replied Arabella. "I daresay it has been some time since I have enjoyed myself so much."

"I am not surprised," said Lady Desmond. "That young gentleman sitting beside you was utterly charming."

"Oh, yes," said Mrs. Claybrook, entering the conversation. "Mr. Macaulay appears to be a very fine gentleman. And he is so very handsome."

"Yes, I suppose one might say he is handsome," said Arabella with studied indifference. "And he is very pleasant."

"Yes, he is," said Lucy. "And he is Charles's dear friend."

"Has Sir Charles known him long?" asked Lady Desmond.

"Oh, for ages," said Lucy. "They were friends at Eton together. Of course, they have not seen each other in some years. Mr. Macaulay prefers town. He seldom goes to the country."

"Macaulay," said Mrs. Claybrook thoughtfully. "I believe I once met a Sir Harold Macaulay in town. Perhaps they are related."

"I cannot say," said Lucy. She looked over at her sister. "Has Mr. Macaulay mentioned any relations?"

Serena shook her head. "Save for his father, of course."

"His father?" said Arabella.

"Yes," replied Serena. "His father is Lord Ravenswood—from Northumbria if I am not mistaken."

"Lord Ravenswood," said Arabella, very much liking the sound of it. "Would Mr. Macaulay be the eldest son?"

"Oh, yes," said Serena, pleased with Arabella's interest. "He is the only son and heir."

"That is most interesting," said Mrs. Claybrook.

"The family is very wealthy," continued Serena. "According to Sir Charles, Mr. Macaulay will inherit a very great fortune. And he has money of his own from a great-uncle. Is that not what Sir Charles told you, Lucy? It was a very considerable sum of money I believe."

Taking her cue, Lucy nodded. "Yes, that is right. I believe it was"—Lucy hesitated, unsure what sum would be sufficient to impress the company—"a great deal of money."

Clearly impressed, all the ladies save Mrs. Woodbury regarded Lucy with keen interest. Arabella tried very hard to pretend that such information did not interest her overmuch, but inside she was filled with excitement. Not only was Macaulay one of the most attractive men she had ever met, but he was wealthy as well.

"Then he is a very great prize indeed," said Lady Desmond. "Imagine a gentleman with such prospects being so handsome and well-spoken. The lady who ensnares him will be very fortunate." She smiled at Serena. "My dear Serena, what do you think of Mr. Macaulay?"

"Oh, I think he is pleasant enough," said Serena blandly.

"My dear girl, I should fancy that you would be more interested," said Lady Desmond.

Mrs. Osborne frowned at this remark. Her son had been diligently seeking Serena's hand for months. Mrs. Osborne did not appreciate Lady Desmond encouraging Serena to consider this upstart newcomer. Indeed, thought Mrs. Osborne, if this Mr. Macaulay were so rich, why did he need to marry a wealthy young lady like Serena Blake? "Wealth is not in itself sufficient for happiness in a marriage," observed Mrs. Osborne solemnly.

Lady Desmond regarded Mrs. Osborne as if she were a fool. "Happiness in a marriage is seldom achieved in any case. A lady had best consider a man's fortune. You may take my word that it is better to be rich and miserable than poor and miserable."

Serena burst into laughter. "So those are the choices? Then I must say I cannot see why everyone is so eager to see me find a husband. I suspect it is the old adage, 'misery loves company.' "

"Well, I still think marriage quite wonderful," said Lucy stoutly.

"As you should," said Lady Desmond. "You are marrying a fine young man as well as a man of considerable property. I do hope you will do as well as your sister, Serena."

"As I am always telling Lucy, that is impossible," said Serena, smiling at her sister. "Charles is a paragon. There are not many others like him."

"Yes, that is certainly true," said Lady Desmond. "It appears to me that there is a dearth of nice young men. Certainly that is the case in our area."

Mrs. Osborne frowned, knowing that Lady Desmond did not like her son Frederick.

"But do tell us what you thought of Mr. Macaulay, Arabella," said Mrs. Claybrook. "It seemed that you and he got on famously."

Arabella smiled. "I thought him quite nice. He is a very interesting gentleman."

"Do tell us what you discussed," said Mrs. Claybrook.

"My dear Mrs. Claybrook, I would not know where to begin. We talked of so many things. He is such a witty and amusing man."

"I do hope the gentlemen do not linger too long," said Mrs. Claybrook, eager to see more of Mr. Macaulay.

Thinking they had discussed Macaulay enough, Serena changed the subject, asking Mrs. Claybrook about her daughter, who had recently given birth to her first child. Only too happy to oblige, Mrs. Claybrook eagerly took up the subject, rhapsodizing about her new grandson, who was, in her opinion, the most wonderful baby who had ever been born in the British Isles.

It was some time before the gentlemen rejoined the ladies in the drawing room. When Trenhaven appeared, every feminine eye was upon him including those of Mrs. Woodbury, who looked up from her knitting. .

Trenhaven looked about the room as he entered it, nodding to the various ladies. Meeting Serena's gaze, he smiled slightly and then turned to gaze attentively at Arabella, who smiled seductively at him.

Serena was not at all pleased by the looks the two of them were exchanging. Rising from her chair, she assumed her role of hostess. "Do come in, gentlemen," she said. "I'm sure you will enjoy some musical entertainment. You must assist me in persuading Lucy to sing."

This announcement was met with acclamation since Lucy was known in the area for her lovely soprano. Serena who always accompanied her sister, walked to the pianoforte. To her surprise, Trenhaven came up beside her. "Yes, Mr. Macaulay?"

"I thought you might need my assistance."

"Your assistance?"

Trenhaven grinned. "In turning the pages. While I am not a musician, I am not too modest to admit that I am an accomplished page turner."

"Really, sir," said Serena, speaking in a low voice, "don't you think that you might go sit beside Arabella?"

"My dear Miss Serena, I sat beside her throughout dinner."

"I did not think that was a particular hardship for you, Mr. Macaulay."

The marquess grinned. "No, it was a most enjoyable experience. Mrs. Lindsay is a delightful dinner companion."

"Is she indeed?" said Serena ill-humoredly.

Trenhaven nearly laughed at her expression. "But you cannot blame me for wishing a change. I've hardly spoken with you. Don't you think I am doing well? I should not doubt that Arabella will be willing to elope with me within a day or two."

"I should think sooner than that," said Serena, "now that I have told her you have a substantial fortune."

The marquess laughed. "So she knows I am heir to this Ravensborough fellow?"

"Good heavens!" said Serena in an alarmed whisper. "It is Ravenswood! Can you not remember the simplest thing?"

"Oh, yes, Ravenswood," said his lordship, enjoying the horror-stricken look on her face. "Dashed silly of me not remembering my own father's name."

"I do hope you are not foxed," muttered Serena. "Charles was to prevent you from drinking too much port."

Adopting a rather befuddled look for Serena's benefit, he grinned. "Charles did his duty. I am not in even the least bit inebriated. However, I must say that your father has a bang-up wine cellar if that port is a sample of it. But if you'd rather I join dear Arabella, I shall do so."

"No," said Serena. "In your condition, who knows what you might say to her. You had best stay with me."

"I would like nothing better, madam," he said.

Serena directed a disapproving look at him as she arrived at the piano. Sitting down on the bench, she looked over at Lucy, who came forward, smiling modestly at the guests. Serena opened the music. She and Lucy had agreed beforehand on the selections, a Scottish ballad and a song from an Italian operetta.

Serena looked over at her sister to see if she was ready to start. Smiling, Lucy nodded, signaling Serena to begin to play. Serena tried very hard to ignore the fact that Trenhaven was hanging over her shoulder, watching the music while she played. Although she was a very competent pianist, Serena could not help but be distracted by his lordship's presence. Despite that, she performed flawlessly.

Lucy, of course, was the center of attention. She sang the moving Scottish ballad with such feeling that Mrs. Osborne and Mrs. Claybrook both dabbed at their eyes with their handkerchiefs. Charles sat watching his fiancée with undisguised adoration as her clear soprano voice filled the room.

When the song was over, the guests clapped enthusiastically. "She is dashed good," Trenhaven whispered into Serena's ear. She looked up at him, nodding. "And you are beautiful, Serena," he said, his gray eyes fixing themselves upon her hazel ones.

Finding his use of her Christian name without the usual "Miss" rather disconcerting, Serena looked down at her hands. She knew she was blushing and she felt rather irked with him. Why would he say such things to her? she asked herself.

Serena somehow managed to play the next song despite his lordship's distracting influence. When the guests demanded an encore from Lucy, Serena rose hastily from the piano seat to announce that it was time for someone else to entertain the company. She called upon Freddy Osborne to play. That gentleman was only too happy to oblige, rising eagerly from his seat to come to the pianoforte.

Relieved to be a member of the audience, Serena sat down in a chair some distance from Trenhaven. The marquess would have liked to have joined her, but the only available seat was beside Arabella, who smiled radiantly at him as he sat down.

The rest of the evening passed quickly. Osborne, who was a talented musician, played for a time. When the musical entertainment was concluded, the guests indulged in conversation until they once again were called to the dining room for a late supper.

Serena was glad that she had no further contact with Trenhaven, who spent his time talking with Arabella. Although Serena had been worried that Mr. Macaulay had consumed too much wine and spirits, he seemed clear-headed enough. Arabella was apparently delighted with him. Mr. Blake, on the other hand, was just as obviously vexed with Charles's friend.

When all the guests had gone, Serena went quickly to bed. Exhausted from the evening, she quickly fell asleep, but awakened in the middle of the night thinking about Trenhaven. As she lay there in the darkness, Serena decided that Mr. Macaulay was, without a doubt, the most vexatious gentleman she had ever met.

12

Having lain awake for hours during the night, Serena finally fell asleep again in the early hours of the morning. After sleeping a few hours, she awakened far later than was her custom. Rising from her bed, Serena noted the time—ten o'clock. There was no sign of Muggins, who usually slept on the rug beside her bed.

The maid Betty entered the room as if on cue. "Good morning, Miss Serena."

"Good morning, Betty," said Serena. "It is very late. I feel like a slugabed. You were a dear to let me sleep."

"You need your rest, miss," said the servant, opening the drapes to let bright sunshine fill the room. "Would you like to wear your blue striped morning dress?"

"That would be fine, Betty," said Serena. Sitting down at her dressing table, she took up her hairbrush and began to brush her dark tresses. "Have you seen Muggins?"

"He is with Miss Lucy and the master."

"Have my father and sister gone downstairs?"

"No, miss," said Betty, "that is to say, Miss Lucy rose some time ago, but the master did not feel well and stayed abed. Miss Lucy is with him."

"What?" said Serena, turning to face her servant. "My father is unwell?"

"Oh, 'tis naught to worry about, miss. A slight stomach complaint. Mrs. Bishop prepared Mr. Blake a draught and he'll be better in a trice."

Serena frowned slightly, not liking to hear that her father was not feeling well. "I must go and see him at once."

After dressing as quickly as possible, Serena hurried to her father's room. There she found Mr. Blake gloomily sitting up in bed with pillows propped behind him. Sitting in a chair beside the bed was Lucy and lying on the floor with a rather doleful expression was the dog Muggins. The terrier raised his head as his mistress entered.

"Papa," said Serena, going to his bedside, "Betty said you are ill."

"It is nothing serious, I assure you," said her father glumly. "Only a touch of indigestion and a headache. There is no need to be concerned."

Serena placed her hand on his forehead. "You do not have a fever. Betty said that Mrs. Bishop gave you something for your stomach."

"That woman was fussing about me as if I were on my deathbed," said Mr. Blake.

"She is only concerned for you, Papa," said Lucy.

"There is no need for concern," said Mr. Blake with uncharacteristic peevishness. "All I need is rest."

"We will both sit with you," said Serena. "I shall get a chair."

"That is not necessary," said her father. "Indeed, what I most want to do is go to sleep."

Lucy rose from her chair. "Very well, Papa. We will leave you. But do ring the bell if you need anything. Come, Serena. I think it best if we allow Papa to rest now."

Serena nodded. "Very well." Leaning over, Serena kissed her father. "Do rest. We will visit you later."

The young ladies left the room followed by Muggins. "Were you with Papa for very long this morning, Lucy?" said Serena as they descended the great staircase that led to the entry hall.

"Half an hour or so," said Lucy. "As you could see, he is not in the best of humors. I believe he wanted only to be left alone. Of course, one cannot blame him if he is feeling unwell."

"I expect it was too much rich food at dinner," said Serena.

Lucy nodded. "I should not be surprised. There was enough food to feed an army. Indeed, I do not know why I should be hungry, but I am."

Since Muggins recognized the words "food" and "hungry," he looked up at Serena, wagging his tail. Serena laughed. "It appears Muggins is as interested in breakfast as you, Lucy."

They proceeded to the dining room where they helped themselves to the chafing dishes arranged on the sideboard. Sitting down at the table, Serena looked thoughtful as she took a bite of toast. "It was a great success last night, was it not, Luce? It appeared that Mr. Macaulay charmed Arabella."

Lucy nodded. "She was very much taken with him. Poor Papa.

Arabella scarcely exchanged a word with him all evening. I believe that is why he is out of sorts today."

"Do you think so?" said Serena. "You cannot believe he could make himself sick over her?"

Lucy shrugged as she took up her knife and fork. "Mrs. Bishop said that she believes Papa fancies himself in love with Arabella. When I told her how Arabella had eyes only for Mr. Macaulay last night, Mrs. Bishop thought Papa would be broken-hearted. She is very worried about him."

"Mrs. Bishop?"

"Oh, yes," said Lucy, matter-of-factly. "I think she is very fond of Papa."

"Do you think so?" said Serena, very much interested.

"Yes, most certainly. She is always so concerned about his health."

"But she is concerned about everyone," said Serena. "She is the dearest woman."

"Yes, indeed," said Lucy. "But she worries that Papa will pine away about Arabella." She frowned at her sister. "I do hope we do not cause more harm than good. How will we feel if he dies of a broken heart?"

"Do not be a goose," said Serena. "No one dies of a broken heart. Or at least I don't believe anyone does. I certainly have not heard of it except for novels."

"No," said Lucy, "but I know I should die of a broken heart if Charles left me for someone else."

"I don't believe one should waste much time worrying about that unlikely possibility," said Serena, taking another bite of toast. "The man is quite mad about you."

"Yes," said Lucy with a sigh. "But that is why I feel a bit guilty about Papa. He seems so fond of Arabella. He was so excited about the dinner party. Did you see his face when she first arrived? And then when Mr. Macaulay usurped her attentions! He was completely miserable."

"I assure you, Papa will recover."

"I hope you are right, Serena." Lucy looked thoughtful. "Mr. Macaulay seemed to like Arabella very much. He is such a charming man and so very handsome. I do hope you do not mind his attentions to Arabella, Serena."

"Why would I mind?" returned Serena quickly.

"It is just that I thought you rather liked him yourself."

"I am keeping my wits about me where he is concerned," said Serena although she was not altogether sure that what she said was true. "I admit he has a certain charm, but I know too much about him. And last night he was acting quite badly. I was worried that he was drunk."

"Oh dear," said Lucy.

"He seemed incapable of remembering that his father's name was supposed to be Ravenswood. He could so easily ruin everything. And he seems to find the whole business frightfully amusing."

"But I do like him. And he is a dear friend of Charles's."

"I am beginning to think that Charles should choose his friends more wisely," said Serena.

"I am sure that Charles is a very good influence on Mr. Macaulay."

"I hope you are right," said Serena, feeding a piece of sausage to Muggins, "but Mr. Macaulay appears to be the sort of man who is not easily influenced."

"Perhaps not," said Lucy. "Anyway, we must be glad that he has agreed to assist us. It seems your plan is working. I must say that I was not in favor of the idea at first, but it does appear that Arabella will desert Papa."

"I am certain of it," said Serena, "as long as Mr. Macaulay does not bungle things." Lucy nodded in reply and turned her attention to her breakfast.

When they were finished eating, Serena and Lucy left the dining room. "What do you wish to do now, Serena? Shall we go for a walk?"

The word "walk" made Muggins let out a short, eager bark. "I am sorry, Muggs," said Serena, "we will go on a walk, but first we must see Mrs. Bishop."

"Mrs. Bishop?"

"Yes, your saying how fond she was of Papa made me think."

"What do you mean?"

"Oh, nothing," said Serena rather mysteriously. "We must talk to her first."

Lucy voiced no objection and the sisters made their way to the housekeeper's rooms. Mrs. Bishop lived in a suite of well-furnished rooms in the west wing of the house. As chief female servant in the Briarly household, Mrs. Bishop had a position of grave responsibility, overseeing much of the household's operations.

An exceedingly competent and clever woman, Mrs. Bishop handled her duties with great skill. She was liked and respected by the other servants, who viewed her as a great authority on just about everything.

Arriving at the door to Mrs. Bishop's rooms, Serena rapped smartly on it. "Come in."

Lucy and Serena entered with Muggins at their heels. Mrs. Bishop was sitting at a desk in her room, perusing a big ledger book. She peered up at the sisters from behind a pair of reading glasses. "Miss Blake and Miss Serena," she said, starting to rise from her chair. It was not customary for the young ladies to visit the housekeeper there, although they did so from time to time.

"Oh, don't get up, Mrs. Bishop," said Serena. "We do not wish to disturb you."

"You are not disturbing me in the least," said Mrs. Bishop, taking her spectacles from her face and smiling at them. She was very fond of both Lucy and Serena, regarding them with a feeling more akin to motherly affection than a servant's regard for her employers. "Do sit down."

Serena and Lucy sat down in chairs across from Mrs. Bishop's desk. "I believe you saw my father this morning, Mrs. Bishop," began Serena. "I am rather worried about him."

"You must not be concerned, my dear. I suspect the master simply ate too much of Cook's excellent dinner last evening. And perhaps he had a bit too much wine. He normally drinks so little."

Lucy and Serena exchanged a glance. The idea that their plan could drive their father to drink caused Lucy to adopt a worried look.

"Papa seemed rather blue-deviled as well," said Serena. "Lucy said that she told you about the dinner—how Mrs. Lindsay appeared enamored of Mr. Macaulay and ignored my father."

"That dreadful woman," muttered Mrs. Bishop. "I fancy she wished to make the master jealous."

"That could be her plan," said Serena, "or she may simply find Mr. Macaulay more attractive."

"More attractive than Mr. Blake?" said Mrs. Bishop in a tone that implied such a thing quite unlikely.

Serena smiled. "Mr. Macaulay is a good deal younger, of course. And persons have led Mrs. Lindsay to believe that he is far richer than Papa and the heir to a title."

Mrs. Bishop directed a shrewd look at Serena. "Persons have led her to believe? Do you mean that Mr. Macaulay is not a rich gentleman?"

Serena laughed. "Indeed not. He is horribly in debt. And he is not the heir to a title."

A look of enlightenment came to Mrs. Bishop's face. She smiled broadly at Serena and Lucy. "There is mischief afoot here. What are you girls about?"

"We have decided to prevent Arabella Lindsay from making Papa miserable," said Serena. "We have arranged for Mr. Macaulay to divert her attention from our father."

"And you believe such a plan will succeed?" said Mrs. Bishop.

Serena and Lucy both nodded. "I was rather skeptical at first," said Lucy, "but if you had seen her with Mr. Macaulay last evening, hanging on his every word and addressing such looks at him!"

"The poor master," said Mrs. Bishop gravely. "She will break his heart."

"I fear so," said Serena. "It cannot be helped. But I know that it is far better to break his heart now and prevent her from becoming his wife."

"Perhaps you are right, my dear," said the housekeeper. "But Mr. Blake will suffer in any case. He is such a good, kind man. If only Mrs. Lindsay had not come to Whitfield."

Serena nodded. "Lucy and I have said that many times, Mrs. Bishop." She rose from her chair. "We have bothered you long enough, Mrs. Bishop. It is time for us to go. I have promised Muggins a walk this morning." Muggins eyed his mistress hopefully and Serena laughed. "Yes, we will go now, Muggs."

Lucy smiled at the housekeeper as she got up. "You are not to worry. All will work out in the end."

"I do hope so, Miss Lucy," said Mrs. Bishop.

The young ladies took their leave of the housekeeper. "Mrs. Bishop is so concerned about Papa," said Lucy as they walked down the corridor.

"Indeed she is," said Serena, a thoughtful expression on her face. "I believe I have realized something for the first time, Lucy. I cannot believe I have been so birdwitted as to not have seen it for all these months."

"Whatever can you mean, Serena?"

"That Mrs. Bishop is in love with Papa."

Lucy stopped dead in her tracks. "Oh, Serena! I know she is fond of him, but in love? That is ridiculous."

"Indeed, it is no such thing."

"Then that is very sad for Mrs. Bishop."

"Sad?" said Serena.

"Don't you think that unrequited love is the saddest thing in the world?"

"I am not so certain that there are not sadder things. Perhaps war and pestilence?"

"Do not vex me, Serena. If Mrs. Bishop is in love with Papa, it is very serious."

"But it is quite wonderful," said Serena.

"Wonderful? I cannot know how you would think that?"

"Don't you see? I have thought for some time that it would be splendid for Papa if he could find a suitable lady to marry. And here she is right under our noses."

Lucy's eyes opened wide in astonishment. "Mrs. Bishop! You cannot be serious."

"We both adore Mrs. Bishop. She is kind and clever and everything a man could wish for in a wife."

"Good heavens!" cried Lucy. "Mrs. Bishop is our housekeeper!" Lucy paused to look about in case some of the servants were nearby. She continued in a whisper. "She may be the best and kindest woman in the world, but she is not a lady! How could you think that Papa could marry her? What would everyone say?"

"What would everyone say if Papa married his housekeeper?" Serena shrugged. "Rather less than if he married Arabella I should think. And Mrs. Bishop is a lady. Do you know of anyone who acts like a lady more than she does?"

"That is not the point," said Lucy. "Acting like a lady does not make one a lady. Why, she is a servant, Serena."

"She is a housekeeper not a scullery maid," said Serena firmly. "And she will make Papa very happy."

Lucy shook her head and regarded her sister as if she had lost her mind. "This is the most addlepated idea, Serena. And even if it were acceptable for Papa to marry Mrs. Bishop, you have forgotten one thing."

"And what is that?"

"That Papa scarcely knows that Mrs. Bishop exists."

"What do you mean? He has the highest regard for her."

"Just as he has the highest regard for his best horse and his favorite armchair. Why, he hardly ever looks at her. I doubt if he could tell you the color of her hair."

"I'm not so certain of that, Lucy," said Serena. "Mrs. Bishop is not an unattractive woman. Indeed, she has very good eyes and an excellent complexion. We have only to get Papa to take notice of her."

"Serena, that is utterly absurd."

"I don't think so," said Serena, mulling over the matter. "Come, let us take that walk. We will discuss it further."

Lucy directed an exasperated look at her sister, but Serena only smiled and walked briskly onward.

13

Arabella sat in a chair in the library of her aunt and uncle's house, reading a novel. Looking up from the book, Arabella glanced at the clock on the mantel above the fireplace. Reflecting that time seemed to be going rather slowly that day, Arabella wearily put aside her book. She looked out the window onto the village green where her aunt was standing chatting with Mrs. Claybrook.

Arabella watched them with a frown. Whitfield was such a dull place, she thought, that it was a wonder that Mrs. Claybrook always had so much to say. Frowning, Arabella looked away from the window.

Of course, considered Arabella, the previous evening at Briarly had not been in the least dull. She smiled as she thought of Trenhaven. Remembering the dinner party, Arabella was pleased at the idea that she had made another conquest. Although Arabella had made a good many conquests in her time, it was always exciting to think about another male succumbing to her charms. The thought made Arabella smile.

"You appear very pleased with yourself, Arabella."

Arabella looked over to see her cousin Freddy enter the room. As always Osborne was dressed in the dandified style he thought marked a gentleman of the first water. Clad in a tight-fitting coat of olive-green superfine, black and yellow striped waistcoat, and buff-colored pantaloons, he sported an elaborately tied cravat. "Freddy, where have you been? I have been so bored sitting here by myself."

"I have been trying to buy some decent snuff." He directed a long-suffering look at her. "And I must tell you that there is no such thing to be found in this village. It is such a trial to be marooned in such a place as Whitfield."

"My dear, I am well aware of that," said Arabella.

"I imagine I shall have to write to my friend Bellamy to send me more of that wonderful blend he found in town." Osborne caught sight of a pile of letters on the table. "Is that the morning post?"

Arabella nodded. "I did not receive even one letter. I fear all my friends have abandoned me."

Not knowing how to respond to his cousin's remark, Osborne made no reply. He picked up the stack of mail and began thumbing through it. "Did you rest well after our evening at Briarly, Cousin?"

"I did indeed," said Arabella. "It was a lovely dinner party. I have not enjoyed myself so much since arriving in Whitfield."

"Well, I had a miserable time. While you were flirting with that Macaulay fellow, I was enduring Serena's snubs. I must say I am losing my patience with the girl."

"I cannot blame you," said Arabella as her cousin continued to look through the pile of letters.

He stopped to regard one note with keen interest. "Why, here is a letter from Bellamy." Tossing the rest of the communications onto the table, Osborne sat down on the chaise lounge opposite his cousin. "I do not doubt old Belly will be trying to put the touch on me once again. How many times must I tell him that I haven't any blunt to spare?"

"Really, Freddy, I believe 'Belly' to be a most unsatisfactory name for anyone."

Osborne grinned as he opened his friend's letter. "It is a rather unflattering nickname, but if you saw him, you would think it most appropriate. He is a very stout fellow, you see."

"I so detest stout men," said Arabella. "A man should be tall and lean like Mr. Macaulay."

Osborne looked up from his letter to frown at his cousin. Since he was neither tall nor lean, he did not appreciate the remark. "I feel you are making a mistake in showing so much interest in Macaulay," said Osborne, continuing to read his letter. "You will have cause to regret it if you toss away your chance with Blake."

Arabella shrugged. "Sometimes I think marrying Blake might be too great a sacrifice for a young woman such as myself. He is so very old."

Osborne did not seem to be attending. "Good God!" he muttered.

"What is it?"

"Bellamy. He writes that he is coming here."

"Coming here to Whitfield? Why on earth would he do that?"

"His creditors are dunning him to death. He says that he must leave town at once and he will arrive on the coach Monday." Osborne frowned at Arabella. "Where on earth will we put him?"

"I have no idea," said Arabella. "This is such a small house. And I assure you that I am not giving up my room for your corpulent friend."

"Father never liked Belly," said Osborne. "He will not be pleased."

"Then tell this Belly that he may not stay here."

"One can hardly do that. We were at school together. I shall speak with Mother. She always thought Belly a good chap. She can talk to Father." He folded up the letter. "It will be good to see the old boy again. And you will like him, Arabella. He never stops chattering and he tells the most droll stories. He knows all the gossip in town."

Arabella brightened. "Indeed?"

"Oh, yes. Belly will keep you amused."

"Then I shall welcome him."

"Yes, it will be good to see him." Osborne frowned suddenly. "Dash it all!"

"What is it?"

"How will I get my snuff if Bellamy is coming here?"

"Perhaps your friend will bring you some."

"I doubt it," said Osborne. "It sounds as if he hasn't a farthing. I wonder how he found the coach fare."

"It is so dreary being poor," said Arabella. "I know I am sick of it. Of course, if Mr. Macaulay is as rich as we're told . . ."

Osborne looked disgusted. "How do we know he is rich at all? I would not doubt that he is as poor as Bellamy."

"Why ever would you think that? Why, he dresses so well and he has such an air of nobility about him. I have had a great deal of experience with rich men of title, Freddy, and I believe I can recognize them by their manner."

"By their manner? That is nonsense," said Osborne. "If you would have seen the fellow dressed in a peasant's smock the way I did, you would not have thought he had such an air of nobility. Has it not occurred to you that there may be some sort of trickery involved here? The man is Mainwaring's friend. He may be in collusion with Mainwaring and the Blake sisters to keep you away from their father. This Macaulay is probably an imposter. I suspect that he is no more the heir to a barony than I am."

"You are being ridiculous," said Arabella. "The man has the manner and look of a nobleman."

"Well, you are a fool if you do not find out more about him.

Let us look up his family in *Debrett's*." Osborne rose from the chaise lounge and proceeded to one of the bookshelves. "It is here somewhere." After rummaging around for a time, he pulled a fat volume from the shelf and returned to his seat. "We will see about this supposed nobleman of yours."

"I'm sure you are quite mistaken if you think Macaulay some sort of pretender."

"We will see," said Osborne, paging through the thick tome. "We are told his father is Lord Ravenswood." After a time, he looked up at his cousin. "Just as I thought. There is no Lord Ravenswood in *Debrett's*."

"You must be mistaken."

"While I admit I am no scholar, I assure you that I can read. There is no Baron Ravenswood in here. See for yourself." Osborne handed her the book and Arabella started to look through it. It was some time before she gave up her search.

"You are right. He is not listed. There must be some mistake."

"There is no mistake. Macaulay is a fraud."

"I shall not assume that is the case simply because this dusty old peerage book does not list his father. It is a very old edition."

"My dear Arabella, what does that signify? Most of these baronies go back to the Conqueror."

"But not all," said Arabella. "I do not think there is enough evidence in the least."

"It is enough for me. You know that Serena and Lucy dislike you. It is they who are putting out the stories about how rich Macaulay is and that he will inherit a title. They think they are being very clever, but we will foil their plot."

Arabella frowned. Her cousin's words did make sense. Perhaps she was allowing a handsome face to cloud her judgment. After all, she thought, it would not be the first time. "Perhaps you are right," she said finally. "I had best not burn my bridges where Blake is concerned. Indeed, I shall call on him today and make amends. And we will discover the truth about Mr. Macaulay."

"Good," said Osborne, relieved that his cousin had returned to her senses. At that moment Mrs. Osborne walked into the library, eager to acquaint her son and niece about her conversation on the green with Mrs. Claybrook.

Serena and Lucy enjoyed their walk nearly as much as Muggins, who found many interesting things to investigate along the way. When they returned to the house, the young ladies went up to check on their father.

Serena was glad to find that Mr. Blake had risen from his bed. Attired in his dressing gown, the master of Briarly was sitting in a chair by the bed reading a book.

"Are you feeling better, Papa?" said Lucy, entering the room.

"A little," said Mr. Blake.

"But you don't feel like leaving your room?" said Serena.

"No, I should think it best if I stayed here. I feel very tired."

"It is a lovely day, Papa," said Serena. "Lucy and I took a walk. We had a pleasant time." She looked down at Muggins, who was standing by her side. "Muggins chased a rabbit. And he very nearly caught it. He was very proud of himself."

"Good old Muggins," said Mr. Blake. The dog wagged his tail.

"Will you be down for luncheon, Papa?" said Serena.

"Oh, I don't think so, Serena," replied her father. "I am not very hungry."

"I shall tell Mrs. Bishop to arrange for some soup for you," said Serena. "She is very concerned about you, you know."

"That is kind of her," said Mr. Blake, "but there is no cause for concern on anyone's part."

"Mrs. Bishop will be very happy to hear that you seem much improved, Papa," said Serena. "Lucy, we should not tire Papa."

"No," said Lucy, smiling at her father, "we will not stay, but you must ring if you need anything at all."

"Of course, my dears," said Mr. Blake.

Serena and Lucy turned to go, but Serena turned back. "I shall inform Mrs. Bishop that you are better, Papa." She paused. "Have you noticed anything different about Mrs. Bishop?"

Mr. Blake regarded his daughter blankly. "Different about her?"

"Why, yes, Lucy and I were just discussing it, weren't we, Luce?"

Lucy, who had no idea what her sister was talking about, felt it best to agree. "Yes, we were."

"Mrs. Bishop has always been a very attractive woman—"

Her father interrupted her. "Mrs. Bishop?" he said.

"You cannot mean you have not noticed the fact, Papa?"

"I must say I have not," returned Mr. Blake.

"Men are so unobservant sometimes," said Serena. "But what I was saying was that Mrs. Bishop has always been a very attractive woman, but lately she has become even more so. There is something changed about her." She looked over at Lucy. "What do you think it is, Lucy?"

Since the elder sister did not really approve of the direction of the conversation, she shook her head. "I'm sure I cannot say, Serena."

"I believe it is a sort of glow. Perhaps there is truth in the rumor that Mrs. Bishop has a beau."

"A beau?" said Mr. Blake, regarding Serena in surprise. "Mrs. Bishop? What nonsense is this?"

"Surely you do not think it so incredible. She is still a young woman."

"Young?" said Mr. Blake. "I should think she is five and forty if she is a day."

"I do not consider that old in the least," said Serena, "especially in the case of someone as vibrant and youthful as Mrs. Bishop."

"Vibrant and youthful?" said Mr. Blake. "Mrs. Bishop?" Lucy nearly burst into laughter at her father's expression.

"Yes, of course. Really, Papa, you must pay more notice to her."

"You say she has a beau? Who is he?"

Since Mr. Blake did not look at all happy at the idea, Serena was encouraged. "Oh, I have no idea. It is only a silly rumor. I should not have mentioned it. I'm sure it is complete and utter nonsense."

"I hope so," muttered Mr. Blake. "I'll not have my housekeeper running about after some man. We won't have such a thing at Briarly. Mrs. Bishop had best give her notice if there is the danger of scandal. What sort of example is she setting for the other servants? No, indeed, I will not tolerate any improper behavior."

"Oh, Papa, I meant nothing of that sort," said Serena, rather alarmed by the direction the discussion had taken. "Do forget that I said anything at all. It was just a rumor. I'm sure there is no truth in it."

"I hope so," said her father.

"We will leave you then, Papa," said Serena. "We shall visit you in the afternoon. I am hopeful that you will feel quite well by then."

After they had left the room and proceeded down the corridor, Lucy erupted into gales of laughter. "Oh, Serena," she managed to say, "it was too funny!"

"What was funny?" demanded Serena.

"Your talking about Mrs. Bishop having a beau! And now Papa thinks her some sort of light skirt!"

"He does not!" cried Serena.

"Did you not see his face? Oh, Serena, if you don't take care,

Papa will sack Mrs. Bishop for impropriety!" This comment made Lucy burst into laughter once again.

Serena looked alarmed for a moment, but then smiled. "From what I have observed, it never hurts for a lady to be thought to have an admirer. I daresay Papa will be looking at her very closely after this."

"I should think he would," said Lucy, still laughing.

Serena folded her arms in front of her and appeared thoughtful. "Mrs. Bishop must have some new clothes. I shall send for Mrs. Norris at once."

"Some new clothes? How will you explain that to Mrs. Bishop?"

"There is nothing to prevent us from giving her a new dress or two, is there?"

"Why, no," said Lucy, "but I think the idea a bad one. Indeed, you know that I feel it quite absurd for you to try to match Papa with his own housekeeper."

"I am very certain that I am doing the right thing," said Serena firmly. "I have a very strong feeling that Mrs. Bishop would make Papa very happy."

Lucy started to protest, but thought better of it. After all, there had never been much point in trying to dissuade her strong-willed younger sister from doing something Serena was determined to do. "I shall not argue with you," she said finally.

"Good," said Serena with a smile and the two young ladies continued on down the corridor.

14

Trenhaven was in a particularly good mood as he climbed into the driver's seat of his stylish high-perch phaeton. Charles, who was following behind him stopped to look up at his friend. "You cannot mean I am to climb up beside you?"

"Egad, Charlie, come on up. Do you expect me to be the driver with you sitting in the back?"

"It is an idea," said Charles with a grin.

"Charlie, come on or I shall go without you."

This threat caused Charles to reluctantly begin his ascent. The marquess reached down, and, grasping his friend by the arm, pulled him up into the seat. "That wasn't so bad now, was it?"

Charles looked down at the ground. "I'm not sure how I'll get down without killing myself."

His lordship laughed. "We will worry about that when we arrive at Briarly." The marquess flicked his reins against the backs of the horses and the black steeds started off, stepping smartly on the gravel drive.

"They are splendid bits of blood and bone," said Charles, alluding to the horses.

"You'll find none finer in all of England," said Trenhaven with unmistakable pride.

"And you drove this phaeton all the way from London?" said Charles. "I should have died of fright up here like this. Your poor valet."

"I don't believe Judd enjoyed the journey overmuch," said the marquess with a smile. "But he survived and it appears he is enjoying his stay at Mainwaring Hall."

"Good. And I do hope his master is enjoying his stay as well?"

Trenhaven glanced over at his friend as the phaeton traveled away from Mainwaring Hall. "I have never enjoyed myself more, Charlie. I cannot know why I ever thought I detested the country. Why, I don't even like thinking about returning to town."

"I expect I know why," returned Charles. "The excellent cuisine of Mainwaring Hall."

His lordship laughed. "While I salute your cook, Charles, I confess that is not the reason."

"I thought not," returned Charles.

At this time the phaeton arrived at the end of the lane that led to Charles's residence. Trenhaven turned the horses onto the road in the direction of Briarly. "Charlie," said the marquess, a thoughtful expression on his face.

"Yes, William?"

"I was wondering. Did you know at once that Lucy was the girl you wished to marry?"

"I'm not sure that I knew that the first time I saw her, if that is what you mean. But it did not take long, I must admit." He directed an inquiring look at his friend. "I believe this has something to do with Serena?"

Trenhaven nodded. "I am quite certain that I wish to marry her."

"Good God, William. Are you sure?"

"Quite sure. If she will have me, I will be her husband." He grinned. "It is rather ironic that I rush off to Somerset because I was so heartily sick of my parents forcing marriageable young ladies upon me. And now I am determined to marry Serena Blake."

"The duke and duchess will be rather surprised, don't you think?"

The marquess laughed. "They will be stunned."

"I do hope they will approve of Serena."

"I daresay they will have to approve of her," said Trenhaven matter-of-factly. "I am more concerned about Serena's approval."

"Indeed?" said Charles. "I find that surprising from the way you were acting at Briarly last evening. It seems you were doing your best to vex her."

"I could not resist," said his lordship. "She looks so adorable when she is provoked."

"Adorable? That is like saying a tigress looks adorable when provoked. My dear fellow, I know Serena better than you and a wise man does not wish to 'provoke' her."

Trenhaven only laughed. "I have never claimed to be a wise man, Charlie."

"Well, if you wish to marry Serena, I think you had best give up this masquerade of yours."

"Indeed not," replied his lordship, "I am enjoying myself far too much for that. And I must do my part to keep my future father-in-law from making a dreadful *mésalliance*." He grinned. "Besides," he continued, "I must earn that one hundred pounds."

Directing an amused look at his friend, Charles shook his head as the phaeton continued on its way.

After luncheon Serena busied herself studying fashion magazines in the drawing room. Lucy, who had a number of letters to write, had retired to her sitting room. When she had completed her correspondence, Lucy joined her sister in the drawing room.

Serena sat on the sofa with Muggins up beside her. On the floor a number of pages ripped from the magazines were strewn about in a haphazard fashion.

"What are you doing, Serena?" demanded the elder of the Blake sisters as she entered the room and saw the papers lying about.

"I am so glad you are here, Luce," said Serena, looking up. "I need your opinion." Leaning down, Serena picked up some of the loose pages from the floor. "I was finding some dresses for Mrs. Bishop." As Lucy sat down on the sofa next to Muggins, Serena thrust the pages into her lap. "What do you think?"

Directing a look of distinct disapproval at her sister, Lucy nonetheless picked up the pages and began to study them. "Good heavens, Serena, this is a ball gown. You cannot think that Mrs. Bishop will go to a ball!"

"Once they are married," said Serena. "But actually I tore that one out for myself. Do look at the morning dress, the one with the bows on the front." Taking the pages from Lucy's hands, she thumbed through them. "Here it is," she said, handing the page back to her sister. "Don't you think this one is perfect for Mrs. Bishop?"

Lucy looked down at the drawing in her hand. It showed a demure young lady attired in a high-waisted pelisse and broad-brimmed hat, who was carrying a parasol. "It is very nice," said Lucy uncertainly.

"I thought we could have Mrs. Norris make this one and one other. We will surprise her."

"Surprise her? How can one surprise someone with a dress? She must have fittings."

"Oh, I have thought of that. I have already taken one of her dresses from her wardrobe when she was away from her room. Mrs. Norris can use that to make the others."

"You cannot mean you have stolen Mrs. Bishop's dress?"

"She was in the servant's hall. No one saw me. And it was that old black dress. She hardly ever wears it."

"Serena, she will notice at once that it is missing. I daresay she does not own so many dresses that she would not miss one. And using an old dress is not the same as having fittings. Mrs. Norris will not like it."

"You worry far too much about details," said Serena. "We will go and see Mrs. Norris this afternoon. Oh, I cannot wait to see Mrs. Bishop's face when she sees her new dresses."

Lucy shook her head. "Serena Blake, I think this a very bad idea. And I fear you are very much mistaken if you believe Papa will transfer his affections so easily from Arabella to Mrs. Bishop."

"We will see," said Serena with a knowing smile.

The butler walked into the drawing room. "Sir Charles Mainwaring and Mr. Macaulay are here, miss," he said, addressing Lucy.

Lucy's face immediately brightened. "Oh, do show them in, Reynolds," She turned to Serena, "Charles is here! How wonderful! And Mr. Macaulay as well."

Serena tried to appear disinterested, but she was hardly indifferent to the idea of seeing Trenhaven. She busied herself with straightening the magazines as the gentlemen entered the room.

"Good afternoon, my darling," said Charles, hurrying into the room.

Jumping up from the sofa, Lucy went to meet her fiancé. "Charles!"

Charles took her hands and kissed her firmly on the lips, causing Lucy to blush.

The marquess, who regretted that he could not greet Serena in the same way, contented himself with a smile and a bow in her direction. Muggins, recognizing his lordship, let out an excited bark, jumped off the sofa, and rushed up to Trenhaven.

"Dear old Muggins," said the marquess, leaning down to rub the delighted canine behind the ears.

At the sight of Trenhaven, Serena experienced a now familiar sensation. As she sat there looking up into his maddeningly handsome face, Serena was well aware that she had lost her heart. Why, she asked herself, did Macaulay have to be such a disreputable man?

"Miss Serena," said the marquess, turning his attention from Muggins to the terrier's mistress. "How good it is to see you again."

"Mr. Macaulay," said Serena in a cool, even voice. "Do sit down, sir."

"Yes, do sit down," said Lucy, taking Charles's arm and leading him to the sofa where they both sat down with Charles sitting next to Serena.

Envying his friend his position on the sofa, Trenhaven could only take a seat in an armchair across from them. He sat there regarding Serena intently.

"We thought we might take you ladies for a ride in William's phaeton," said Charles. "I daresay the Prince himself does not have such a fine vehicle."

"I daresay you are right, Charlie," said his lordship, smiling at his friend.

"And, Serena, you will be most interested in the horses." Charles looked across at the marquess. "Serena is the best judge of horseflesh in the county. She is in great demand at the horse fair. Everyone is always asking her to take a look at a horse before they buy it. Serena can tell a right one with a glance."

Trenhaven raised his eyebrows slightly. "Indeed, Miss Serena? That is an uncommon ability for a lady. I shall be most eager to hear your assessment of my blacks."

"I shall be eager to see them, sir," said Serena.

Charles could not fail to note the way in which his friend was gazing at Serena and how that lady seemed very much interested in Trenhaven. "And where is Mr. Blake?" said Charles.

"I fear Papa is indisposed," said Lucy. "He did not feel well this morning. He is much better now. I fear something he ate last evening did not agree with him."

"Everything I ate agreed with me well enough," said Charles. "That was a wonderful dinner. I thoroughly enjoyed myself."

"I am glad," said Lucy, placing her hand on his. "I hope you enjoyed yourself, Mr. Macaulay."

"I do not know when I have enjoyed myself more, Miss Blake," replied the marquess. "The food was marvelous and the company"—he paused to smile in Serena's direction—"the company was as fascinating as anyone would find in London."

"It did seem that you found Arabella Lindsay quite fascinating, Mr. Macaulay," said Serena.

"Oh, I did," said Trenhaven, pleased at the look of displeasure on her face. "She is utterly charming and so beautiful." He noted with some amusement that this remark elicited a frown from Serena. "I cannot imagine a more pleasant way to earn one hundred pounds than to court such a lovely lady as Mrs. Lindsay."

"You did very well, Mr. Macaulay," said Lucy. She looked over at her sister. "Don't you think Mr. Macaulay did a splendid job?" When Serena made no reply, she continued. "Arabella quite ignored Papa last evening. I fear that may be why he was not feeling well this morning. He was very upset."

"That is too bad," said Charles, "but surely it is better for him to find out her true colors now."

"That is what Serena always says," replied Lucy. "I do hope she is right."

"Of course I am right," said Serena firmly. "We cannot allow Papa to marry someone like Arabella. He must marry someone who will love him and care for him. I must tell you gentlemen of my plan."

"Oh dear," said Lucy. "Serena has a new scheme. You must both help me talk her out of it. It is quite outrageous."

"It is not outrageous in the least. Lucy thinks me quite addlepated, but I see nothing wrong in trying to interest our father in another lady who would be a much more suitable wife and companion for him."

"Why, that is a good idea," said Charles. He smiled fondly at his future bride. "Why do you object to it, my dearest?"

"I do not object to the idea of father finding someone else. But I cannot approve of Serena's idea," replied Lucy. "Serena, tell the gentlemen whom you have chosen for father."

"I shall be happy to do so. It is Mrs. Bishop."

"Mrs. Bishop!" cried Charles, very much astonished.

"Who is Mrs. Bishop?" said the marquess, his interest piqued by his friend's reaction to the announcement.

"She is our housekeeper," said Lucy.

His lordship's eyebrows arched in amusement. "You have decided that your father should marry the housekeeper, Miss Serena? That is quite extraordinary."

"Serena, what can you be thinking?" said Charles. "A gentleman does not marry his housekeeper."

"I daresay such a thing has occurred from time to time in the annals of British history," replied Serena. "And I cannot think there is anything so very shocking about it if the housekeeper is as exemplary a person as Mrs. Bishop."

"Really, Serena," said Charles, "I am sure Mrs. Bishop is a very fine woman, but this will not do at all. The idea is absurd."

"It is not absurd," said Serena stubbornly. She looked at Trenhaven. "I imagine you find it ridiculous as well, Mr. Macaulay."

"I should not dare to think any idea of yours ridiculous, Miss Serena," said his lordship.

Not knowing how to take this remark, Serena regarded him questioningly.

"Well, I can see there is no point in arguing about the matter," said Charles. "One learns quickly not to argue with Serena. It is always quite futile. Let us speak no more of Mrs. Bishop. Would you not like to take a ride?"

"That would be wonderful," said Lucy. "Shall we, Serena?"

"I should be happy to do so," said Serena, rising from the sofa. Lucy rose as well and the gentlemen got quickly to their feet. "Give us but a few moments to make ready," said Serena.

The gentlemen nodded and Lucy and Serena took their leave with Muggins following at their heels. When they were alone, Charles shook his head. "Can you imagine Serena wishing her father to marry the housekeeper? What a scandal that would be if he did so."

Trenhaven shrugged as if the matter did not interest him. Walking over to a landscape painting that adorned the wall, he appeared to study it.

"You don't care?"

"Care about what, Charles?"

"Care that Serena has the idea to make the housekeeper her stepmother. It does concern you, you know."

The marquess looked at his friend. "It does?"

"Indeed, if Mrs. Bishop married Mr. Blake and you married Serena, that would make her your mother-in-law."

"And with you married to Lucy, we would be brothers-in-law." He grinned. "I can see there are many disturbing aspects to marrying into this family, Charlie."

Charles laughed. "Do be serious. What would His Grace think of Mrs. Bishop? And the duchess? We must discourage Serena in this."

"I cannot see why you are so concerned. Do you think Mr. Blake, a man who is infatuated with Arabella Lindsay, will be content with his housekeeper? Or is his housekeeper so very alluring?"

"Mrs. Bishop? 'Alluring' is scarcely a word I would use to describe her. She is a nice, matronly sort of woman, but she is no beauty."

"Then there is nothing to worry about."

"I hope you are right," said Charles. "Mrs. Bishop would be my mother-in-law as well."

"You could do far worse, I assure you. My mother wishes me to marry Lady Charlotte Cavendish and her mother is a veritable gorgon! Now there is a mother-in-law to give one pause. I should not worry about nice, matronly Mrs. Bishop. Oh, here are the ladies."

Serena and Lucy entered the drawing room followed by Muggins. Now attired in pelisses and bonnets, they appeared ready for an outing.

Wearing a pale green pelisse decorated with silk rosettes and a fetching leghorn hat, Lucy looked fashionable and extremely pretty. Charles hurried to offer her his arm.

Trenhaven was only vaguely aware of Serena's sister. His attention was focused only on Serena, who looked splendid dressed in a pelisse of gray kerseymere trimmed with ruby velvet. Atop her head was a stylish bonnet of ruby velvet adorned with ostrich feathers.

Serena took his lordship's arm and the four of them left the drawing room. Once outside, Serena caught sight of Trenhaven's magnificent black horses. Walking over to them, she studied the horses appreciatively. The groom Roberts was standing at the horses' heads. "Roberts, have you ever seen such horses?"

"Nay, Miss Serena, I've not seen any to compare with the like of these two." He patted one animal's sleek neck.

Serena smiled at the marquess. "They are exceptional, Mr. Macaulay."

Trenhaven, who was exceedingly proud of his horses, could not help but be pleased. "I am happy to hear your opinion, especially now that I know you are the best judge of horses in the county."

Serena smiled up at him. Then having a disquieting thought, she frowned. "Mr. Macaulay?"

"Yes, Miss Serena?"

"I must ask you something." Taking his arm, she led him a few steps away so that Roberts would not hear them. She spoke in a low voice. "However could you afford such horses? And that phaeton?"

"Do not concern yourself about that," said his lordship, suppressing a smile.

"Charles has told me your financial situation," said Serena, regarding him seriously. "It is quite mad of you to buy such things."

"I know that I am something of a spendthrift."

"Something of a spendthrift?" She shook her head. "Charles has said you are hopelessly in debt. Seeing these horses and this phaeton, I can see why."

"I must ask Charles to cease gabblemongering about my affairs."

"You must act more sensibly, Mr. Macaulay. A man in your position should never have bought horses like these. If you were wise, you would consider selling them. Perhaps you might take them to the Whitfield horse fair. It is on Saturday. You would get a very good price."

"Sell my horses?" said Trenhaven. "I should just as soon ask you to sell Muggins." Hearing his name mentioned, the terrier looked eagerly up at his lordship. "No, I'll not sell these beauties for any price."

Serena frowned. "But you must act sensibly."

"I am not accustomed to acting sensibly," said his lordship, looking down into Serena's hazel eyes. Seeing her worried expression, he had a strong urge to take her into his arms and cover her delectable lips with his own. With admirable self-control, he restrained himself. "Now I will not hear anything more about my prodigal behavior. Come, I wish to take you for a ride. You must see what my blacks can do."

"Very well," said Serena. She looked at the horses again. "Do you think I might drive them?"

"Drive them?" The marquess was taken aback by the request.

"Oh, do not fear, I am a tolerable whip, I assure you."

He hesitated only a moment. "Very well. If you wish."

She smiled. "Thank you, sir."

Trenhaven helped Serena ascend up into the seat of the high-perch phaeton. Going to the other side, he climbed up beside her and handed her the reins. "Charles, I suggest you assist Miss Blake into the carriage so we may be off."

Charles had been so intent upon Lucy that he had not even noticed his friend and Serena get into the phaeton. He regarded them in surprise.

"Yes, do get in," said Serena. "I am eager to get started. Mr. Macaulay is allowing me to drive. Is that not good of him?"

"I hope I will not regret it," said his lordship good-naturedly.

"You would regret it if you let *me* drive," said Charles, handing Lucy up into the carriage seat behind the driver and then getting in himself. "I would make a mess of it, but Serena could drive a four-in-hand blindfolded."

"Not blindfolded," said Serena, smiling brightly at his lordship. "Shall we go?"

Trenhaven nodded and Serena started off. Muggins trotted happily alongside. It did not take long for the marquess to see that he had nothing to worry about with Serena at the ribbons. She drove with skill and confidence. The blacks performed flawlessly as usual. "They are wonderful," said Serena.

"So are you, Miss Serena," said his lordship.

These words and the tone in which they were said rather disconcerted Serena who was glad she had the horses to see to. "Don't be ridiculous, sir."

He laughed. "Where did you learn to drive?"

"Papa taught me. I had my own pony cart when I was eight. I've never driven any horses to compare with these."

"Nor have I," said his lordship. "They are the best horses I have ever had." He grinned. "So do not tell me to sell them."

"Very well, I shall not." She glanced over at him. "But you must not go any further into debt."

"I am touched that the idea of me in debtor's prison distresses you so much, Miss Serena."

"I am distressed at the idea of anyone in such difficulty, Mr. Macaulay," said Serena, keeping her eyes on the road and the horses.

"Yes, of course. You are right, Miss Serena. It is time for me to start acting more responsibly. Indeed, my father is always telling me I am a wastrel."

"Your father? Oh dear, is he very angry with you?"

"He is furious with me."

"Because you are in debt?"

The marquess nodded. "That is part of it. I suppose I am not the best of sons, plaguing him as I do. He suffers enough with his gout."

"Gout?" said Serena. "You must speak to Mrs. Bishop about that. She has an excellent treatment for gout."

"This Mrs. Bishop seems to be a most useful person."

"Oh, she is," said Serena. "You must meet her. I know you will like her. We will ask her about gout when we return." Serena slowed the horses. "We probably should start back. We have gone far enough."

"I'm not sure that I wish to return," said the marquess. "I enjoy sitting here next to you."

Serena thought it best to ignore this remark. "I shall turn around there at the crossroads."

Trenhaven nodded. When Serena arrived there, she pulled the horses up. "What is it?" said Charles. "We're not stopping? Lucy and I were having such a lovely time."

Serena looked back at them. "I think it best if we go no farther." She urged the horses ahead and then skillfully maneuvered them into a turn. They were soon heading back toward Briarly.

"A turn worthy of a skilled coachman," said his lordship.

"Thank you," said Serena.

"You are quite extraordinary, you know, Serena Blake."

"Really, sir, I suggest you reserve your flummery for Arabella."

Trenhaven smiled at her. He was about to assure her that he truly meant what he said when the sight of another vehicle approaching diverted him. "Here comes your friend Osborne."

Serena frowned. There was Freddy driving his curricle toward them. "He is so completely odious. Let us snub him royally."

The marquess smiled. "I shall be happy to."

Keeping the horses at a decorous trot, Serena continued on. As they neared Osborne's curricle, he raised his hat in greeting. Keeping her eyes straight ahead, Serena pointedly ignored him, guiding the blacks swiftly by his vehicle.

"Serena," cried Lucy, glancing back at Osborne, "that was very rude."

"I know," said Serena, smiling at his lordship. "I cannot imagine what came over me." Trenhaven smiled in return as the phaeton continued on toward Briarly.

15

After dinner that evening, Mr. Blake excused himself very early, saying that he had a headache and wished to go to bed. When he had gone, Serena and Lucy sat down in the drawing room. "I am worried about Papa," said Lucy. "He seems so discouraged since Arabella took little notice of him at the dinner party."

"He will come round in time," said Serena. "And I do not doubt that Mrs. Bishop will soon distract him."

Lucy regarded her sister with a long-suffering look. "Oh, not that again, Serena! It appears it is impossible to dissuade you from that ridiculous idea."

"But Mrs. Bishop is quite perfect for him. Oh, I know her pedigree is not of the first water, but she has a good many other virtues. And in regard to her family, did she not once mention that she is related to Sir Edward Chatham?"

"Very distantly related," said Lucy with a frown. "I believe she is his second cousin twice removed or something of that kind. She has never met him."

"But she is related nevertheless. We will have to remind Papa of the connection. And Mrs. Bishop is so very clever. I believe Mr. Macaulay was very glad to have her treatment for gout."

"Serena, do you not think her treatment rather severe? I cannot imagine that Mr. Macaulay's father will relish the idea of a strict vegetable diet. And those poultices! They sounded quite horrible."

"It was very good of Mrs. Bishop to write down the recipes for them. And she gave Mr. Macaulay a good many herbs to send to his father. I do not doubt that the old gentleman will show marked improvement very soon."

"I do not dispute that Mrs. Bishop is well versed in herbal medicines," said Lucy, "but that hardly qualifies her to marry Papa."

"What an old stick you are, Lucy," said Serena good-naturedly.

She folded her arms in front of her and smiled. "Mr. Macaulay appeared very pleased with Mrs. Bishop's advice."

"I daresay he was only being polite."

"Oh, I don't believe so. I am convinced that he was perfectly sincere." Serena smiled. "It was a very pleasant afternoon, was it not?"

"Oh, it was lovely," said Lucy. "I so enjoyed riding in Mr. Macaulay's phaeton. But I enjoy anything if I am in Charles's company."

"Yes, I am aware of that," replied Serena.

"It seems that you are very fond of Mr. Macaulay, Serena."

Serena frowned. "I confess I do like him, Luce."

"If only he were more suitable," said Lucy.

"Yes," replied Serena glumly.

Lucy regarded her sister closely, surprised that Serena had admitted her interest in Macaulay. "You will keep in mind that he is unsuitable, won't you, Serena? Do not forget what Charles has said about him. You would not be happy with such a man."

"Good heavens," said Serena, "I have no intention of running off with him. Indeed, I believe he is far more interested in Arabella than he is in me."

Lucy was unsure how to reply. She was worried that her sister had lost her heart to Charles's friend. While Macaulay seemed like a nice gentleman, Lucy was concerned that he was a fortune hunter. After all, Charles had warned her that he was.

Despite Serena's statement that Macaulay was more interested in Arabella, it seemed to Lucy that he was paying a good deal of attention to her sister. And Charles's friend must know that Serena had a considerable fortune. "Well, let us talk no more of Mr. Macaulay," said Lucy. Since Serena was quite agreeable to this suggestion, the conversation turned to other matters.

Although Serena had said that she had no intention of running away with Trenhaven, as she lay in bed that evening, she found the idea rather appealing. Remembering being seated beside him in the phaeton, Serena thought of his broad shoulders and handsome face.

When they had arrived back at Briarly, Trenhaven had jumped down quickly from the vehicle and had assisted her down from the driver's seat. Serena reddened at the recollection of his hands on her waist as his strong arms lifted her down.

As she lay there in the dark, she could not help wondering what it would be like to have such a man for a husband. Her face grew hot as Serena envisioned Trenhaven sharing her bed, touching her in intimate ways, and covering her with kisses. Serena sighed aloud, wishing suddenly that he was there with her so that she could bury herself in his embrace and give herself to him entirely.

Alarmed at her disturbing thoughts, Serena tried hard to force Trenhaven from her mind. It was a very long time before she was able to do so, finally falling into a fitful sleep.

In the morning Serena rose early. In the light of day it was easier to focus on other matters. After breakfast, she and Lucy busied themselves with household duties.

Mr. Blake, while not in the best of moods, did not seem altogether gloomy. He no longer had a headache, which he attributed to Mrs. Bishop's headache draught that she had given him before he went to bed.

By luncheon, Mr. Blake seemed almost cheerful. Serena noted with great satisfaction that he mentioned Mrs. Bishop several times while they were dining. She was particularly pleased that he asked if she or Lucy knew anything more about Mrs. Bishop's reputed male friend. The topic, Serena observed, greatly interested her father.

After luncheon Lucy and Serena went to work in the garden. The sky was dreary and overcast and the air rather cool. Serena thought it the perfect day for gardening. She and Lucy, assisted by the head gardener and Muggins, busied themselves with separating a number of perennials that had outgrown their places in the border.

An avid gardener, Serena liked nothing better than to spend an afternoon in Briarly's splendid gardens. She was so occupied with what she was doing that she scarcely noticed the arrival of one of the footmen.

"Miss Lucy, Miss Serena," said the servant, a gangly youth of fifteen.

"Yes, Harry?" said Lucy.

"Mrs. Bishop has sent me to fetch you. There are guests for tea."

"Guests for tea?" said Lucy, hopeful that the guests in question would include Sir Charles Mainwaring.

"'Tis Mr. Frederick Osborne and Mrs. Osborne and Mrs. Lindsay."

Serena, who had been kneeling in the flower bed, rose to her feet. "Oh, blast," she muttered.

"Oh dear," said Lucy, handing her spade to the gardener. "We must go in at once."

Serena nodded, thinking it inadvisable to leave her father alone with Arabella for long. "You will have to carry on without us, Johnson," she said, addressing the gardener. "Come, Lucy, we must hurry."

Going inside, the two sisters went up the back staircase to their rooms. After changing from their gardening clothes, they hurried to the drawing room. There they found a very happy Mr. Blake engaged in conversation with Arabella. Mrs. Osborne sat beside her daughter smiling benevolently at Mr. Blake. Osborne was seated in an armchair nearby, staring idly at one of the paintings on the wall.

When the young ladies entered the room, Osborne and Mr. Blake got to their feet. "Ah, girls," said Mr. Blake, "we are most fortunate to have guests for tea."

"Indeed," said Serena, smiling blandly at the guests.

"How good to see you," said Lucy. "How nice that you can stay for tea."

The young ladies seated themselves with the others and the gentlemen returned to their seats. "Mr. Blake has told us that you girls were working in the garden," said Arabella, directing a smile at Serena and Lucy. "I do envy you. I so miss the garden I had in Brussels. The roses were quite lovely. Of course, they could not rival the rose garden at Briarly." She smiled at Mr. Blake. "I know that Mr. Blake has a particular interest in roses."

This remark accompanied with Arabella's fond smile seemed to delight Mr. Blake as much as it irritated Serena. It appeared, she thought, that Arabella was trying to make amends for ignoring Mr. Blake at the dinner party.

"Oh, yes," said Serena's father. "I am quite devoted to my roses. We have so many varieties."

Arabella, while she was fond of receiving roses from masculine admirers, thought flower gardening a rather boring subject. She did her best to look enchanted as Mr. Blake began to talk about the various roses he had.

Mrs. Osborne, who was a great flower gardener herself, entered the conversation. She and Mr. Blake and his daughters talked for a long time about roses and other flowers while Arabella tried to listen and waited for an opportunity to change the topic.

When Mr. Blake mentioned that he had received a fine rose specimen from a London acquaintance, Arabella had her chance. "A London friend of my cousin's will be coming to Whitfield very soon. Freddy, do tell Mr. Blake and the girls about your friend Bellamy."

Everyone looked expectantly at Osborne, who was glad to receive some attention. "Yes, my friend Bellamy will be staying with us. He is a good fellow and he knows everyone in town." He smiled at Serena. "Perhaps he knows Mainwaring's friend Macaulay."

"One cannot know everyone," said Serena. "London is a very great metropolis."

"Indeed," said Osborne, "but Bellamy has a good many friends in the first circles of society. Since Macaulay is such an illustrious fellow, I should not be surprised if they are acquainted." This remark was said with a good deal of sarcasm, making Serena frown ominously at Osborne, who continued undaunted. "I was surprised when I did not find Macaulay's father listed in *Debrett's*. And I searched the volume quite thoroughly. There was no Baron Ravenswood. Don't you think that curious, Serena?"

"I think it curious that you devoted time to paging through *Debrett's*, Freddy."

"You cannot blame me, Serena," said Osborne. "I do not meet that many sons of peers. I was so excited at the prospect of having such a noble acquaintance that I rushed to my uncle's peerage book."

"He was not in *Debrett's?*" said Mr. Blake. "That is odd. I shall have to take a look myself."

"Perhaps your edition was rather old," said Serena.

"But why would that matter?" said Osborne. "Certainly there would be some Lord Ravenswood to be found."

"Perhaps Lord Ravenswood received his title recently," said Serena, searching for a reasonable explanation. She looked over at her sister. "Did not Mr. Macaulay say that his father was recently elevated to the peerage?"

Lucy looked blankly at her for a moment before replying. "Oh, yes, I believe he did say something of the sort."

"Yes," said Serena, speaking more confidently. "I remember now. Mr. Macaulay's father was a war hero. His title was recently bestowed upon him."

"A war hero?" said Osborne. "That is very interesting. I shall ask my father. Certainly the colonel will know of this Ravenswood."

"I believe Lord Ravenswood was a naval hero," said Serena. "The colonel may not be acquainted with him."

"I shall ask him," said Osborne, smiling at Serena in a manner that implied he thought she was speaking humbug.

Serena managed to smile in return, but she thought Freddy Osborne the most loathsome man she had ever met. Fortunately the conversation turned to other subjects as Mrs. Osborne began to speak of a naval admiral who was married to a cousin of hers.

Barely attending, Serena found herself thinking that things were going very badly. It seemed that Arabella and her cousin thought Macaulay an imposter. No wonder Arabella was there that afternoon renewing her pursuit of their father.

The news that Osborne's friend Bellamy was coming to Whitfield was even more distressing. What if Bellamy was acquainted with Macaulay and would reveal that he was an impoverished ne'er-do-well? It would be disastrous! As the servants entered with tea, Serena decided that they must find some way to renew Arabella's interest in Macaulay.

16

Although both Trenhaven and Charles would have liked to have called at Briarly that afternoon, Charles had a good many commitments and could not get away. There were a number of matters relating to the estate that could not be put off. A conscientious landlord, he spent the day with his steward and various tenants discussing some rather pressing problems.

The marquess assured his friend that he need not feel he was neglecting his duties as host by going about his own business for one day. Trenhaven would find ways to occupy himself, he told Charles.

Left to his own devices, his lordship decided to attend to a matter he had put off since arriving in Somerset. Sitting down at the desk in the library, Trenhaven wrote a letter to his parents. It took him some time to compose this missive, since he was not sure what to say to the duke and duchess. His anger had long since cooled toward them and he was now rather ashamed of himself for causing them distress.

The marquess stared at the paper for some time before dipping the quill pen into the ink and starting to write. He apologized to the duke and duchess for his abrupt departure from town and explained that he was in Somerset with Charles.

Trenhaven paused, considering what to say next. Then he continued, "I am sure that I will astound you with my news," he wrote. "You will doubtless consider it quite ironical since my leaving London was prompted by my reluctance to marry, but I have met a wonderful young lady here. Her name is Serena Blake and she is the sister of Charles's fiancée, Lucy. I am determined to marry her and I hope I will have your blessing. The Blake family is one of the wealthiest and most respected families in the west country. I hope you will have no objection to such a connection for I am very much in love with her. I have reason to hope that she returns my affection and I intend to ask for her hand." He stopped again, knowing that these lines would cause a sensation in the ducal residence.

He continued on, describing Serena and her father and sister. Noting Serena's concern for the duke's gout, he included Mrs. Bishop's remedy for the condition. When he had finished, he folded up the missive and then sealed it with wax. He then wrote another shorter letter to his sister.

Trenhaven gave the letters to his valet to be posted in the village. With them was a small parcel containing Mrs. Bishop's herbs that was to be sent to the duke. While his lordship's servant Judd did not reckon that such errands were part of his normal duties, he was more than happy to oblige his master.

His letter writing having occupied most of the afternoon, Trenhaven joined Charles for dinner. The master of Mainwaring Hall talked endlessly about drainage of fields, improvements to farm cottages, and the corn harvest. Since such things did not normally interest his lordship, he found his mind wandering. He thought instead about Serena. Remembering how beautiful she looked when she was driving the phaeton, he reflected that she was a most remarkable woman.

"I daresay I am boring you, William," said Charles.

"Boring me? Not in the least."

"Good. I do wish I hadn't had to meet with these blasted fellows this afternoon. We might have gone to Briarly."

"I would have liked that," replied the marquess.

"I imagine you would have," said Charles with a smile. "You are quite smitten with Serena, aren't you?"

"I confess that I am."

"I do think that she seems rather taken with you."

Trenhaven smiled. "She is concerned about my intemperate drinking and spendthrift ways."

"Yes, poor girl. She's probably quite distraught, believing she is in love with such a scoundrel."

"So you think she could be in love with me, Charlie?"

"I would not be surprised. But, my dear William, when are you going to tell her who you are?"

The marquess shrugged. "It is a bit awkward, Charlie."

"Indeed, but it will be a dashed site more awkward as time goes on."

"Well, I shall tell her soon, Charlie. Now what else did you have to decide this afternoon as lord of the manor?" This question diverted Charles and he began to discuss his meetings once again.

Shortly after dinner, a servant interrupted Trenhaven and the baronet, who had retreated to the drawing room. "Excuse me, sir," he said, addressing Charles. "There is a letter for Mr. Macaulay come by messenger from Briarly." The servant extended a silver salver with a folded paper on it.

"From Briarly?" The marquess took up the letter. "Thank you."

The servant bowed and left.

"What is it, William?"

Opening the missive, Trenhaven looked first at the signature at the end. "Serena Blake," it said. "It is a letter from Serena."

"The devil," said Charles.

The marquess eagerly scanned the contents of the communication, which was written in an elegant spidery hand. He looked up at Charles. "Unfortunately, it is not a love letter. I shall read it to you. 'Sir, a matter of some urgency causes me to write to you. I fear Freddy suspects you are not who we have said you are. Not finding your father's name in *Debrett's*, odious Freddy has concluded you are some sort of imposter. I have told him Lord Ravenswood is a naval hero recently elevated to the peerage. Should you meet Freddy, I hope you will speak convincingly of this matter.

'Lucy and I thought that you and Charles might take us to the horse fair tomorrow. We will be ready at ten o'clock. I am sure that we will see Freddy and Arabella there and we can set things right. Serena Blake.'" Trenhaven smiled at his friend. "There is a postscript, 'I do hope you are not acquainted with a gentleman named Bellamy who resides in London. He is an old school friend of Freddy's and he is coming to Whitfield. If you know him, we are doomed.'" Trenhaven laughed at the last sentence.

Charles grinned at his friend. "So your father is a naval hero? That is very exciting. And do you know this fellow Bellamy?"

The marquess shook his head. "The only Bellamy I know is old Lord Bellamy. He is nearly seventy."

"Good. Then we are not doomed."

Trenhaven laughed again. "Not doomed for that reason in any case."

Charles smiled and poured a glass of wine for his friend.

The Whitfield horse fair was a monthly event that was always eagerly awaited by local residents. Since it attracted a good many visitors from throughout the county, the fair transformed Whitfield into a bustling, exciting place.

While the main attraction of the fair was the buying and selling of horses, there were a good many other things going on. Merchants of all kinds set up booths on the village green, selling a wide assortment of merchandise and food. Most times itinerant performers came to the village for the fair and it was common to see jugglers, musicians, or a puppet show.

There was also a horse race for sporting enthusiasts. Whitfield residents enjoyed the sport of kings as much as any Englishmen and the monthly races were always well attended.

Being a devoted equestrian, Serena Blake never missed the horse fair. She liked nothing better than to look at all the animals and exchange horse talk with their owners.

That morning there was a good deal of activity at Briarly as members of the Blake family made ready for the fair. Lucy was very excited even though she did not share her sister's passion for horses. Lucy's passion was reserved for Charles, and the idea of accompanying him to the fair made her very happy.

Mr. Blake, too, was eager to attend the fair. Although he loved horses as much as his daughter Serena, Mr. Blake was more interested in the fact that Arabella Lindsay had mentioned that she would be there.

All of the Blakes were ready early and they assembled in the drawing room to await the arrival of Charles and Trenhaven. "You girls look lovely," said Mr. Blake, viewing his daughters with paternal pride.

"Thank you, Papa," said Lucy. She looked quite attractive in a pelisse of pale blue silk and matching bonnet.

Serena looked equally lovely attired in a green and white striped spencer worn over a green dress. A French bonnet trimmed with green satin completed the picture. "And you look very handsome, Papa," said Serena, noting that her father had dressed with particular care. The fact did not please Serena since she knew very well that his attention to fashion that morning was due to his desire to impress Arabella.

"It is a lovely day for the fair," said Lucy, glancing toward the windows where bright sunshine could be seen.

"Oh, yes," said Mr. Blake. "I do not doubt that there will be a great crowd to see the race since there is a fine stallion coming from Taunton. He will be a match for Tom Baker's Midnight. I am told there is heavy wagering. I've put a small sum on Midnight myself. Best to bet on Whitfield's own by my way of thinking."

Serena appeared thoughtful at the mention of wagering. She had forgotten that a good deal of money often changed hands at the races. Serena frowned, remembering that Charles had informed them that his friend Macaulay was quite addicted to gaming. The horse race would probably be an irresistible temptation to him.

The butler arrived in the drawing room. "Sir Charles Mainwaring and Mr. Macaulay," he intoned.

The gentlemen entered the room. Catching sight of Serena, Trenhaven smiled. She smiled in return, her eyes meeting his. "Good morning, Mr. Macaulay, Charles."

"Good morning, Miss Serena," said Trenhaven. Somewhat reluctantly he turned his gaze from Serena to her father and sister. "Miss Blake, Mr. Blake."

Mr. Blake nodded rather coldly at the marquess. Since the dinner party, the master of Briarly was disinclined to like Charles's friend.

"I say it is a bang-up day," said Charles, going over to take Lucy's hand and kissing her on the cheek. "I have told William that he has a great treat in store for him. The Whitfield horse fair!"

"I do not doubt that such a provincial event will seem very dull for you, Mr. Macaulay," said Serena.

"I do not believe so, Miss Serena," returned the marquess with a smile. "I am looking forward to it. Charles tells me that I will see some very fine horses."

"And that you will," said Charles.

"I daresay we must not dillydally," said Mr. Blake. "If we do not get started, we may not be in time for the race." He offered his arm to Serena. "Come, my dear."

Serena took her father's arm and the two of them led the others from the drawing room. Once outside, Mr. Blake eyed Trenhaven's high-perch phaeton with disapproval. He thought the vehicle ridiculous although he noted that the horses were of exceptional quality. "I do not see how we will all ride in that," he said.

"Oh, there is room for all of us," said Charles, smiling at Lucy who clung to his arm. "We don't mind a bit of a squeeze. Mr. Blake, you will ride with Lucy and me. Serena can ride up with William. Will you drive us again, Serena?"

"I should like that very much," said Serena, "if Mr. Macaulay does not object."

"I have no objection, madam," said his lordship amiably.

While Mr. Blake did not know if he approved of his younger daughter riding up on the high seat with Charles's friend, he had no qualms about her abilities as a driver. Therefore, he made no remark, but climbed into the phaeton. Lucy and Charles followed, the three of them sitting very close together.

Trenhaven helped Serena up into the driver's seat and then he climbed up himself. The marquess handed her the reins.

"Thank you, sir," said Serena, taking them from him.

The phaeton pulled out, traveling away from the house at a decorous pace. "You are a dashed good whip," said Trenhaven.

"Thank you, Mr. Macaulay," said Serena.

Trenhaven looked back at their passengers, who seemed a bit too crowded for comfort. Lucy, who was sitting in the middle did not seem to mind. Indeed, she seemed particularly pleased at the arrangement. She chattered merrily to Charles as Mr. Blake stared at the landscape. Trenhaven returned his attention to Serena. "Lucy and Charles seem to be enjoying themselves," he said. Then leaning toward her and speaking in a low voice, he continued. "I don't believe your father likes me."

Serena smiled. "That is because you paid so much attention to Arabella. But you must not allow that to deter you. When you see her at the fair, you must be particularly charming."

"I shall do my best," said his lordship, regarding her with amusement.

Serena turned the horses onto the road to the village. "Do you know Freddy's friend Bellamy?" she asked Trenhaven.

"No, I do not know him," returned his lordship.

"Good," said Serena, very much relieved. "We would be quite undone if he knows your true identity."

"I daresay we would be indeed," said the marquess with a smile. "I shall try to convince this Osborne that I am who we say I am. I have given considerable thought to my father's illustrious naval career. Should Osborne ask me, I shall be ready for him."

Serena glanced over at him, not liking his bantering tone. She frowned at his grinning countenance. "I hope you will not make a muddle of things. Sometimes I fear that you do not seem to take this matter seriously enough," said Serena.

"I shall endeavor not to disappoint you, madam," replied Trenhaven, directing a look of such intensity at her that she blushed and looked away.

Serena concentrated on the horses. She was finding Trenhaven's close proximity very disturbing. "There is something I wish to tell you, Mr. Macaulay."

"Yes, Miss Serena?"

"There is a horse race at the fair."

"Charles has told me all about it. Some interloper horse from

Taunton will challenge Whitfield's own Midnight. I had not expected such exciting sport. I am very fond of racing."

"There is a good deal of money being wagered on the race," said Serena, speaking in a low voice. "I do hope you will be sensible and refrain from betting. You know that you are in such grave trouble already."

The marquess could not help but burst into laughter.

"What is so funny?" called Charles from the backseat.

"Nothing at all," said Trenhaven, looking back at his friend. Glancing back at Serena, he smiled, but she was keeping her eyes firmly on the road.

When they arrived in the village, they found it a beehive of activity. The excellent weather had brought out a great number of people, who milled about patronizing the vendors and looking at the horses.

After entrusting the phaeton to the care of a young man at Whitfield's stables, Trenhaven and the others joined the cheerful throng. Serena took her father's arm as they wound their way through the crowd. "Ah, look, there is young Freddy and Mrs. Lindsay," said Mr. Blake with sudden animation.

Looking ahead Serena caught sight of Arabella. She was wearing a stylish primrose outfit. Atop her blond curls was a charming leghorn hat. Arabella was walking with Osborne.

Recognizing Mr. Blake, Arabella started off in their direction, pulling Freddy with her. "Mrs. Lindsay is coming toward us," said Mr. Blake, his voice filled with eager anticipation. He walked toward them with Serena at his side.

"My dear, Mr. Blake," said Arabella as they met. "How fortunate to meet you here." She smiled pleasantly at Serena and Lucy. "Dearest Serena and Lucy. I am so pleased to see you."

Mr. Blake stated that he was very happy to see Mrs. Lindsay again and polite greetings were exchanged. The marquess, mindful of his role, directed a bold look at Arabella, who noted his attention with some satisfaction.

Although Arabella had been convinced by her cousin to be wary of the man, one could not deny that Macaulay was a terribly handsome man. Standing there, Arabella could not help take note of the difference between the two gentlemen and apparent suitors. Indeed, it was hard to ignore the fact that Mr. Blake was old enough to be her father, while Trenhaven was dashing and very appealing. Mr. Blake stood there regarding her earnestly while Macaulay smiled in his roguish way.

Osborne nodded coolly to Serena and the marquess. "How very

nice to see you, Serena," he said. "Good day to you, Lucy, and to you, Mainwaring." Osborne looked at Trenhaven. "And to you, Macaulay."

His lordship nodded, directing a look of aristocratic disdain at Osborne. "Osborne," he said.

"Uncle tells us that there are some very good horses here today," said Arabella. "We were just going to look at them. Perhaps we might all go."

"Yes, that would be splendid," said Mr. Blake. "I am looking for a new hunter."

"And so am I," said Trenhaven, stepping forward. "Perhaps you would like to accompany me, Mrs. Lindsay. You might help me select one."

"I, Mr. Macaulay?" said Arabella. "I am no judge of horses."

"Yes," said Mr. Blake. "For that you would want Serena. She knows more about horses than anyone."

"Oh, I should not wish to trouble your daughter, Mr. Blake. She has had to tolerate my company on the ride here." He offered his arm to Arabella, who hesitated only briefly before tucking her arm under Trenhaven's.

Serena could not help frowning. She found it very irksome to watch Arabella flirting with the marquess despite the fact that she knew she should be pleased. Her father looked rather crestfallen as Trenhaven set off with Arabella. He and Serena and the others followed them with Freddy sticking close to Serena like a great oafish puppy.

There were a number of fine-looking horses assembled on the green. Serena was somewhat diverted when she caught sight of a beautiful bay gelding. "Oh, look, Papa. He is a fine fellow. What about him?"

"What?" said Mr. Blake, watching Trenhaven and Arabella in a forlorn manner.

"You said you are looking for a new hunter. Look at the bay. Is he not beautiful?"

Mr. Blake only nodded absently, but Osborne spoke with enthusiasm. "That is a splendid animal. You do have an eye for horses, Serena."

Ignoring Osborne, Serena propelled her father over to the horse and its owner. While Serena and her father scrutinized the gelding, Charles and Lucy, who had little interest in horses, wandered off in the direction of a man on stilts and a juggler. Osborne, however, stuck close by.

Serena noted that Trenhaven had escorted Arabella toward a

group of horses some distance away. Mr. Blake regarded their retreating forms glumly. "What do you think, Papa?" said Serena.

"What?"

"What do you think?" repeated Serena with a trace of impatience. "About the horse?"

"Oh, yes, the horse," said Mr. Blake, running his hand along the animal's withers in a desultory fashion. "Very nice."

"Yes, I do believe this is an excellent horse, Mr. Blake," said Osborne.

"Would you like to make an offer for him, sir?" said the horse's owner, deciding that Mr. Blake appeared to be a serious customer.

"No, I don't think so," said Mr. Blake. "Come, Serena, I should like to see that tall chestnut over there. Macaulay and Mrs. Lindsay are looking at him. Now that is a fine animal. I'll not allow Macaulay to buy him out from under my nose. He said he is looking for a hunter. Come, my dear."

Serena could only take her father's arm and go off in the direction of Arabella and Trenhaven with Osborne close behind. Coming toward the marquess and his fair companion, Serena noted that Arabella appeared to be enjoying herself immensely. She was regarding his lordship with a fond and decidedly flirtatious look.

"It seems you have found a right one, Arabella," said Osborne, eyeing his cousin with undisguised disapproval.

"Mr. Macaulay seems to like him very much," said Arabella, "but I can see nothing particularly out of the ordinary. He does have nice brown eyes though."

Trenhaven laughed with apparent delight at this remark.

Serena frowned, but said nothing. Her attention was taken by the horse, a tall chestnut stallion with a handsome blaze on his face. Despite her young years, Serena had been involved in a good number of horse trades. Keenly interested in the chestnut, she feigned indifference. "I admit he is not a bad-looking creature," she said, patting the animal's neck.

"You'll not see a finer horse anywhere, miss, than my Achilles," said the owner, coming forward. He was a tall, burly man in a respectable-looking coat and buff-colored pantaloons. "I've had several offers for him today, but I must have at least one hundred pounds."

"One hundred pounds?" said Mr. Blake. "That is a goodly sum for an untested animal."

"Untested? Nay, sir, he's been ridden to the hounds many a time. And a fine jumper he is. You'll see no better in the county."

Trenhaven examined the horse's legs and hooves with expert hands. "He seems fit enough," he said.

"Indeed, sir," exclaimed the owner. "He is fit and game as any that ever walked on four legs."

Mr. Blake stared solemnly at the stallion. "I shall give you one hundred for him."

"I'll give you one hundred and ten," said Trenhaven.

Mr. Blake frowned and Serena regarded the marquess with disapproval. How could he bid against her father? And where would he get one hundred pounds? It was ridiculous.

"One hundred and twenty," said Mr. Blake.

"One hundred and thirty," replied his lordship.

Mr. Blake was growing red with anger. "One hundred and fifty," he snapped. "That is my final offer."

Everyone looked expectantly at Trenhaven. "Since it is clear that Mr. Blake is determined to have him, I shall not disoblige him. The stallion is yours, sir."

Serena's father glowered at the marquess, uncertain whether he should be relieved or furious that the younger man had dropped out of the bidding. He had the feeling that Trenhaven had bested him, forcing him to pay too much for the animal and making him look foolish in Arabella's eyes.

"It is a very fine horse, Papa," said Serena. "I know you will be pleased with him."

"That you will, sir," said the owner. "You'll never regret buying my Achilles, I'll warrant."

Mr. Blake nodded although he wondered if he didn't already regret the purchase. While he made the final arrangements about the sale with the owner, Serena stood with Arabella, Osborne, and Trenhaven. At that moment she was very dissatisfied with all of them.

"I would have liked to have had that horse," said Trenhaven, "but it was very clear Mr. Blake wanted him more."

"Was it not clear that my father wanted him when he first made his offer?" said Serena.

"Oh, perhaps so, Miss Serena," said the marquess, "but one can't tell at first. I've bid on a good many horses that I really didn't care about. It is so hard to resist when one sees a good-looking animal." Trenhaven glanced over at Arabella when he said this as if to imply that Arabella was herself a "good-looking animal."

Arabella smiled delightedly. "You were kind to allow Mr.

Blake to have the horse, Mr. Macaulay. He would have been so disappointed."

"Yes, how very kind of you, Mr. Macaulay," said Serena sarcastically.

Trenhaven smiled at her. "Well, perhaps I shall find another horse."

"I shall be very glad to assist you," said Arabella.

"You will not wish to miss the race," said Osborne, pulling his watch from his pocket. "It will be starting soon."

"Oh, yes," said Arabella, "I adore horse races!"

"Have you placed your wager on the race, Macaulay?" said Osborne. "There is still time if you have not done so."

"I fear I've sworn off wagers," said Trenhaven, directing a meaningful glance at Serena.

"That is so admirable," said Arabella. "I daresay you would do well to emulate Mr. Macaulay, Freddy."

"Then you never wager?" said Osborne, finding that concept hard to imagine.

"Oh, it is not that I have not placed my share of improvident bets in the past," said the marquess, suppressing a smile as he noted Serena's expression. "But I have resolved to turn over a new leaf in deference to my father's wishes."

"What a good son you are, Mr. Macaulay," said Arabella.

"I am certain Lord Ravenswood must think himself a fortunate man," said Osborne. "I am told your father is an eminent war hero."

"Indeed so, Osborne," said the marquess. "He was with Nelson at Trafalgar, you know. And he commanded the flagship *Excelsior* during the Battle of Iberia. I am certain you know about that famous encounter." Trenhaven spoke very convincingly although the Battle of Iberia had been invented for the occasion.

Although neither Osborne nor Arabella had ever heard of it, they did not like to admit their ignorance. They found it more prudent to nod as if they knew what the marquess was talking about. Osborne frowned, wondering whether Macaulay was a great humbug or whether there was any chance that he might be telling the truth. He decided that it would be best to be civil to the man just in case he turned out to be the son of a peer and a war hero.

Trenhaven then offered his arm to Arabella in a most solicitous fashion, saying that he would like nothing than being allowed to watch the race in her charming company. Arabella seemed happy to assent, and the two of them started off, leaving Serena and Osborne there waiting for Mr. Blake.

"It appears Macaulay finds Arabella very attractive," said Osborne.

"It seems the feeling is mutual," replied Serena.

"Yes," said Osborne, frowning darkly in their direction. "What woman would not find the heir of a wealthy peer attractive? And his father a great war hero as well. I shall ask my father about this Battle of Iberia."

"That is a good idea, Freddy," said Serena. "Doubtless the colonel knows all about it."

Mr. Blake joined them looking very unhappy. "Where is Arabella?"

"Oh, she has gone off with Mr. Macaulay to see the race, Papa," said Serena, knowing that information would irritate her father.

"He dragged her away, Mr. Blake," said Osborne. "There was scarcely a thing Arabella could do about it. I daresay she would have preferred to stay with us." Although Osborne realized how lame this sounded, he thought it best to attempt to placate Mr. Blake.

"I suppose it is time for the race," said Serena's father. "We had best be on our way."

Serena took Mr. Blake's arm and the three of them walked off in the direction Trenhaven and Arabella had gone.

The journey back to Briarly from the fair was not altogether pleasant. Mr. Blake was in a rare bad temper. He insisted that his daughters ride beside him in Trenhaven's phaeton, forcing Charles to climb up beside the marquess in the driver's seat.

This arrangement did not please anyone save Mr. Blake. Lucy was crushed that she could not sit next to Charles and his lordship was very disappointed at not having Serena up beside him. Serena had looked forward to driving Trenhaven's fashionable vehicle back to Briarly so she was likewise disappointed.

Tied to the back of the vehicle, the chestnut stallion trotted smartly behind them. When Serena ventured the opinion that Achilles was a lovely horse, her father only frowned and made it clear that he did not wish to discuss the animal's virtues.

There were a number of awkward silences with Lucy being the only one to talk much. She chattered on about the juggler and the mince pies she had tasted, but neither Serena nor Mr. Blake expressed much interest.

Charles and Trenhaven deposited their passengers at Briarly's front door, and since Mr. Blake seemed in such an ill humor, they took their leave. Mr. Blake glumly escorted his daughters into the house and then excused himself, saying he must attend to business in the library.

At dinner that evening, Serena's father made it very clear that he felt Charles's friend an impertinent fellow. Serena expressed no disagreement although Lucy ventured the opinion that Mr. Macaulay seemed a very nice young man. A look from her father told Lucy that she had best not waste any more words defending Charles's friend.

Early the next morning Lucy entered her sister's room. "Are you awake, Serena?"

"I daresay I am awake now," said Serena.

Lucy, who was dressed and eager to begin the day, sat down on the bed beside her sister. Muggins rose from his rug and wagged his tail. "I do think everything is going splendidly, don't you?"

Serena yawned. "I am not sure what you mean."

"It seemed to me that Arabella quite snubbed Papa yesterday. I believe she likes Mr. Macaulay much better. I think Papa is quite vexed with her."

"He is vexed with Mr. Macaulay," said Serena. "I fear that he still believes Arabella to be some sort of angel."

"That could be," said Lucy, "but Charles and I were discussing the situation yesterday afternoon. I believe I have a very good idea."

"I shall be very happy to hear it," said Serena sitting up in bed.

"Tomorrow afternoon we will call upon the Osbornes. I will send word to Charles that he and Mr. Macaulay should happen by at the same time. It will appear to be a coincidence."

"I thought I was the devious member of the family," said Serena, very much interested.

"That will give Mr. Macaulay the opportunity to be charming again to Arabella. And we will suggest an excursion."

"An excursion?"

"Yes," said Lucy. "Charles and I thought it would be good to provide another opportunity for Mr. Macaulay and Arabella to be together. You and I and Papa could go."

"But where would we go?"

"Charles had the best idea. He thought we might go to Glastonbury Abbey."

"Indeed?" said Serena with a thoughtful expression. "That is an excellent idea."

"Yes, I think Charles very clever to think of it. It is so romantic and beautiful. Arabella will fall in love with Mr. Macaulay if she has not done so already. Don't you think it a splendid idea?"

"Yes," said Serena although she did not particularly like the idea of Arabella falling in love with Trenhaven. "It is a very good idea, Luce. I do not doubt that Arabella will be very eager to go on such an expedition."

"Oh, yes," said Lucy. "I am convinced she will like the idea. I expect Papa will be eager to go as well when he hears that Arabella will be accompanying us."

"Yes," said Serena, "and Papa will have another opportunity to see Arabella's true colors."

Lucy rose from the bed. "Exactly so. But do get up, Serena. You must not be a slugabed. It will soon be time to go to church."

Lucy left the room. Rising from her bed, Serena rang for her maid and began to dress.

17

When the stagecoach from London arrived at Whitfield Monday afternoon, one passenger descended from his perch high atop the coach. Tired from his journey and eager to have his feet upon the ground once again, Roger Bellamy viewed Whitfield with great happiness.

Taking up the quizzing glass that hung on a satin ribbon around his neck, he studied the village street. "How very quaint," he pronounced aloud.

"Your bag, sir," said the coachman's assistant, tossing his carpetbag down to him.

After catching it easily, Bellamy began to saunter down the street. He had visited Whitfield once before a few years ago. He had stayed more than a fortnight, even though in Colonel Osborne's eyes, he had worn out his welcome after two days.

There was not much activity in the village, but those few persons on the street regarded young Bellamy with interest. He was a tall, heavyset young man with carroty red hair which was, for the most part hidden by his tall beaver hat.

Very much the fashionable gentleman, Bellamy wore a coachman's topcoat over a pea-green coat, apricot waistcoat, and ivory pantaloons. Always wishing to appear at the height of fashion, Bellamy suffered the discomfort of his very high collar and elaborate cravat.

Arriving at the Osborne residence, Bellamy put down his bag and rapped on the door. The maid who answered his summons regarded him questioningly.

"I am Mr. Bellamy," he said grandly.

"Oh, yes, sir. Master Frederick is expecting you, sir."

Stepping inside, Bellamy took off his hat and topcoat and handed them to the servant, who led him into the library where Osborne sat writing a letter. "Mr. Bellamy is here, sir," said the maid.

Osborne looked up. "Belly, old man," he said rising to his feet and extending his hand.

Bellamy took the proffered hand and shook it enthusiastically. "Freddy, you old devil. My, you look well. Life in the provinces agrees with you."

"Agrees with me? By God, I cannot say why that should be the case. I detest it here. But do sit down. Would you like a glass of sherry?"

"That would be splendid," said Bellamy.

Osborne poured him a glass from a carafe on the library table. "So they hounded you out of town."

"That they did," said Bellamy, sitting down near the fireplace. "I daresay that I was being dunned at every turn. I barely escaped with my life. I certainly hope your parents will not mind me staying here."

"As luck would have it, my parents are visiting my uncle in Taunton. They will not return for several days."

This news cheered Bellamy immeasurably. "Do tell me how you are getting on. I am eager to hear about your pursuit of this heiress of yours."

"You would better oblige me by not mentioning the subject."

"Oh dear," said Bellamy, taking a sip of his sherry. "You cannot mean that the lady has refused you?"

"I have not made an offer for her, although I daresay she would refuse me if I did. I have come to believe she quite detests me. Why only the other day I drove directly by her and received the cut direct."

"Poor Freddy," said Bellamy. "But are there no other heiresses to be found who might show better judgment?"

Osborne shook his head. "Unmarried ladies of fortune are very rare in Somerset."

"As they are in town," said Bellamy. "I, too, have been most unlucky where the fair sex is concerned. There was one lady, a widow. She was more than forty and she was quite stout and bad-tempered, but she had a tidy fortune. I did everything I could to win her and, my dear fellow, it was monstrous hard spouting lovesick drivel to such a dreadful woman. Oh, well." Bellamy looked forlorn as he took another drink of sherry.

"I say, Belly, I have been so eager for you to arrive. First of all, have you brought any more of that splendid snuff you sent me?"

"Oh, I did not come empty-handed. I brought some in my bag. It is Prinny's favorite blend, you know."

"What a good fellow you are," said Osborne. "And now I have another question. Do you know of a man named Macaulay? William Macaulay is the name."

"I don't believe so," replied Bellamy. "No, I am sure I have never made the acquaintance of anyone by that name."

"His father is purported to be a certain Lord Ravenswood."

"Ravenswood?" Bellamy shook his head. "No, I have not heard of him."

"I believe Macaulay to be an imposter," said Osborne. "He is wooing my cousin Arabella."

"But I thought your cousin was to marry that Mr. Blake, the rich squire."

"That is what I thought, but the silly creature will very likely ruin her chances by flirting with this Macaulay. I had hoped you knew him."

"No, that is a pity," said Bellamy. At that moment Arabella entered the room.

"I was told our guest had arrived," said Arabella.

The gentlemen rose to their feet. Bellamy, who had never before met Arabella, stared at her with undisguised admiration.

"Arabella," said Osborne. "May I present my friend Bellamy? Bellamy, this is my cousin, Mrs. Lindsay."

"Mr. Bellamy," said Arabella, smiling her most dazzling smile and extending her hand.

Bellamy took it eagerly. "Your devoted servant, ma'am," he said.

"I have been telling Belly about Macaulay," said Osborne. "Unfortunately, he is not acquainted with him."

"Freddy says you know everyone in town, Mr. Bellamy," said Arabella. "I had thought you might have met Mr. Macaulay."

"One cannot know everyone," said Bellamy, "although I am acquainted with many people in society."

"If Belly has not heard of him, I cannot believe that Macaulay is a person of any consequence."

"I do wish you would not refer to Mr. Bellamy by that nickname, Freddy," said Arabella.

"It is a dashed silly nickname," said Bellamy, grinning.

Osborne started to make a comment, but the appearance of the maid interrupted him. "Miss Serena and Miss Lucy are here. I have shown them to the drawing room."

"They are here?" said Osborne quite astonished. He had not expected that Serena and Lucy would ever call on them.

"This is interesting," commented Arabella.

Osborne rose from his chair in some agitation. While he had told himself that he had no chance with Serena, her arrival brought a tiny ember of hope to him.

"I shall be glad of meeting these ladies," said Bellamy languidly. "Freddy has written so much about them." Bellamy was always eager to meet young ladies, especially unmarried ones who had large marriage settlements to commend them. Now that his friend Freddy had apparently given up on winning Serena Blake, it occurred to Bellamy that he might have a go at the prize.

Sensing his friend's thoughts, Osborne frowned. "If you have the idea that you might charm Serena Blake, Belly, I warn you that you will be disappointed."

"Why such an idea is the farthest thing from my mind, Freddy," protested Bellamy.

Leaving the library, they made their way to the drawing room. Serena and Lucy were seated upon the sofa. "What an unexpected pleasure," said Osborne.

"Yes," said Arabella, hurrying to the young ladies to greet them with a kiss on the cheek. "My dear Serena and dearest Lucy." Arabella took a seat in a chair near them while the gentlemen remained standing.

"Good afternoon," said Serena, smiling pleasantly. Noticing Bellamy, she regarded him with interest.

"My dear friend Bellamy has just now arrived from London," said Osborne. He made the introduction and Bellamy bowed very low over first Lucy's and then Serena's hand.

"Osborne has written to me so much about you ladies," said Bellamy. "But I was totally unprepared to find two such beauties. Indeed, I see before me three of the loveliest ladies in the kingdom. Should you all come to town, you would create a sensation."

Serena smiled at Bellamy, although she thought him a rather absurd young man. She noted with amusement his rather wild-looking red hair and dandified clothes. "I do hope you will enjoy your stay in Whitfield, Mr. Bellamy."

"Oh, I know that I shall," said Bellamy.

"We should not like to take up too much of your time," said Lucy. "We have come to issue an invitation."

Osborne regarded her in some surprise, for he had not expected the Blake sisters to invite him to anything. Of course, he reasoned, Mr. Blake was probably behind it.

Lucy continued. "Serena and I thought that it would be such great fun to go to Glastonbury Abbey. We thought we might go on Thursday. I do hope you will accompany us. My father is very knowledgeable about the abbey's history. He will be going with us, of course. And, Mr. Bellamy, you are welcome as well."

"Yes, Mr. Bellamy," said Serena, "you should not come to our vicinity without visiting it."

"I should like that very much, Miss Serena," said Bellamy.

"What a capital idea," said Osborne even though he thought Glastonbury Abbey a dull old ruin.

Arabella appeared very enthusiastic. "I do think that sounds quite wonderful."

"It will be a great lark," said Lucy. "Do you think you can come?"

"Yes, I am sure that I could," said Osborne. "What do you think, Arabella?"

"Oh, I should dearly love to go and Thursday is excellent."

"Good," said Serena. Before she could say something further, the maid once again entered the room.

"Excuse me, sir," she said, addressing Osborne. "Two gentlemen are here. Sir Charles Mainwaring and Mr. Macaulay."

"Why, this is the day for visitors," said Osborne. He had certainly not expected them to appear at his door. After all, there was no love lost between Charles and him. Still, reflected Osborne, it would not be incredible for Macaulay to wish to call on Arabella.

"Do not turn them away on our account, Freddy," said Serena. "Lucy and I cannot stay."

"Show them in, Ellen," said Osborne.

The maid returned in a moment with the gentlemen. Charles entered the room first. He brightened at the sight of his beloved Lucy. "My dear Lucy," he said. "I did not expect to find you here."

"Oh, we were just leaving, Charles," said Lucy.

"We will escort you back to Briarly," said Charles, happy at the prospect.

Trenhaven followed his friend into the room. Serena noted that he looked very dapper in his perfectly cut coat. He smiled at her, causing the now familiar quiver of excitement to run through her.

"Good afternoon, Freddy," said Charles, smiling amiably at Osborne. "Arabella."

"I should like to introduce my friend Bellamy," said Osborne. "He has just arrived from town. Sir Charles Mainwaring and Mr. Macaulay, may I present Mr. Bellamy?"

Charles and Trenhaven both nodded in Bellamy's direction.

The marquess was happy to see that he had never before cast eyes on Osborne's friend.

While Bellamy nodded politely to Charles and Trenhaven, it took all of his self-control to refrain from revealing the astonishment he felt at that moment. There standing before him was the Marquess of Trenhaven!

While his lordship did not know Bellamy, that gentleman knew him very well. After all, Trenhaven was one of society's most eminent members. Bellamy, who was not admitted to the best drawing rooms, had had many occasions to view Trenhaven from afar. He had never dreamed that he might one day actually meet the illustrious marquess.

"We called to invite Freddy and Arabella on an excursion," said Lucy. "We are going to Glastonbury Abbey on Thursday. I hope that you and Mr. Macaulay will accompany us."

"Glastonbury Abbey on Thursday?" said Charles. "That would be fine. You would like to see Glastonbury, would you not, William? They say it is where King Arthur had his court."

"I think it is a splendid idea," said Trenhaven. He smiled at Arabella. "I do hope you are going, Mrs. Lindsay."

"Yes, I am very excited at the prospect, Mr. Macaulay," said Arabella, meeting his gaze and smiling brightly.

Serena did not fail to note how Arabella was looking at the marquess. She frowned. "I fear we must be going," she said rising to her feet. "Truly, Charles, there is no need for you to escort us back to Briarly. I could not bear to think of you cutting short your visit on our account."

"Oh, we should be going anyway," said Charles. "Mr. Bellamy has just arrived. I daresay he is too tired for visitors. We will go. It seems we will all meet Thursday for our adventure."

"Yes," said Lucy, getting up from the sofa. "It is not such a long time away. We will arrange everything. Do you think you could come to Briarly by eleven o'clock on Thursday? It would be more convenient to leave from there."

"We will be there," said Osborne.

The arrangements made, Lucy and Serena took their leave. Charles and Trenhaven followed them.

When they had gone, Bellamy sat down on the sofa. "My God," he said.

"What is the matter?" said Osborne, alarmed at his friend's expression.

"Are you unwell, Mr. Bellamy?" said Arabella.

"No, indeed. It is just that I recognized your Mr. Macaulay."

He grinned at Osborne. "It seems you were right to think he is not what he seems."

"Whatever do you mean, Belly?"

"I mean that the man whom you know as Mr. Macaulay is none other than the Marquess of Trenhaven, the son of the Duke of Haverford."

"Don't be absurd," said Osborne.

"Yes, that is quite impossible," said Arabella.

"Might you have a copy of *Debrett's?*" said Bellamy.

"In the library," replied Osborne. "I shall fetch it."

He returned shortly with the volume, which he handed to Bellamy. Paging through it quickly, Bellamy found what he was looking for. "There he is, His Grace, the Duke of Haverford. And there is his son. See for yourself, Freddy."

Osborne took the peerage book. The name of the duke's son was listed. "William Arthur Macaulay Savage, Marquess of Trenhaven," Osborne read it aloud. "Damn me, I cannot believe it!"

Arabella took the book from her cousin and studied the entry. "But he did not know you, Mr. Bellamy."

Bellamy smiled again. "We have not been introduced, ma'am. And I confess I do not find myself in such rarified circles as his lordship. But I know well who he is. Yes, that gentleman was Lord Trenhaven. There is no doubt of it. Indeed, there was talk of his lordship leaving London. No one knew where he went."

"So he came to Whitfield," said Arabella. She smiled suddenly. "And Freddy thought him an imposter."

"He *is* an imposter," said Osborne.

"The Marquess of Trenhaven," said Arabella. "Do you think anyone else knows who he is?"

Osborne shook his head. "I cannot say. Although if he felt it necessary to come here incognito, perhaps he wished to prevent everyone from knowing who he is."

"Were I a marquess, I should wish everyone to know it," said Bellamy.

"A marquess," repeated Arabella, looking rather wistful. "And he is the son of a duke."

"Are you imagining yourself a duchess, Arabella?" said Osborne, frowning at his cousin.

"And why not?" said Arabella. "Lord Trenhaven is not indifferent to me." She turned to Bellamy. "He is not married, is he, Mr. Bellamy?"

"Indeed not, Mrs. Lindsay. The marquess is the greatest prize in town. I daresay every eligible lady in all of London has set her cap for him."

"Now, Arabella, do not get ideas," said Osborne. "You must know it is hopeless to think you might ensnare a marquess who will one day be a duke. If you were wise, you would turn your attentions to Blake."

Arabella did not deign to reply. "I hope you gentlemen will excuse me," she said. "I must see to Mr. Bellamy's room."

Rather surprised at his cousin's unexpected domesticity, Osborne nodded. When she had gone, Osborne demanded that his friend tell him every detail he knew about the Marquess of Trenhaven.

As his lordship walked away from the Osborne house, he had no idea that his identity had been revealed. He looked forward to the walk back to Briarly with Serena at his side. The four of them passed through the village with the gentlemen leading their horses.

Lucy was in high spirits, thinking her plan to go to Glastonbury Abbey a brilliant one. She leaned heavily on Charles's arm as they walked away from the house. "When Serena first thought of the idea to make Arabella turn from Papa to someone else, I thought it would not work. But Mr. Macaulay has been splendid. Do you not agree that he has been quite wonderful, Serena?"

Serena glanced at the marquess, who was smiling at her. Looking back at her sister, she nodded. "I will say that he has done his part well enough."

Sensing that her sister was not altogether pleased with the situation, she made no reply. Then turning her attention to Charles, Lucy pressed his arm and regarded him with an adoring expression.

Finding herself walking beside Trenhaven, Serena found that once again his closeness was rather discomfitting. She tried hard to appear indifferent.

"If I did not fear that I would be thought immodest," said Trenhaven, continuing to smile at Serena, "I should say that I have acted my part brilliantly."

"I doubt it was so difficult for you, Mr. Macaulay. I daresay you have a great deal of practice charming ladies in town."

"Perhaps," he said with a smile. They walked on a little in silence. "Your father must think me a dreadful villain."

"I must confess he does not have the highest opinion of you, sir. He was quite vexed about the horse."

"Indeed? I should not have bid against him. You must tell him that I would be happy to buy the horse from him at the price he paid."

"You have quite forgotten yourself, Mr. Macaulay," said Serena, frowning at him. "You would pay my father for the horse? Where, pray, would you find the money?"

"Yes, that is always the difficult part," said the marquess with an amused look. "I fear I did forget myself. I was dashed fond of that chestnut. I am sorry to irritate Mr. Blake. I should be happier if he thought better of me, but if I am to take his lady love away from him, I cannot expect him to be pleased."

"No," replied Serena. "Knowing my father, he will not forgive you."

"That could be a problem," said his lordship, imagining Mr. Blake as his father-in-law."

"What do you mean?" said Serena.

"Oh, nothing," said Trenhaven. "It is only that I cannot be happy thinking that such a fine gentleman as your father despises me. But under the circumstances, I suppose that is how it must be. But I shall look forward to our journey to Glastonbury Thursday. And even though your father will hate me, I shall do my level best to win Arabella."

Serena cast a sidelong glance at him. "It seems you get on so well with her. I'm sure you will enjoy yourself."

"Enjoy myself? Oh, I doubt it." He smiled. "I shall hardly be happy paying my attentions to Arabella when I should much prefer paying them to you."

Serena looked down in surprise. "Don't say such absurd things, Mr. Macaulay."

"I am perfectly serious," replied the marquess. As his gray eyes met her hazel ones, Trenhaven found it hard to resist the impulse to take her into his arms. "Oh, I realize I cannot hope that you might regard me with favor, knowing as you do my many failings. But if I were a different man, without ruinous debts and strong defects of character, might you dislike me less?"

"I do not dislike you, sir," said Serena, knowing well the nature of her true feelings. She regarded him earnestly. "But you are not a different man, and your faults are grave indeed."

Trenhaven appeared thoughtful. "Serena," he said, "there is something I must tell you."

"Yes, Mr. Macaulay?"

Before he could reply, the marquess was interrupted by Charles. "William, I was just telling Lucy about that dreadful man who taught us history at school. You know, the old fellow who talked incessantly of King Arthur. I cannot remember his name."

"Whittaker," said Trenhaven.

"Yes, of course," cried Charles. "Whittaker! What a detestable man. But he did know everything about King Arthur. He wrote a book on the subject. I have it in the library. We will have to find it when we return. He often mentioned that Arthur was buried at Glastonbury. They say his ghost wanders about at night."

Charles continued on, talking about King Arthur and his knights. Trenhaven had no opportunity to renew his private conversation with Serena, a fact that disappointed both of them. As they continued on, walking toward Briarly, Serena found herself wondering what Mr. Macaulay had intended to tell her.

18

On Thursday morning the sky was gray and overcast, threatening rain. Despite that neither Serena nor Lucy considered changing the plans for the trip to Glastonbury. After all, the arrangements had been made and the food had been packed into baskets.

Mr. Blake had viewed the trip with mixed emotions after having learned that Trenhaven would accompany them. Having developed an antipathy toward that gentleman, he had no desire to spend at entire day in his company, especially when Arabella would be there as well.

Although Mr. Blake had been very much disheartened by Arabella's apparent preference for Mr. Macaulay, he had not given up hope. Knowing that the day's excursion would provide him with an opportunity to engage Arabella's affections once again, Mr. Blake was determined to do his best to impress her. He dressed with particular care, wearing a new coat and pantaloons. He even submitted himself to the agony of whalebone stays beneath his waistcoat in order to improve his figure.

Mr. Blake was not the only person to pay great attention to his appearance that morning. At the Osborne residence, there was a good deal of activity as Arabella, Osborne, and Bellamy made ready.

Since learning of Trenhaven's true identity, Arabella had thought of nothing else but how she might ensnare the marquess into matrimony. She was certain he was not immune to her charms. Indeed, his attentions to her had made that very obvious.

Still, Arabella was realistic enough to know very well that it might not be easy getting Trenhaven to propose marriage. After all, a man of his station generally chose a wife from the ranks of the aristocracy. Yet, Arabella reminded herself, there were numerous instances of gentlemen falling in love with ladies of far lower birth than she. As Arabella sat in front of her dressing table arranging her blond locks, she smiled confidently and imagined herself a duchess.

Osborne, on the other hand, had given up his pursuit of an advantageous marriage with Serena Blake. He consoled himself with the idea that being married to the willful Serena would make any man's life miserable. He was well rid of her, he concluded.

As he dressed that morning, Osborne wished he had not agreed to go to Glastonbury. Having seen the ruined abbey several times, he had no desire to see it again. Nor did he relish the idea of giving Serena more opportunities to snub him. And marquess or no, "Mr. Macaulay" was not someone Osborne wished to see again.

In a small, cramped room down the hallway from Osborne's, Bellamy cheerfully attended to his morning ablutions. Splashing cold water on his face from the basin, he smiled into the mirror and then took up his shaving tackle.

While his friend Osborne was dreading the day's activities, Bellamy was filled with eager anticipation. He had not expected Whitfield to be so fascinating. Why, he had scarcely arrived when he had been introduced to the Marquess of Trenhaven. He had only dreamed of such a thing in town. Now he would be spending an entire day in Trenhaven's company.

Bellamy began to whistle as he sharpened his razor on his leather strop. He felt as though he was to have a change in his fortunes. Certainly if one could become friendly with such an illustrious personage as the Marquess of Trenhaven, some good could come of it. Smiling again, he began to shave.

Arabella, Osborne, and Bellamy arrived at Briarly at the predetermined hour. They were led to the drawing room where Mr. Blake welcomed them. Smiling warmly at Arabella, he complimented her on how splendid she looked.

Arabella did look beautiful. She had selected her best outfit, a peacock-blue spencer over a matching dress and French bonnet. She thought she looked every bit as grand as any lady in London society.

Lucy and Serena joined the guests a short time later. They, too, had dressed carefully. Lucy wore a peach-colored pelisse over an ivory dress, while Serena's elegant pelisse was claret in color and adorned with satin bows.

The magnificence of the ladies caused Bellamy to erupt into a stream of compliments and proclaim himself a lucky man indeed to find himself in such company. For her part Serena eyed Bellamy with amusement. He was wearing the pea-green coat he had worn the day before, but his neckcloth was tied in an even more elaborate style, puffing out from his neck in such a way as to remind Serena of the sails of a ship. While she found his exaggerated style of dress rather ridiculous, Serena found something oddly likable about Bellamy as he chattered on.

Charles and Trenhaven arrived a few minutes later to join the others in the drawing room. "Now everyone is here," said Lucy, going over to stand beside Charles.

"Yes," said Mr. Blake. "We had best be going. One cannot know when the weather will change. I should not like to be viewing the ruins in the rain."

"Indeed not, sir," said Bellamy. "I should think it most expedient to commence our journey at once."

"Then let us go," said Mr. Blake, offering his arm to Arabella. Charles smiled brightly at Lucy and led her toward the door.

Trenhaven smiled at Serena. "Do go on, gentlemen," he said, addressing Osborne and Bellamy. "I shall escort Miss Serena outside." Osborne did not look too pleased, but he and Bellamy nodded and made their way to the door. "Good morning, Serena."

"Good morning, Mr. Macaulay."

"You look wonderful."

"You are too kind, sir," replied Serena, feeling rather weak under Trenhaven's gaze.

"But where is Muggins?"

Serena smiled. "He has been banished to the kitchen. Freddy has a horror of him. And Muggins has such an aversion for Freddy. I daresay Muggs was disappointed that he could not come with us, but it is for the best. But, we must not dally here, sir, or the others will wonder where we are."

"I should like nothing better than to dally with you, Serena," said his lordship, regarding her with a look that made her blush.

"Mr. Macaulay!" said Serena, taking his arm and propelling him toward the door. "I hope you will not forget that it is Arabella you are to charm."

"I have not forgotten," said the marquess with a smile.

When they joined the others outside, they found Mr. Blake was giving instructions. "I think it best if I accompany the ladies in my carriage," he said. "You young gentlemen may ride in Charles's carriage."

Although keenly disappointed at the idea that he would not be riding with Lucy, Charles took his future father-in-law's pronouncement in stride. "I say, sir, you are the fortunate one, traveling with three beautiful ladies."

"Yes, I am," said Mr. Blake, holding fast to Arabella. "Age has its privileges. Now I believe we should be off." He assisted the ladies into the carriage and then climbed in himself, happily sitting next to Arabella.

The carriages started off on the journey. Trenhaven found himself sitting beside Charles. Across from him was Bellamy with Osborne next to him. The marquess noted with some satisfaction that Osborne seemed in a particularly foul mood. Folding his arms in front of him, Osborne stared sullenly out the window.

Bellamy on the other hand was in the best of spirits. In response to Charles's query as to how he liked Whitfield, Bellamy expounded on the many delights of such a picturesque small village.

Since it was scarcely more than seven miles on a fairly decent road, the journey from Briarly to Glastonbury usually took only about an hour and a quarter to complete. Trenhaven, while preoccupied with thoughts of Serena, found the time passed very quickly. He was kept amused by Bellamy, who had a droll sense of humor and a host of anecdotes about his life in London.

Serena found the ride considerably more tedious. Sitting across from Arabella, she did not enjoy watching her father cast fond glances in that lady's direction. The conversation was rather desultory with Lucy doing most of the talking.

Serena was glad when they reached the end of their journey and the carriages pulled up near the ruins of Glastonbury Abbey. After descending from the vehicle, Serena stared at the ruins. Although she had been here many times before, Serena was always moved at the sight of the what was left of the medieval abbey. Once one of the richest monasteries in England and the heart of a thriving medieval town, the abbey was destroyed by King Henry VIII in the sixteenth century.

Supposing it to be one of the most romantic places in England, Serena loved Glastonbury. Turning from the abbey ruins, she looked out at Glastonbury Tor, a hill rising sharply from the land. Atop the tor was the ruined tower of the Church of St. Michael. Serena knew well that according to legend, the Holy Grail was buried beneath the waters of a spring on the hill.

Legend also had it that King Arthur and Guinevere were buried beneath the abbey ruins. The idea intrigued Serena, who loved the Arthurian legends. Looking from the tor back to the ruins, she thought wistfully of Camelot.

"It is beautiful," said Lucy, smiling at Arabella. "Don't you think so, Arabella?"

"There is not much to see, is there?" replied Arabella, clearly unimpressed.

By this time the gentlemen from the other carriage joined them. Charles hurried to Lucy's side, eager to link arms with her. "I do hope it doesn't rain," said Charles. "It does look as if it could." He glanced over at Trenhaven. "Dashed fine ruin, don't you think, William?" he said.

The marquess smiled. "An excellent ruin to be sure."

"I concur wholeheartedly, sir," said Bellamy. "I have seen a good many ruins, but this is as fine a ruin as any I have seen."

Serena could not help but laugh at this comment. "I am glad you like it, Mr. Bellamy. You must allow my father to tell you all about it. He is an expert."

"Are you, Mr. Blake?" said Bellamy.

Mr. Blake modestly brushed aside his daughter's compliment. "I fear I know only what I read in my guidebook, Mr. Bellamy. But I will tell you that there are only two intact buildings left, the kitchen and the abbot's barn. I find the kitchen most interesting." He turned his attention to Arabella, hoping to escort her about the site.

To his great displeasure, he found that Arabella had made her way to where Trenhaven was standing. Having taken his arm, she looked up at him with a flirtatious smile. The marquess appeared quite pleased with her attention.

"Perhaps you would like to come with me, Mrs. Lindsay," said Mr. Blake hopefully. "I mentioned to young Bellamy about the abbot's kitchen. It is there." He pointed in the direction of an octagonal building.

"Oh, I shall be along with Mr. Macaulay," said Arabella.

Serena noted her father's crestfallen look. It appeared that Arabella was not in the least interested in Mr. Blake. Apparently, she had transferred her interest entirely to Trenhaven. Lucy and Charles had gone off from the others, wandering around the ruins. Mr. Blake and Bellamy started toward the kitchen with Serena and Osborne following close behind.

Since he found the place exceedingly dull, Osborne adopted a bored expression as he walked through the old abbey. Only a small section of the original structure remained. There were parts of walls, but no roof of any kind. Uninterested in history, Osborne did not like thinking about the Middle Ages. The idea of King Arthur and his knights had little appeal as well.

There was one aspect of the outing that provided Osborne with some interest and that was Arabella and Trenhaven. Glancing back every now and then, Osborne noted that the two of them seemed to be getting on famously. They appeared determined to stay far enough away from the others so that they could hold a private conversation.

Osborne thought his cousin Arabella a fool. Now that he knew Trenhaven's true identity, he was certain that Arabella was very much mistaken in assuming that she could charm him into marriage. Considering himself a man of the world, Osborne was well aware of the direction such flirtations usually went. A cynical young man, he did not believe they led to marriage.

Therefore, Osborne could summon no enthusiasm for Arabella's ambitions. Had he truly believed she might succeed, he might have been supportive, for it would be a very grand thing to have a cousin married to a marquess even if he were someone Osborne detested.

Serena was likewise interested in Trenhaven and Arabella. Like Osborne, she kept glancing in their direction. Her father did so as well. Imagining that Arabella was exchanging intimacies with the marquess, his displeasure grew greater. Arabella seemed blithely unaware of Mr. Blake's anger. She made no effort to join him and the others, preferring to linger with Trenhaven.

"Father, do tell Mr. Bellamy about the legend of how the Holy Grail was buried," said Serena, hoping to divert her father for a time.

Mr. Blake told the story, but without the usual zest he had for the tale. Bellamy listened with interest, while Osborne's mind wandered.

"Dashed fascinating, Mr. Blake," he said when Serena's father concluded his narrative. "I do enjoy such stories. The Holy Grail and the knights of the Round Table. Stirring stuff, what?"

Osborne nodded absently, while Mr. Blake turned to see Arabella and Trenhaven. To his surprise, they were gone. "Excuse me," he said. "I shall return in a moment."

Turning, he strode off, leaving Serena, Freddy, and Bellamy standing beside the abbot's kitchen. "Do excuse me as well," said Serena, hurrying off after her father.

Osborne watched them go. "Poor old Mr. Blake. The man is making a great cake of himself over Arabella."

"Well, your cousin is a dashed pretty girl, Freddy. It seems Trenhaven is very much taken with her."

Osborne shrugged. "Arabella believes she will persuade him to marry her. I fear she will regret it." He frowned and then the two of them started off after Serena and Mr. Blake.

* * *

While anyone seeing Trenhaven with the lovely Arabella might have deduced that he was a very lucky fellow, the marquess did not feel in the least fortunate. Although Trenhaven could not deny that Arabella was a very desirable and beautiful woman, it was Serena whom he wanted. Remembering his assignment to preserve Mr. Blake from the fate of marrying Arabella, the marquess did his best to appear enthralled with his companion. When Arabella batted her eyelashes and spoke in a seductive voice, Trenhaven appeared to find her irresistible.

Leading him behind one of the ancient stone walls and out of the view of the others, Arabella directed a bold look at the marquess. "I must confess, Mr. Macaulay, that I find you a very handsome man."

"And I find you very beautiful, Mrs. Lindsay."

"Perhaps you might call me Arabella."

"Very well, Arabella."

"And I hope I might call you William."

"Yes, of course."

She looked around and then smiled at him. "A place like this can make a lady quite forget herself. It is so romantic. I think of Lancelot and Guinevere."

"Yes, one would," said Trenhaven.

Arabella needed no further encouragement. "Oh, William, I am so in love with you." Then throwing her arms around his lordship's neck, she pulled him to her and kissed the astonished marquess full on the lips.

"Macaulay!"

A loud masculine voice caused the marquess and Arabella to spring apart. There stood an enraged Mr. Blake and behind him was Serena. "Mr. Blake!" cried Arabella.

"Macaulay, what is the meaning of this?" Mr. Blake purpled with rage. "How dare you take advantage of this lady in such an infamous manner. What sort of man are you?"

"It was all perfectly innocent, I assure you," said Trenhaven.

"Innocent? Do you take me for a fool, sir?"

"Now, Papa," said Serena, coming up beside him, "do not excite yourself."

"Good heaven! You are here, Serena? You witnessed this?"

"Do take care, Papa," said Serena, worried at his overwrought expression.

"Yes, do calm yourself, Mr. Blake," said Arabella.

"Had I not come by, I daresay the fellow would have taken more liberties," said Mr. Blake.

Arabella, who would have been very happy had such a prospect occurred, frowned. "Mr. Blake, you need not worry. Mr. Macaulay is a gentleman."

"Is he?" said Mr. Blake. "He does not act like a gentleman. You are a villain, sir!"

"Mr. Blake!" cried Arabella. "Do not speak to Mr. Macaulay in such a way. This does not concern you, sir."

Mr. Blake looked at her with a pathetic expression. "I had once thought that you were fond of me."

"Then you were mistaken, sir," she replied sharply.

"Yes, I suppose I was," said Mr. Blake in a weak voice.

Serena was frightened by her father's tone. She had never heard him so utterly disheartened. "Papa . . ." She started to take his arm, but he pulled away.

"I am going to the public house in the village. You do as you please."

"Papa!"

Mr. Blake did not reply, but hurried off toward the nearby houses.

Serena regarded both Trenhaven and Arabella angrily, but she could think of nothing to say to either of them. Most of her anger, she realized, must be reserved for herself. It was she who had arranged for her own father to be humiliated in such a disgraceful manner.

"Is something wrong?" Lucy's voice made Serena turn around. There stood her sister and Charles, worried expressions on their faces. Bellamy and Osborne were coming up behind them. "Where is Papa going? What happened?" said Lucy.

"Oh, there is nothing to worry about," said Serena. "Papa wished to go to the village."

Trenhaven stood there awkwardly. Watching Mr. Blake walking briskly away, he wished that he had never agreed to assist Serena with her scheme.

19

Riding home in the carriage, Serena reflected that the trip to Glastonbury Abbey had been a disaster. Shortly after her father had stalked off to the public house in Glastonbury, it had started to rain and the idea of the picnic lunch had to be abandoned.

The inclement weather had forced them to join Mr. Blake in the pub even though Serena had been well aware that her father wished to be alone. Fortunately, Mr. Blake had sufficiently recovered his composure by the time the others found him.

Luncheon had been an awkward affair with most of the company having little to say. After they had eaten, Serena had suggested that they return home.

The journey back to Briarly had not been a pleasant experience for Serena. She had felt exceedingly uncomfortable sitting across from Arabella and her father. Mr. Blake had sat with his arms folded across him, saying nothing. Arabella, on the other hand, had chatted on about Glastonbury and other topics as if nothing were the matter.

Serena was very glad when the carriage turned into the lane leading up to Briarly and finally came to a stop in front of the main entrance to the country house. Charles's carriage stopped at Briarly as well, but Charles and Trenhaven did not linger. Saying that they must go on to Mainwaring Hall, Charles paused only to allow Osborne and Bellamy to disembark. After a few polite words, they were on their way.

Arabella, Osborne, and Bellamy were quick to take their leave as well. When everyone had gone, Mr. Blake retired to his rooms, saying he felt very tired and was not sure whether he would join them at dinner.

After changing into a simple muslin dress, Serena came downstairs. "Jim," she said, addressing a footman who was passing through the entry hall, "where is Muggins?"

"I have not seen him, miss."

"Would you please fetch him for me? I shall be in the drawing room."

"Very well, miss, Miss Serena," he replied.

Serena went into the drawing room and sat down on the sofa. Sighing, she rested her head in her hands and thought that it had been a dreadful day. The image of Arabella in Trenhaven's arms kept coming back to her. The sight of them together had jarred her terribly. A bitter smile crossed Serena's face as she reflected how well she understood how her father must feel.

When Lucy entered the drawing room a short time later, she found her sister staring glumly at the fire. She took a seat in an armchair across from her. "Serena, do tell me what happened at Glastonbury Abbey. It must have been something terrible, for you and Papa both are very upset."

Serena looked over at her. "Papa came upon Mr. Macaulay kissing Arabella."

"Oh dear!" cried Lucy. "Are you certain?"

"I saw them as well," said Serena. "Papa was furious!"

"No wonder he is so blue-deviled. But then what happened?"

"Papa told Macaulay he was a villain. And Arabella said that it was no concern of his. Then Papa said he had thought she was fond of him. She replied that he was mistaken."

"Oh, poor Papa," said Lucy. "He must be heartbroken."

Serena nodded. "I fear he took it very ill. But we are rid of her. We have succeeded in that." She frowned again. "I am not now sure that we have done the right thing."

"But we should be glad that Papa will not marry her," said Lucy. "Indeed, I am happy about that. And in time I am sure that Papa will realize he is better off without a wife like Arabella. She is such a horrid, fickle creature. I daresay she will be very unhappy to learn that she has thrown Papa aside for a man who has no money." Lucy looked thoughtful. "Do you think Mr. Macaulay kissed Arabella to earn the one hundred pounds or because he wanted to kiss her?"

"I do not know, nor do I care why he kissed her," said Serena crossly.

Noting her sister's unhappy expression, Lucy felt it wise to say nothing more on this topic. She was well aware that her sister had developed an unfortunate *tendre* for Mr. Macaulay. It seemed he was as unscrupulous as Charles had said.

"I am certain all will be well in the end," said Lucy.

"I hope you are right, Lucy," said Serena.

"Oh, I know I am," replied Lucy firmly. She then decided to

change the subject. "I did think Mr. Bellamy rather amusing, did you not?" said Lucy.

Serena smiled. "I did think so. He is rather silly, but seems a good-hearted young man. Yes, I thought him quite pleasant even if he is Freddy's friend."

"I believe Freddy has given up on you, Serena," said Lucy.

"I am relieved of that," said Serena. "I daresay Papa will not regard him quite so fondly now that Arabella has turned out so badly."

"Yes, I expect you are right," said Lucy. She looked down at a letter she was holding and then looked over at her sister. "It just occurred to me, Serena. Now that Mr. Macaulay has completed his work and Arabella has abandoned Papa, we must pay Mr. Macaulay his one hundred pounds."

"I daresay we must," said Serena. "I shall write to Mr. Hayton at the bank to send it to me from the money Uncle Oliver left us."

"Yes," said Lucy. "I suppose it is money very well spent."

Serena made no reply to this remark, but frowned. "I wonder where Muggins is. I asked Jim to fetch him," said Serena. At that moment Jim entered the room, but Muggins was not with him. "But where is Muggins, Jim?"

"We have not yet found him, Miss Serena."

"Not found him?" said Serena. "Was he not in the kitchen?"

"No, miss. He was not there. Tom and Peter are searching for him. It does not appear that he is in the house."

"I do not like him roaming about," said Serena, in some irritation. "Someone should have seen to him."

"We will find him, miss," said the footman.

When he had gone, Serena rose from her seat. "I shall go and look for Muggins. Perhaps he is sleeping under a bed somewhere."

"I shall help you," said Lucy, getting up from her chair.

The two young ladies left the drawing room and proceeded through the house, calling the dog's name. After having no luck in the house, Lucy and Serena fetched their hats and cloaks to look outside.

They walked along their usual path, but there was no sign of the terrier. Finally they returned to the house. "Do not fear," said Lucy. "Muggins will come back when he has a mind to do so."

"I am sure you are right," said Serena. Yet as she entered the house, she could not help but worry. Muggins had never run off before.

Mr. Blake did come to dinner much to the relief of both of his daughters. Serena's father, while hardy in a cheerful mood, seemed a bit less depressed.

The main topic of conversation at dinner was Muggins and his unfortunate disappearance. Knowing how much Serena loved the dog, Mr. Blake did his best to reassure his younger daughter that Muggins would undoubtedly return.

After dinner Lucy and Serena once again set off on a walk about the estate, searching for Muggins. When he could not be found, they returned quite discouraged. Deciding that it had indeed been a wretched day, Serena went to bed early. Between her worries about the dog and her memory of seeing Trenhaven kissing Arabella, it was some time before she fell into a troubled sleep.

The following morning Trenhaven joined Charles for breakfast in the dining room at Mainwaring Hall. "Good morning, old man," said the baronet, filling his plate from the sideboard.

"Good morning, Charlie," returned the marquess, taking up a plate and examining the contents of the various chafing dishes.

When they were seated at the huge mahogany table, Charles smiled at his friend. "I hope you slept well, William."

"It was the first night I did not sleep well. I kept thinking of Serena's expression when she saw me with Arabella. That was the most damnable luck."

Charles grinned. "At least Mr. Blake was turned against Arabella. I believe he now realizes what sort of woman she is."

His lordship smiled ruefully. "I imagine he believes he knows what sort of man I am. Good God, how will he accept me as a son-in-law?"

"I should be more worried about Serena," said Charles. "Indeed, kissing Arabella was going a bit far."

"I have told you that it was she who kissed me. She is apparently quite enamored of me or of the great estate I will inherit from Baron Ravenswood. The whole business is an absurd farce."

"I quite agree, William," said the baronet, taking a bite of his boiled egg. "I do hope you will be able to extricate yourself from Arabella's clutches. She is doubtlessly making wedding plans as we speak."

"Then she will be very disappointed. But it is Serena who I am concerned about. I must go and see her to explain what happened yesterday. I do not doubt that she misconstrued the incident."

"One could not blame her," said Charles with another smile. "We will go to Briarly this afternoon."

"This afternoon? I should think this morning would be better. We might pass by on our morning ride."

"Very well, we will do so, but I cannot guarantee that we will be received."

Trenhaven seemed willing to take the chance and the two friends continued with their breakfast.

Osborne and Arabella sat in the modest dining room of the Osbornes' residence, eating breakfast. Since Bellamy was accustomed to keeping town hours, he had not yet risen.

Osborne was in a decidedly ill humor for he was exceedingly vexed with his cousin for throwing away her chance to become mistress of Briarly. On the way back to Whitfield the previous day, he had made his opinion very clear to Arabella much to her vexation.

Taking a piece of toast, Arabella frowned at her cousin. "You will not be so disappointed with me, Freddy, when I am Lady Trenhaven."

"Lady Trenhaven?" said Osborne. "You are deluding yourself."

"I find it quite offensive that you cannot think that Trenhaven would wish to marry me. I do not find the possibility so unlikely."

"We will see," said Osborne. "For my part, I think you were completely bird-witted to toss Blake aside. The man was utterly besotted with you. And he is as rich as a nabob."

"But Trenhaven is richer. And he is a marquess. One day he will be a duke. I would be a duchess." There was a gleam in Arabella's eyes as she imagined herself attired in ermine and coronet.

"Well, I cannot help thinking you have made a serious mistake," said Osborne, taking up his teacup.

Having a good deal more confidence in herself, Arabella only smiled and took a bite of toast.

20

Trenhaven and Charles arrived at Briarly shortly before eleven o'clock. One of the grooms hurried out to take their horses as they dismounted. Lucy met them at the front door.

Very pleased to see Charles, she greeted him with a kiss. "Charles! I did not expect you! Good morning, Mr. Macaulay."

The marquess tipped his hat. "Good morning, Miss Blake. I hope you will forgive us for calling at this hour."

"Oh, I am so pleased to see you both," said Lucy, ushering them inside. "I am in need of company. Papa has taken to his bed with a cold. He is quite miserable."

"But where is Serena?" said Charles.

"She has gone riding. She has been out all morning looking for Muggins."

"Looking for Muggins?" said the marquess.

"He has run off," said Lucy. "We all expected he would be back this morning. Serena is quite beside herself with worry. She so dotes on Muggins. Of course, I love him, too. He is such a darling."

Charles, who did not share this opinion of the bullterrier, wisely remained silent. "I do hope Serena has not gone off alone."

"But she has. I told her to take one of the grooms, but she sent them all out to search for Muggins, saying they could cover more ground if they went separately. She promised she would not go far."

"Did she say where she was going?" said Trenhaven.

Lucy nodded. "She said that she would take the Somerton Road. I am sure she will be home soon."

"Perhaps we should go in search of Serena, William," said Charles. "We could look for Muggins."

"I shall go," said the marquess. "Why don't you stay with Lucy? Tell me how to find this Somerton Road."

While Charles did not like to have his friend go off by himself, the idea of having some time alone with Lucy seemed very appealing. After receiving directions, the marquess took his leave, going out of the house and mounting his horse once again.

Riding away from the house, Trenhaven turned his horse in the direction of Whitfield. Following Charles's instructions, he found the Somerton Road without difficulty and proceeded along it. Although the road on which he was now traveling was taking him through some marvelously picturesque countryside, his lordship was so intent on his thoughts of Serena that he took little notice of the scenery. After traveling nearly two miles, he caught sight of her.

Serena was dressed in the crimson riding habit that she had been wearing when he had first met her. Trenhaven smiled, thinking her a splendid sight atop her fine gray mare.

Recognizing Trenhaven, Serena regarded him in surprise. She had not expected to see him there. As she neared him, she felt her pulse quicken. Yet she cautioned herself to act sensibly. After all, she reminded herself severely, it was only yesterday that she had discovered him embracing Arabella.

"I am glad to have found you, Serena," he said, coming up alongside her. "I was at Briarly and your sister told me where you had gone. I do not think it wise for you to ride so far alone."

"Good day, Mr. Macaulay." Serena thought of saying that she was quite capable of riding a few miles from her own home by herself, but she was stopped by the look of genuine concern on his face. "You have been to Briarly, sir? Then you know that Muggins is missing."

The marquess nodded. "You have had no luck finding him, I see."

Serena shook her head. "No, I have not found him." She looked very concerned. "When he had not returned home this morning, I was very worried. I fear something has happened to him."

"There is no need to think of that," said Trenhaven. "A dog will roam when he has the chance."

"Yes, I suppose that is true," said Serena, directing a meaningful look at the marquess.

Trenhaven frowned. "Serena," he said, "I should explain about yesterday."

"I don't know what you could mean, sir," she said.

"Dammit, of course you do. I know you were not too pleased with me when you saw me kissing Arabella."

"I do not know why you would think that, Mr. Macaulay. Indeed, I should commend you for your success. My father has given up Arabella. I no longer have to worry about having her for my stepmother. I am most grateful to you and I shall be happy to pay you the one hundred pounds you are owed. I imagine you found it a very pleasant way to earn such a sum."

"Surely you cannot think I am fond of Arabella?"

"It seemed you were fond of her when you kissed her."

"I did not kiss her," said the marquess. "She kissed me. I was taken by surprise, I assure you." He regarded her seriously. "Upon my honor, there is another lady whom I would much rather kiss."

Serena looked down at the reins in her hands. "Mr. Macaulay, I wish you would not say such things. Indeed, I think it best if we returned to Briarly. Perhaps someone has found Muggins."

While the marquess had no wish to return to Briarly now that he was alone with Serena, her mention of Muggins returned him to the somber fact of the dog's disappearance. "You did not find anyone who had seen him?" said Trenhaven.

She shook her head glumly. "I spoke with several people. They all said that they would look for him. I daresay everyone now knows that he is missing. We should be going back." Serena urged her horse forward. The marquess turned his horse and came up beside her.

"You must not worry, Serena, I am sure you will find Muggins."

"I do hope so," said Serena. "I am so fond of him."

"I shall do everything I can. Charles and I will look everywhere."

"That is very kind of you, Mr. Macaulay," said Serena. They rode on for a time until Serena espied a man walking down a narrow lane toward the road. "It is Mr. Henderson. Perhaps he has seen Muggins," she said, pulling her horse to a stop and waving to the man.

Henderson, a gaunt, elderly fellow in a farmer's smock and broad-brimmed hat came toward them. "'Tis Miss Serena," exclaimed the farmer, doffing his hat respectfully. "How very good to see you, miss."

"Good morning to you, Mr. Henderson," replied Serena. "I am hopeful that you might assist me. Do you know my dog, Muggins?"

He scratched his chin. "Nay, miss, I do not believe I do."

"He is a bullterrier, brindle in color. He is wearing a leather collar with his name inscribed on a brass medallion. He has run off and I am looking for him."

"Run off? Miss Serena? 'Tis a pity," replied the farmer. He cast an interested glance at Trenhaven. Thinking that the young gentleman accompanying the squire's daughter was a grand-looking man, he wondered who he might be and whether he might be a marital prospect for Serena.

"You have not seen Muggins, have you, Mr. Henderson?"

"Nay, miss, but my grandson told me this morning that he saw a strange dog with Jack Griggs. Perhaps that was your dog, miss."

"Did your grandson describe the dog he saw?" said Serena hopefully.

"Nay, miss. I was not so interested to ask. But you may wish to ask Griggs about him."

"Thank you very much, Mr. Henderson. We will see Griggs at once. Good day to you. Do give my good wishes to Mrs. Henderson. I hope she is well."

"Oh, very well, miss," said the farmer, pleased at Serena's interest. "Good day, miss." He looked up at Trenhaven. "Sir."

The marquess nodded in reply and the man walked off down the road. "Do you know this Griggs, Serena?"

She nodded. "I do indeed. He is a horrible man who has an uncommon interest in fighting dogs. You cannot think he has stolen Muggins?"

Trenhaven shook his head. "It does not seem likely. Perhaps he has found him. He may be taking him back to Briarly. Do you know where he lives?"

She nodded again. "It is not far. Follow me, sir."

Serena turned off the road onto a narrow path that led across a stream and through a woods. In a short time the path opened up into a clearing. Soon they came upon an untidy thatched cottage. Chained to the back of it were two bullmastiff dogs, who barked furiously as they approached.

"Mr. Griggs," called Serena. "Are you there?"

When there was no answer, Trenhaven dismounted. Going up to the cottage door, he rapped upon it. After what seemed to the marquess a long time, a dirty, disheveled middle-aged man appeared at the door. "What you want?" said the man. His speech was slurred and there was a reek of alcohol about him.

"We are looking for a dog," said the marquess.

"You want to buy a dog?" replied the man, staring at Trenhaven with bloodshot eyes.

"No, I am looking for a lost dog, a bullterrier belonging to Miss Serena Blake."

Serena had by this time dismounted from her horse. She approached the man. "Mr. Griggs, my dog Muggins is lost. We were told that you were seen with a new dog. Perhaps you found Muggins."

"I found naught, miss," said Griggs. "Nay, I've not seen your dog."

"You did not find a dog?"

"Nay, miss."

"But Henderson's grandson saw you with a strange dog," persisted Serena.

"That were my brother's dog, miss. He's tied there in back." He gestured toward the back of the cottage where the dogs were chained.

Serena regarded Griggs with a frown. He was a ne'er-do-well who was universally disliked in the parish. "I hope you are telling me the truth, Mr. Griggs," said Serena.

"'Pon my honor, miss, I do tell you the truth. I've nay seen your dog. Should I see him, I'll bring him to you." He paused. "I expect there be a reward for him who finds the dog."

"Yes, there is a reward," said Serena. "Five pounds."

"Five pounds?" said Griggs. "'Tis a generous reward indeed. I'll keep a wary eye out for him, miss. Good day to you." He started to close the door, but Trenhaven shoved it open. Pushing past Griggs, he stepped into the cabin. "See here, sir," protested Griggs. He looked around the filthy cottage, but Muggins was not there. "You've nay right to come into a man's home uninvited, sir," Griggs said indignantly.

The marquess did not deign to reply, but walked back out. "Muggins is not inside," said Trenhaven, addressing Serena.

"So you think I'm a liar," said Griggs, scowling at his lordship. "There's nay dog here. Are you satisfied?"

Making no reply, Trenhaven took Serena's arm and walked to the horses. He assisted her up onto her sidesaddle. "Do you think he has Muggins somewhere?" said Serena, looking down at the marquess.

"I don't know, but, don't worry, if he does, I should think the reward will make him bring him back to Briarly."

Serena smiled. "I hope so."

Smiling in return, Trenhaven had an almost overpowering urge to pull Serena down from her horse and into his arms. Instead, he mounted his own horse. As they rode off, Trenhaven regretted the fact that the path was too narrow to allow him to ride beside her. He had so much to say to her.

The marquess was glad when they reached the road and he could position his horse next to hers. "Serena?"

"Yes, Mr. Macaulay?"

"Don't you think that you might call me William?"

She nodded. "Very well, William."

Trenhaven smiled. "I must tell you something, Serena," he began. She looked over at him expectantly. Before he could begin to speak, there was a shout in the distance. They looked up to see Charles riding toward them.

"There is Charles," said Serena.

"Yes," said the marquess, thinking his friend's appearance most untimely.

"Here you are!" said Charles as he came up to them. "I have come from Briarly. I was having a very pleasant chat with your sister, Serena, when your father came down to the drawing room."

"But he is ill!" said Serena.

"He was not too ill to come down. It seems one of the servants informed him that I was there and that William had ridden off to find you. He was not at all pleased to say the least. I regret to say, William, that Mr. Blake considers you a dreadful reprobate. You are not welcome at Briarly and you are not to speak to his daughters."

"Oh, he is being quite unreasonable," said Serena.

"Indeed he is," said Charles. "But I said I would go and find you and bring you back immediately. I suggest we make haste to return to Briarly before Mr. Blake sends for the constable."

Serena and Trenhaven exchanged a glance, but there was nothing to do, but to go on to Briarly. Then, because Mr. Blake had made it very clear that the marquess was unwelcome there, Charles and Trenhaven took their leave of Serena and rode back to Mainwaring Hall.

21

The following afternoon, Serena and Lucy sat in the drawing room. Lucy worked on her embroidery while her sister attempted to read a novel. Her mind kept wandering, however, and she would stare thoughtfully into space. Lucy could not help but notice her sister's preoccupation. "I know how worried you are about Muggins," said Lucy, directing a sympathetic look at Serena as she tied a French knot.

Serena, although very worried about her dog, had been actually thinking about Trenhaven. She nodded. "I am not convinced that that horrible Mr. Griggs did not take Muggins. They say he buys and sells fighting dogs. I cannot bear to think what might happen to Muggs."

"Oh, Serena, you must not think of that. No, indeed, I am certain dear Muggins will turn up soon. Someone will find him. I daresay everyone in the parish is looking for him."

This remark did little to encourage Serena, who glumly returned to her book. A few moments later one of the footmen entered the room. "Mrs. Claybrook is here, Miss Lucy," he said.

Lucy looked over at her sister. "Oh dear, I don't suppose we could refuse to admit her."

"Why not?" said Serena. "I have no wish to see that woman. Tell her we are not receiving, Reynolds."

"No, wait," said Lucy, motioning to the servant. She frowned at her sister. "I do think we should see her, Serena. Mrs. Claybrook will think us very rude if we do not."

"Oh, very well," muttered Serena, "but do not expect me to be polite to her."

"You must be civil, Serena," cautioned Lucy. "Do promise me you will be polite to her."

"Oh, dash it," said Serena. "Yes, I will mind my manners. Have no fear. Yes, do show Mrs. Claybrook in, Reynolds."

When Mrs. Claybrook entered, she smiled warmly and announced that she could not stay long. Seating herself beside Serena on the sofa, she expressed her great dismay at hearing that Serena's beloved pet was missing. She then inquired about Mr. Blake. After expressing great concern upon hearing he was in bed with a cold, Mrs. Claybrook turned the conversation to the reason she had come. "I have heard the most exciting news. I thought you girls would wish to know. It is about Arabella."

At the mention of the name, Serena could not help but frown. "Arabella?" said Lucy.

"Yes," replied Mrs. Claybrook. "The rumor is that she is going to marry Mr. Macaulay."

"What?" said Serena, regarding their guest in astonishment.

"You cannot mean that Mr. Macaulay has asked Arabella to marry him?" said Lucy.

"Oh, he has not yet made an offer for her, but she expects he will do so shortly."

"I should think Arabella is rather premature in speaking of marriage if Mr. Macaulay has not yet asked for her hand," said Serena.

"Perhaps," returned Mrs. Claybrook, "but Arabella told me that Mr. Macaulay has spoken to her in such terms of affection that there is no mistaking his intentions. And she told me that on Thursday when she accompanied you to Glastonbury Abbey, Mr. Macaulay made so bold as to kiss her."

"Or she made so bold as to kiss him," said Serena. "Truly, Mrs. Claybrook, I fear Arabella will be very much disappointed in this. She would be wise to say nothing further about it."

"Indeed?" said Mrs. Claybrook, surprised at Serena's reaction.

"It would seem far more prudent for a lady to say nothing until she is actually engaged," said Serena.

"You cannot fault Arabella for wishing to share such good news, and, of course, she has only informed her most intimate acquaintances. And she has said she is quite certain Macaulay is very much in love with her. I am so pleased for her. After all, he is such a wealthy young man with such worthy expectations. Arabella will be a very grand lady married to Mr. Macaulay."

Both Serena and Lucy stared at Mrs. Claybrook. Lucy was unsure how to respond and Serena was so irked that she did not trust herself to say anything. Mrs. Claybrook was gratified to see that she had quite confounded the Blake sisters. Smiling, she rose from the sofa. "I must be going, my dears. I have a good many calls to make. Do give my good wishes for a speedy recovery to Mr. Blake."

"Thank you, Mrs. Claybrook," said Lucy, rising politely. "I shall be happy to do so."

When their visitor had gone, Serena could not hide her exasperation. "That woman will be spreading this all over the village, Lucy. She will be telling everyone that Arabella is to marry Mr. Macaulay."

"Then she will feel very foolish when he does not," replied Lucy. "You cannot believe that Mr. Macaulay would wish to marry Arabella?"

"Don't be a goose," said Serena. "And I daresay Arabella would not wish to marry him if she knew the truth about him."

"I'm sure you are right," said Lucy.

Serena nodded resolutely. "I believe it is time for us to inform Arabella of the truth about Mr. Macaulay."

"Oh, Serena," cried Lucy. "I don't think that would do at all."

"Let us go to the village and see her," said Serena. "Come, Lucy, fetch your bonnet. And do wear your cloak. It is rather chilly. I shall tell Reynolds to have the carriage brought round."

"Serena, you know Papa would be very upset to hear that we are calling on Arabella."

"I have no intention of telling him," said Serena, leaving the drawing room. Lucy could only sigh and follow.

Arabella sat in the library of her aunt and uncle's house writing a letter. After penning a few sentences, Arabella stopped to stare thoughtfully out the window. All day she had been distracted by her thoughts of Trenhaven and the memory of the excursion to Glastonbury.

Thinking of the marquess, she could not help reflecting upon the prospect of being married to such a man. To be a rich and titled lady would be a fine thing indeed. The fact that Trenhaven was a handsome and virile young man was an added and much appreciated bonus.

Putting her pen down, Arabella rested her chin on her hand. How should she proceed to get him to ask for her hand? she wondered. Yesterday she had told Mrs. Claybrook that she expected him to make her an offer of marriage. It had seemed a good idea to allow the word to go out. After all, rumors so often turned out to be true. And Trenhaven had been paying so much attention to her that Arabella had suspected that he had fallen in love. He had not been the first to do so, Arabella reminded herself.

"Excuse me, Mrs. Lindsay." Arabella looked up to see the maid had entered the library. "Miss Serena and Miss Lucy Blake are here. They wish to see you. I have shown them to the drawing room.

Arabella could not hide her surprise. She had certainly not expected the misses Blake to call. "I shall see to them at once," she said, rising from her chair.

When she entered the room, she found Lucy and Serena standing there with very serious expressions on their faces. "How good of you to call," she said in her sweetest voice. "Do sit down. Would you like some refreshment? Tea perhaps?"

"We cannot stay," said Serena, directing an icy look at Arabella. She sat down on a worn leather sofa. Lucy took a seat beside her. "There is something I wish to say to you, Arabella."

Arabella sat down across from Serena. "Yes, Serena?"

"Mrs. Claybrook called at Briarly a short time ago. She told us that you are putting it about that you are to marry Mr. Macaulay."

"I am hopeful of doing so."

"But he has not made an offer for you."

"No, he has not," said Arabella, "but I am sure that he will."

"I cannot know why you think so," said Serena, frowning at her.

"I should think you might have some idea," replied Arabella. "After all, you were at Glastonbury. You witnessed a rather indiscreet moment. I fear Mr. Macaulay was quite carried away. He said a good many things to me that gave me cause to know his feelings. Unless he is an utterly unprincipled bounder, I should think marriage is the next logical step."

"I fear you will be very disappointed, Arabella," said Serena. "I am here to tell you that Mr. Macaulay is not the man you think him to be."

"Indeed?" said Arabella, regarding Serena with keen interest.

"I have a confession to make. Mr. Macaulay is not the son of Lord Ravenswood. There is no such person. He is not a peer's son and he has no money at all."

"What do you mean?" said Arabella. When Serena had started to speak, Arabella had assumed she was going to announce that Macaulay was really Lord Trenhaven. It appeared that Serena was unaware of the fact.

"You must know that Lucy and I did not approve of my father's interest in you."

"I should have been blind if I did not realize that," said Arabella. "Indeed, I knew from the first that you did not think me worthy of your father."

"I confess I did not want him to marry you," replied Serena

matter-of-factly, "but it was his happiness I was thinking about. That is why I invented the story about Mr. Macaulay's wealth and family."

"You invented it?"

Serena nodded. "I thought that you would shift your affections from my father to Mr. Macaulay if you thought him wealthy and a peer's son. It seems I was right."

Arabella stared at Serena. "This is unbelievable."

"I am telling the truth. Mr. Macaulay is a friend of Charles's. When he arrived at Mainwaring Hall, Charles wrote to tell us about him. He has no money. Indeed, he is hopelessly in debt. He agreed to go along with this charade because I am paying him to do so."

"What?" cried Arabella in astonishment.

Serena nodded. "He was paying attentions to you for the sole purpose of earning the one hundred pounds I agreed to pay him."

While this information stunned Arabella, she remained remarkably calm. "You are a despicable creature, Serena Blake," she said. "And you are not much better, Lucy," she said, looking over at Serena's sister. "So you think Mr. Macaulay cares nothing for me? Is that it?"

Serena nodded.

Arabella laughed. "You are very much mistaken."

"He has no fortune, Arabella," said Serena. "There is no point in your pursuing him."

"You fancy that I am the worst sort of fortune huntress," said Arabella. "Yes, I know what you think of me. You were so very sure that I only cared for your father's fortune. Well, I am sorry that you think so little of me. I had great regard for your father. Had not Mr. Macaulay come along, I might have wished to marry him." Arabella rose to her feet and adopted a melodramatic pose. "I am in love with Mr. Macaulay. I do not care if he is as poor as a church mouse. I would gladly marry him if he had nothing more than the clothes on his back."

Serena was taken aback by this pronouncement. She got up from the sofa and Lucy followed. "You cannot expect me to believe anything so absurd."

"Absurd?" cried Arabella. "I assure you, Miss Serena Blake, that I love Mr. Macaulay. I cannot expect you to understand. Everyone knows you are the most cold-hearted girl. You have never cared a fig for any man. But you are both completely mistaken about me and you should be ashamed. Now I suggest you leave here at once." With these words Arabella burst into tears and fled the room.

Serena and Lucy stood there for a moment. Then they hastily departed. Once inside the carriage and on their way back to Briarly, Lucy shook her head. "Oh, Serena, you cannot imagine that we were wrong about Arabella? What if we were? What if she is not the horrid mercenary person we always thought her?"

Serena frowned. Could she have been mistaken about Arabella? She did not think so, but she had to acknowledge that Arabella had sounded convincing. Suddenly, she was not so sure. What if she were in love with William? What if Arabella was telling the truth in saying she did not care that he had no money. "I cannot bear to think that we were wrong about her," Serena said finally.

"We had never thought that she might have fallen in love with Mr. Macaulay. It was so cruel making her think he cared for her." She looked intently at her sister. "I know it is you he loves."

"Oh, Lucy, how can you know that?"

"Why, Charles has told me. He is very much in love with you. And I believe you love him as well."

"I scarcely know him, Lucy."

"That does not signify in the least. Are you in love with him?"

Serena nodded. "I suppose I am. I love him very much. Oh, Lucy, I did not think I could fall in love, but I love William just as you love Charles."

"My poor Serena. What are we to do? Mr. Macaulay is so unsuitable. Papa despises him. And I daresay we could never tell Papa the truth about what we did. And Mr. Macaulay has no money and there are those debts of his to be considered. And then his drinking—"

"Lucy, do not talk to me of his faults. I am well aware that he is not a man I should think of marrying."

"No, you could not marry him, Serena. I told Charles as much. Oh, it is quite a muddle, is it not? But it never occurred to me that Arabella might not care that Mr. Macaulay didn't have any money. But she said that she wished to marry him even though he had no money at all. If we have been wrong about her, we should indeed be ashamed of ourselves."

Serena made no reply. Feeling very miserable, she pulled her cloak tightly about her and glumly watched the passing landscape from the carriage window.

*   *   *

An hour after Serena and Lucy departed from the Osborne house, Freddy returned home, accompanied by Bellamy. While his houseguest retired to his room for a time, Osborne went in search of his cousin. He found her in the library.

"Ah, Arabella, there you are. Bellamy and I have just come from a ride. I must say old Belly is growing rather tiresome. I do hope he can be persuaded to leave before the Colonel and Mother return."

"I doubt if he ever intends to leave," said Arabella ill-temperedly.

Osborne sat down beside his cousin on the worn leather sofa. "Is something wrong, Arabella? You do not seem very cheerful."

"It is only that I have had a visit from those horrid Blake sisters."

"They called here?" said Osborne in surprise.

She nodded. "It appears you were right in thinking that Serena and Lucy were trying to trick me."

"Whatever do you mean?"

"They had arranged for Trenhaven to divert me from their father. According to Serena, she was paying him one hundred pounds to do so."

"What the devil!" cried Osborne. "That is utterly absurd. Why should the Marquess of Trenhaven agree to such a scheme? And take a hundred pounds? I daresay Serena is deceiving you, Arabella."

"Serena and Lucy do not know who Macaulay really is. Apparently Charles and he are playing some sort of game with them as well. I believe that Trenhaven is amusing himself with this charade."

"Egad, this is dreadful. And now you have lost that idiot Blake. I told you you were a fool to think your Trenhaven would marry you. It is obvious this is all some sort of joke to him."

Arabella nodded grimly. "I fear you are right, Freddy. But I shall have my revenge, I assure you."

"How?"

"I don't know," replied Arabella, "but I will not allow those wretched girls to best me. Nor will I let Trenhaven make a fool of me."

Osborne would have said something more, but Bellamy entered the room at that moment. Unaware of the serious discussion he had interrupted, Bellamy began to chatter about the weather while Arabella and her cousin exchanged frowns.

22

Trenhaven sat in Mainwaring Hall thinking of his own unhappy situation. When he had last seen Serena, he had not had the opportunity to tell her the truth and ask for her hand in marriage. Three days had gone by since then. On each of those days he had ridden to Briarly, attempting to see her. Each time he had been refused admittance.

Charles had been unable to help because the baronet had apparently caught the same cold that had sent Mr. Blake to bed. Confined to bed himself, he could not call at Briarly to attempt to make matters right.

Restless without his friend's company and irritated at his inability to see Serena, the marquess paced about Mainwaring Hall. He spent the day idly wandering about the house, growing more frustrated with each passing hour.

At luncheon, the marquess ate by himself in the cavernous dining hall. Thinking constantly of Serena, he wanted desperately to speak with her.

Visiting Charles in his bedchamber after luncheon, Trenhaven ventured the opinion that he should attempt to call at Briarly once again. Charles was adamantly opposed to the idea, knowing that his friend would be turned away again. He could only advise Trenhaven to be patient and wait until he was fit enough to see Mr. Blake himself.

Leaving Charles to get more rest, the agitated marquess decided to take a ride. Once on horseback it was impossible for Trenhaven to avoid making his way toward Briarly. Arriving there some time later, he jumped down from his horse and went to the front door.

Opening the door, the butler eyed his lordship with disfavor. Reynolds was tired of turning the young gentleman away. "I am sorry, sir, but no one is at home. I shall tell the master you have called."

To Reynolds' great surprise, Trenhaven pushed him aside and

boldly walked into the house. "It is of vital importance that I see Miss Serena," he said.

"I am sorry, sir," said the butler. "I must insist that you leave, sir."

"I shall only take a few moments of her time. Do tell her that I am here."

"I cannot do so, sir," said the servant.

"You will tell her I am here," said his lordship, adopting an imperious tone. "Do so at once!"

The butler was unsure what to do. He did not like to argue with a gentleman as well-dressed and regal as Trenhaven. Still, his master had forbidden Mr. Macaulay from darkening his door. "I am so very sorry, Mr. Macaulay," he said apologetically, "but the master would have my head if I let you in."

The marquess frowned. He was not an unreasonable man and he was not insensitive to the servant's situation. Still, he knew he had to see Serena. "I will not leave," he said in a loud voice. "I will see Miss Serena."

Reynolds looked at a loss for what to do. Fortunately a feminine voice came to his assistance. "It is all right, Reynolds," said Serena, appearing in the entry hall. The marquess noted she looked lovely in a print dress with a ruffled collar. "I shall speak to Mr. Macaulay here at the door."

"Surely I might come in for a moment. You cannot expect me to stand at the doorstep like a common peddler," said his lordship.

"Papa has said you are not to be admitted." She looked at the butler. "I shall speak to Mr. Macaulay outside, Reynolds."

"But, Miss Serena—"

"I assure you it is all right, Reynolds," said Serena, stepping outside.

"Serena, you cannot know how much I wanted to talk to you. I have so much to say to you."

Serena frowned. "I have something to tell you. I spoke to Arabella a few days ago. She claims to be in love with you."

"That is balderdash. You know she cares nothing for me."

"But what if she does? Oh, William, I am very much afraid that I was mistaken about her. I told her that you had no money. I explained that you were not the son of a peer and that we had arranged for you to pay your attentions to her. She said that she did not care that you were as poor as a church mouse. She wanted to marry you anyway."

"What do I care about her anyway?" said the marquess impatiently. "It is you I care for, Serena. You must know that I am in love with you."

"But what about Arabella?"

"What about Arabella? My God, I do not concern myself with her in the least."

"How can you be so heartless? She may be in love with you. Don't you care if you break her heart?"

"What would you have me do? Marry her? If she has conceived a misguided affection for me, I am heartily sorry. But it is you I love, Serena. I want to marry you."

"Oh, William, how could I marry you now with this wretched Arabella business? She has had it bandied about the village that you will marry her."

"Arabella be damned," muttered his lordship, taking Serena into his arms. Pulling her to him, he fastened his lips upon hers. Serena, although shocked by such behavior, could only put her arms around the marquess and return his kiss with a passionate longing that delighted the marquess.

"What are you doing! Unhand my daughter, sir!"

Trenhaven and Serena sprang apart. Mr. Blake stood in the doorway attired in his dressing gown. His face was livid with rage. "God in heaven! Is no woman safe from you, sir!"

"You don't understand, Mr. Blake, I wish to marry your daughter."

"Marry my daughter? Do you think I would allow Serena to marry a debauched libertine like you? Are you mad? Get off my property, sir, or I shall call my servants and have you bodily thrown out!"

"Mr. Blake, you must allow me to explain. About what happened at Glastonbury—"

"Enough!" shouted Mr. Blake. "I do not want to hear another word from you." He then collapsed into a fit of coughing.

"Oh, Papa!" cried Serena, going to him. "You are still not well! You must return to bed!" She regarded Trenhaven imploringly. "You must leave."

"Serena, I—"

"I beg you, William, do go!" By this time several burly servants had appeared behind Mr. Blake.

"I am sorry, Mr. Blake," said Trenhaven. "You are ill. I shall take my leave. But before I go, I must tell you that I do intend to marry Serena."

Mr. Blake regarded him incredulously. "Did you not hear what

I said, sir? I would never allow you to marry Serena." He started coughing again.

"But, sir."

"Get out!" said Mr. Blake.

"William, I do think it best for you to leave," said Serena, clutching her father's arm.

The marquess looked as though he would say something further, but the look in Serena's eyes, made him reconsider. "Very well, Mr. Blake. When you are well, we will talk again."

"We will not talk again, sir," Mr. Blake managed to say between his bouts of coughing. "And I forbid my daughter to see you. You will never see her again. Get out of my sight!"

"Papa," said Serena, "you are overwrought. You must get back to your bed at once. And you must go, Mr. Macaulay. I beg of you."

"Very well, Serena," he said. He looked at Mr. Blake. "Good day to you, sir. I will take my leave."

Mr. Blake, who was, by this time, quite red in the face and feeling weak, made no reply. Serena and the servants helped him back into the house.

The marquess stood for a time looking at the door to Briarly as if uncertain what to do. He finally mounted his horse with great reluctance.

As he rode off, Trenhaven looked back at the house. He could not imagine how things could have gone so badly. Mr. Blake had made it very clear that he was not to see Serena again.

The marquess frowned. He was filled with frustration at the memory of Serena's lips on his. Thinking of how her body had pressed against his filled him with longing, and he was determined to have Serena for his bride.

But what would he do about Mr. Blake? he asked himself. He could not blame that gentleman for thinking him a bounder. After all, Serena's father had found him kissing Arabella just a few days before. His lordship could easily imagine what Mr. Blake had thought when he had come upon his daughter in his embrace.

Trenhaven's frown deepened. It seemed he had a very thorny problem. He could not marry Serena without Mr. Blake's consent unless he carried her off to Gretna Greene. As he made his way toward Mainwaring Hall, Trenhaven appeared thoughtful. He was resolved to marry Serena Blake and father or no, he would do so. "I will marry her," he said aloud as he continued on.

Arriving back at Mainwaring Hall, Trenhaven was greeted by

Charles's butler. "I hope you had a pleasant ride, Mr. Macaulay," he said. "Sir Charles is resting in his room."

"I should like to see him if I could."

"I fear, sir, that the master is asleep. Perhaps later, sir."

The marquess nodded. He wanted very much to talk with his friend about Serena. Having nothing to do, Trenhaven went to the library where he paced about, stopping now and again to pull a book off one of the shelves, glance at it briefly, and then replace it.

Some time later one of the servants informed Trenhaven that Charles had awakened and would be happy to see his friend. The marquess eagerly made his way to Charles's room where he found the baronet sitting up in bed reading a book. "Poor Charlie," said his lordship, sitting down in a chair next to the bed. "I expect you feel wretched."

Charles closed his book and smiled. "No, I feel much better now. But this cold is a dashed nuisance. The doctor has said I must stay in bed. I fear you will have to dine alone."

"Do not concern yourself about that. You must only think about feeling better."

"I hope you are finding ways to amuse yourself. I'm told you took a ride."

The marquess nodded. "I went to Briarly. Oh, I know you said I shouldn't, but I could not help myself. I had to see Serena. Unfortunately, I also saw Mr. Blake. It was a disaster, Charlie."

As Trenhaven described what had happened, Charles shook his head. "What damnable luck, William."

"Indeed," said his lordship. "Serena's father thinks me the worst sort of lecherous rake. He has forbidden her to see me. So what am I to do, Charlie, carry her off to Gretna Greene?"

Charles smiled. "I should not advise that. But, my dear William, Mr. Blake is not an unreasonable man. You must be patient. It will take some time to sort this matter out. I warn you, you must tread carefully with Mr. Blake. He can be a very stubborn man. And he is doubtlessly very upset over this business with Arabella."

"I should not be plaguing you with my problems, Charlie," said Trenhaven, rising to his feet. "You should not be talking. You need your rest. I shall return later." The marquess took his leave, going to his room to change for dinner.

Trenhaven ate his meal in the vast dining hall attended by the servants. He found himself growing rather depressed as he ate the various courses of food. He found himself drinking a good deal of wine.

When the meal was over, the marquess sat, rather morosely drinking his wine while the servants brought out some of the baronet's best port. As he thought about Serena and her father, Trenhaven drank another glass.

As he pondered what now seemed a most unhappy situation, Trenhaven had the feeling that it might not be a bad idea to get drunk. Since the servants at Mainwaring Hall were very happy to supply his lordship with all the wine and spirits he could possibly want, he was well on the way toward a blissful state of intoxication.

As it grew later, Trenhaven rose from his chair. He felt lonely and the silence of the enormous dining room seemed oppressive. "I think I shall go out for a bit of air," he announced.

Once outside the house, the marquess walked around the grounds. After a time, he made his way to the stables. The grooms on duty were rather surprised to see their master's friend wandering about at that time. "Might I be of service to you, sir?" said one of the servants.

"I should be obliged if you would saddle a horse for me."

"Now, sir?" said the groom, very much surprised. He noted that his master's guest was hatless and not attired for riding. " 'Tis rather late, sir."

"I should be obliged if you would saddle a horse for me," repeated the marquess in a stronger tone.

The servant shrugged. "Aye, sir. 'Twill be but a moment."

When the man returned a short time later with the horse, Trenhaven climbed into the saddle. "Thank you," he said, addressing the groom.

"I shall be happy to accompany you, sir. It is dark."

"I am not afraid of the dark, I assure you," returned his lordship, kicking the horse's sides and riding off.

"Don't go far, sir," cautioned the groom, but Trenhaven only urged the horse into a canter and rode swiftly away from the house. The cool air seemed to clear his lordship's head and he felt better as he rode along. Although he was vaguely aware that he was on the road to Whitfield, the marquess did not really care where he was going.

Having not realized how far he had gone, Trenhaven appeared surprised when he arrived at the outskirts of the village where the Stag's Head Tavern stood open for business. The only establishment of its kind in Whitfield, it was a popular meeting place. As the marquess rode by, he heard laughter and talk coming from the tavern. Pulling up his horse, he tied it outside the tavern and went inside.

Looking around the place, his lordship noted a number of patrons enjoying the Stag's Head's famous ale or potent cider. The tavern's proprietor approached the marquess as he seated himself at one of the tables. Trenhaven ordered some ale and the proprietor hurried off to bring him some.

After downing two flagons of the strong brew, the marquess found himself feeling very light-headed. He barely noticed when two gentlemen sat down at his table. "Why, if it isn't Mr. Macaulay," said one of them.

Trenhaven stared at the man, not recognizing him at first. "Osborne," he said finally.

"And Bellamy, sir," said Osborne's companion. "What luck finding you here, sir." Bellamy grinned at the marquess. "It is very good to see you. But where is Sir Charles?"

"He is ill," said Trenhaven, taking up his flagon and downing some more ale.

"That is a pity. I do hope it is not serious," said Bellamy.

"No, not serious," said Trenhaven, his speech slurred by alcohol.

"I so enjoyed meeting you, sir," said Bellamy. "Indeed, I had not expected to find such excellent company in such a place as Whitfield."

Osborne leaned over to his friend. "The man is drunk, Belly," he said in a low voice. "There is no need to fawn over him. He'll not remember it."

Bellamy appeared insulted. "I'm not fawning over him," he whispered.

"Well, gentlemen," said Trenhaven. "what are you drinking? I'll stand you a round or two."

"That is very good of you, sir," said Bellamy, eagerly motioning to the tavern keeper.

Once they had their drinks, Osborne lifted his in a toast. "To the ladies."

"To the ladies," said Trenhaven, raising his glass and taking a deep drink. He hoisted his flagon of ale. "And to the most beautiful, most wonderful lady of all, Miss Serena Blake."

At this Bellamy and Osborne exchanged a glance. While his lordship was drinking again, Bellamy raised his eyebrows at his friend. "He makes no mention of your cousin, Freddy," he whispered.

Osborne scowled. So it was Serena he was interested in. He wished his foolish cousin had been there to hear him. Trenhaven was, by this time, hardly aware of his companions. Finishing his ale, he pounded the flagon on the table. "Proprietor," he called. "More ale for these gentlemen!"

The tavern keeper hurried to bring more of the brew. The marquess took a deep drink. Putting down the flagon, he stared bleary-eyed at Osborne and Bellamy for a moment. Then suddenly he put his head down on the table and collapsed into an unconscious state.

"Sir," said Bellamy, reaching across the table to pull on Trenhaven's sleeve. "Mr. Macaulay."

"Drunk as a lord," said Osborne, directing a smug smile at his friend.

Noting the condition of one of his patrons, the tavern keeper hurried to the table. He was well aware that Mr. Macaulay was a distinguished gentleman of quality and friend of Sir Charles. Like everyone else in Whitfield he had heard that he was a wealthy young gentleman who was heir to a peerage. "It appears Mr. Macaulay has had a trifle too much to drink. Someone will have to see him back to Mainwaring Hall."

"Do not worry yourself about that, Lockwood," said Osborne, addressing the tavern keeper. "My friend and I will take care of Mr. Macaulay."

The proprietor nodded, happy to allow the young gentlemen to see to his customer. "Are we to take him back to Mainwaring Hall, Freddy?" said Bellamy. "It is late. There might be footpads about."

"I have no intention of going to Mainwaring Hall at this hour. We'll take him home. Come on then." The two of them rose. With some difficulty, they lifted Trenhaven's inert body. Then, putting his arms around their shoulders, they pulled and dragged his lordship out of the Stag's Head and into the street.

Fortunately it was not very far to the Osborne residence. Opening the door, the maid was quite shocked to see her young master and his friend supporting the unconscious form of the gentleman she immediately recognized as Mr. Macaulay. "What is wrong, sir?" said the maid. "Shall I fetch Dr. Fletcher?"

"No, Susan," said Osborne, pulling Trenhaven inside. "You may go to bed. There is nothing wrong with Mr. Macaulay that a night's sleep won't cure."

"I see, sir," said the maid, who quickly left after catching a whiff of alcohol.

"What is going on?" said a feminine voice. Arabella appeared in the hallway attired in her dressing gown. Seeing the marquess, her eyes grew wide. "Is he drunk?"

Osborne nodded. "Since you are so eager to marry the fellow, I thought you should see what you would be getting."

"Freddy, you are brilliant!"

"What?" Osborne stared uncomprehendingly.

"Bring him up to my bedchamber."

This command caused Bellamy to raise his eyebrows once again and direct a curious look at his friend. "What do you mean, Arabella?"

"Do as I say," said Arabella. "Bring him upstairs."

Bellamy and Osborne obediently started to haul Trenhaven up the stairs. Once inside Arabella's room, Osborne paused to look inquiringly at his cousin. "Now what?"

"Put him in the bed, you goose," said Arabella. "And undress him. Take off all his clothes."

"Egad, Arabella!" cried Osborne. "What are you about?"

"Don't be a simpleton," said Arabella. "This is a great opportunity. In the morning his lordship will wake up next to me in bed. You and Mr. Bellamy will discover him. How can he help but marry me?"

Osborne and Bellamy deposited the marquess on the bed where he slumped over in a lifeless heap. "I suppose it might work," said Osborne, dubiously.

"Of course, it will," said Arabella excitedly. "After compromising me in such a fashion, he will have to marry me."

Osborne looked at his friend. "You must swear to never tell a soul about this, Belly."

Bellamy nodded solemnly and the two of them set about undressing Trenhaven.

When the marquess awakened in the morning, he had a splitting headache and a feeling of disorientation. When he opened his eyes, he found himself staring at an unfamiliar room. Turning over, Trenhaven realized with a start that there was someone else in the bed. He regarded the blond head that was visible above the bedclothes in bewilderment. It took him a moment to recognize her. Arabella Lindsay! "My God!" he said aloud.

Arabella, who had been lying awake for some time, opened her eyes. "Good morning, my darling," she said.

Trenhaven recoiled as if she were a poisonous snake. "What is going on?" Sitting up in bed, he realized with a start that he was naked. "Good God!"

"Whatever is the matter, my love?" said Arabella.

At that moment there was a rap at the door. "Arabella!" called a masculine voice. "Arabella! It is I, Freddy. It grows very late." The door opened and in walked Osborne followed by Bellamy.

Arabella pulled the bedclothes about her bare shoulders. "Freddy! Mr. Bellamy!"

"What in the name of heaven is going on!" cried Osborne in a thunderous voice. "Macaulay! What is the meaning of this, sir?"

"I haven't the foggiest idea," said Trenhaven, swinging his legs over the side of the bed. "Where are my clothes?" Espying them on the chair nearby, he reached over and snatched up his pantaloons and drawers. He started to dress.

"You mustn't be angry, Freddy," said Arabella in a melodramatic voice. "I am only human, you know."

"Mustn't be angry?" shouted Freddy. "What would my father say? My mother will die of the scandal! Macaulay, I demand an explanation!"

"I haven't an explanation," said Trenhaven irritably as he pulled on his clothes.

"But, Freddy, you don't understand!" said Arabella. "William promised to marry me. We are betrothed."

Trenhaven turned to regard her in some astonishment. "I fear, madam, you are mistaken. I never promised to marry you."

She looked stricken. "But you did! You cannot mean that you lied in order to"—here she appeared to flounder for words—"in order to take advantage of me. How could you, sir? I am a respectable woman. If you do not marry me, I am ruined!" At that point Arabella burst into tears.

Trenhaven stood up and took up his shirt from the chair. As he put it on, he scowled. "If I ruined you, madam, I have no recollection of it."

"Oh, William! How could you be so cruel?"

"And I have no intention of marrying you!"

"See here, sir," said Osborne. "Are you so unprincipled to care nothing for this lady you have dishonored? You are a scoundrel, sir!"

Trenhaven grabbed his coat and hastily put it on. "I will say nothing more to any of you," he said, heading toward the door.

"See here, Macaulay," said Osborne. "You cannot think you can desert my cousin after your shameful escapade?"

"Stand aside, Osborne," said the marquess, raising his fist in a menacing fashion.

Osborne and Bellamy hesitated only a moment before moving from the door, allowing Trenhaven to leave. When he was gone, Osborne shook his head at Arabella. "I fear your little plot might have failed, cousin."

"I think not," said Arabella. "He'll not escape me now. Now get out, both of you!"

Osborne hastily departed with Bellamy following close behind. As he went down the stairs, Bellamy reflected that his visit to Whitfield was a good deal more interesting than he had expected.

23

Since she had spent much of the night lying awake worrying, Serena was glad to see the light of dawn peek through the draperies of her room. Eager to be up, she rose and dressed in a somber gray morning dress.

Throwing a shawl about her shoulders, she made her way downstairs and out to the garden where she glumly surveyed the perennial border. The sky was gray and cloudy, reflecting Serena's mood.

Serena wandered about the garden paths, hoping to find solace in her beloved flowers. After occupying herself for a time snipping spent flowers from some of the plants, she sat down on a bench.

Serena had never been a person given to gloomy reflection. Yet now everything seemed so miserable. First, of course, she had lost her beloved pet Muggins. After almost a week she was abandoning hope of seeing him again. Then yesterday's incident with Trenhaven had been an utter disaster.

A sigh escaped Serena as she thought of the marquess. She knew she was very much in love with him, and he had declared his feelings, saying he wished to marry her. That her father had forbidden her from seeing him again was unbearable.

While Mr. Blake had always been such a fond and permissive father, Serena had no doubt in her mind that he was very serious about this matter. No, Serena told herself, he would never permit such a marriage.

Serena sat for a long time brooding about the unfortunate state of affairs until she was joined by her sister. "There you are," said Lucy. "Reynolds told me you were in the garden and that you have been for hours."

"Oh, Lucy, I am so unhappy."

Sitting down on the bench beside Serena, Lucy placed a comforting arm around her sister's shoulders. "My poor dear," she said. "I know everything seems a frightful muddle."

"It is indeed," said Serena. She looked over at Lucy. "Is Papa better this morning?"

"Yes," said Lucy. "He is much better. I just saw him. Mrs. Bishop was sitting with him." Lucy smiled. "I do believe he is taking notice of her. Yesterday he told me that it was very odd that he had never realized what an attractive woman she is. So you see? Your plan may be succeeding. And I confess, while I was so opposed to it at first, now I realize I would be quite content to see Papa marry Mrs. Bishop. She is a fine person and she would make him a good wife."

While Lucy had hoped this admission would please her sister, she was disappointed to see that Serena only frowned. "I fear I cannot be so happy for Papa when he is determined to make me miserable."

"Serena, you must not be so hard on him. I daresay it must have been quite shocking for Papa to find Mr. Macaulay kissing you. You know he thinks Mr. Macaulay to be the most odious sort of Don Juan. He does not know anything about how we were paying him to court Arabella. And how could we tell him the truth?"

Serena nodded. "He should think Mr. Macaulay even worse if he knew that he had agreed to such a thing. And he would never forgive us. But what am I to do, Lucy? I love William. I wish to marry him. Indeed, if Papa does not change his mind, I shall elope with him."

"Serena!" cried Lucy. "Do not even say such a thing! Elope with him? That is an utterly crackbrained idea. You know Charles has said he had no money. How would you live?"

"I have my money from Uncle Oliver," said Serena.

"But you will not have full control of that until you are five and twenty. You must be sensible, Serena. Do not do anything in haste. Oh, look, there is Mrs. Bishop."

The housekeeper was coming toward them, a bright smile on her face. "My dear girls, the oddest thing has happened. Tom Jefferies has come round with a parcel from the village. He said it was for me from Mrs. Norris. You can imagine my surprise when I opened it and found two lovely dresses. I thought it was a mistake and the dresses were for you or Lucy, but they are too large. Indeed, they appear to be exactly the right size for me."

"Tom Jefferies," muttered Serena. "He cannot do the simplest task without bungling it. He was supposed to bring the dresses to me." She rose from the bench and smiled at the housekeeper. "The dresses are a gift from Lucy and me."

"A gift?" Mrs. Bishop looked bewildered.

"We do so little for you, Mrs. Bishop," said Serena, "and you do so much for us. Lucy and I wanted to give you a gift to show our appreciation for your good and dedicated service. We thought of the dresses. I hope you like them."

The housekeeper seemed overwhelmed. "They are lovely. I am very touched." Mrs. Bishop embraced first Serena and then Lucy. "How lucky I am to live here at Briarly."

"It is we who are lucky," said Lucy.

"Yes, we are," said Serena. "Now let us go in. You must try on the dresses so we may see how they look."

"Very well," said Mrs. Bishop, quite eager to do so. Smiling broadly, Mrs. Bishop accompanied the young ladies into the house.

While Serena was being diverted by Mrs. Bishop and her new dresses, Trenhaven rode up to Mainwaring Hall. His head throbbing, he dismounted and handed the reins to an awaiting servant, who eyed him with keen interest.

The marquess entered the great country house and made his way to his rooms. His valet Judd, while surprised to see his master in such a strange, disheveled condition. "My lord!" he cried, forgetting for the first time to address the marquess as Mr. Macaulay. "You are not ill?"

Trenhaven was feeling too wretched to notice his servant's lapse. "I am only suffering the effects of the immoderate use of wine and ale, Judd."

The valet appeared relieved. Knowing that the marquess had been out all night, Judd had been worried. While his lordship had often stayed out all night when in town, he had been keeping very early hours during his sojourn to the country. Judd had been starting to think that his young master had met with foul play.

"And we don't have Cook to make her remedy, sir," said Judd. "But I believe I know what is in it. I shall ask Sir Charles's cook to make it."

"That would be good of you, Judd. And I should like a bath more than anything."

"Of course, sir."

"Do you know if Charles is feeling better?"

"Aye, sir. His man has told me he is very much improved."

"Good," said Trenhaven. Judd went about his duties while the marquess sat down on the chair, rubbing his forehead, and reflecting that things could hardly have been worse.

Charles, who was now feeling much better, had been very concerned when he heard that his friend had gone off during the evening and had only returned that morning. The baronet hurried to Trenhaven's room. "William? Are you all right?"

The marquess looked up at Charles as he entered the room. Sitting there in the chair and feeling awful, Trenhaven was not particularly glad to see his old friend. "I am in no danger of dying, I will say that," said his lordship. He smiled ruefully. "Although considering the way I feel, I should not think dying so dreadful a prospect."

"Come, come, old man, what is the matter?" Charles pulled another chair up beside the marquess and sat down. "You look frightful. My servants tell me you were out all night."

Trenhaven shook his head. "Charlie, I was so damned drunk I scarcely knew what I was doing. I rode to Whitfield. I went to the tavern. Osborne and his friend were there. I drank some ale and then I can't remember another thing.

"This morning I awakened in a strange bed. There I was in the condition God made me and there beside me in a similar state was Arabella Lindsay."

"Good God!" The baronet's mouth dropped open in astonishment. "You cannot mean that you and Arabella . . . ?"

"I don't think so," said Trenhaven. "Upon those occasions when I have spent the night with a lady, I assure you I have had a vivid recollection of it."

"But then how did you come to be there?"

"I suspect Freddy Osborne would have the answer to that. He and his friend Bellamy entered the bedroom to find us in flagrante delicto, so to speak. At that point Arabella claimed that I had promised to marry her."

"So you believe Freddy and Arabella arranged this to force you to marry her? It is an audacious plot, I must say. It seems Arabella is most anxious to marry you, William. While I do not wish to minimize those obvious virtues that make so many females find you irresistible, I do not doubt that it is your alleged status as Ravenswood's heir that interests Arabella. Egad, if she only knew who you really are!"

"Yes, she must be very eager to be Lady Ravenswood." A strange look came to Trenhaven's face as he suddenly remembered Serena's words. "But wait a moment, Charlie. Serena told me that she informed Arabella that I am not the heir to a peerage, that I am penniless and in debt."

"She told her that?" said Charles in some alarm.

Trenhaven nodded. "She told her everything. Even about how I was part of a scheme to divert her from Mr. Blake to me."

"And what did Arabella say?"

"According to Serena, she replied that it did not matter and that she wished to marry me regardless."

"By my honor," said Charles, "this is a queer affair. I would have thought Arabella would have come after you with a pistol when she learned the so-called truth. You cannot imagine that she is truly in love with you?"

"No, I cannot," said the marquess. "But, Charlie, let us speak no more of it for now. I am in need of a bath and my head feels as if it might explode."

"My dear William, I shall leave you. Do get some rest."

Trenhaven smiled. "I thought you were the one needing the rest."

"Oh, I am almost completely cured, William," said the baronet. "Now do lie down. I shall see you later." His lordship nodded as his friend took his leave.

24

In the afternoon, Mr. Blake felt well enough to leave his rooms and venture down to the drawing room. Fortified with chicken soup that Mrs. Bishop had made with her own hands, he was eager to speak to Serena.

Mr. Blake had spent the morning in sober reflection. That Serena was fond of the dastardly Mr. Macaulay was quite appalling. Of course, Serena's father blamed Trenhaven exclusively for the lamentable state of affairs. Mr. Blake was well aware that there were a good many men who lacked principles where women were concerned. Being a gentleman of high moral character himself, he had little patience with rakes and libertines.

As he entered the drawing room, Mr. Blake thought about Charles's friend. Frowning, he found himself wishing that Charles had never brought the fellow to Somerset. Had he remained in London, things would have been very different.

Serena's father walked over to the window and stared out at the grounds in front of the house. Thinking of Arabella, he frowned again. It was odd, he realized, how quickly his feelings for her had changed. He had been so enamored of her, but she had obviously cared nothing for him. He had been an old fool, he told himself. His daughters had been right in disliking her.

Mr. Blake thought suddenly of his housekeeper. It was funny how he had taken so little notice of her even though she had worked at Briarly for almost five years. He should have thought of marrying someone like her, an older, more mature woman with a kind heart.

Folding his arms across his chest, Mr. Blake grew thoughtful. Yes, if he were to remarry, it should be to someone like Mrs. Bishop. Indeed, he thought suddenly, if he wanted a wife like Mrs. Bishop, why could he not marry the lady herself? He quickly dismissed such an outrageous idea. She was his housekeeper and the gulf between them was far too wide. A slight smile came to his face. He could imagine what Serena and Lucy might think if he announced he wished to marry Mrs. Bishop!

"Papa, you should be in your room resting."

He turned around to see Serena enter the room. "Good afternoon, my dear. I am much better. Mrs. Bishop has been a vigilant nurse. I was tired of lying in bed. I thought I could sit here for a while. It is a warm day."

"Then do sit down, Papa. I fear you will have a relapse if you do not rest. You are still coughing."

"But I am much better, I assure you," returned Mr. Blake, sitting down on the sofa. "And my throat is not in the least sore."

"I am glad of that," said Serena, coming to sit beside him. She looked over at him. "I am sorry to have so distressed you yesterday, Papa."

"It was not you that distressed me, my dear. No, indeed, it was Macaulay. He was at fault. "I am well aware of that."

Serena shook her head. "Papa, you misjudge him. I know you do not wish to hear this, but I must tell you that I am in love with Mr. Macaulay."

"Now, now, Serena, you may believe you are in love with him. I know how a young girl may have her head turned by such a fellow."

"No, Papa, I truly love him. I wish to marry him."

"Serena, I have made it very clear that that is out of the question."

"Papa, I am quite in earnest when I say that I am determined to marry Mr. Macaulay."

"And I am equally in earnest when I say that you will not marry him. You scarcely know the man, Serena. Perhaps you are blinded to his true character by the fact that he will inherit a title and fortune."

"Good heavens, Papa," cried Serena, "do you think that I would care about a man's fortune or title? In truth, Mr. Macaulay has neither." Having blurted out these words without thought, Serena instantly regretted them.

"What do you mean, Serena? Macaulay has neither fortune nor title?"

Serena hesitated a moment before plunging ahead. "Oh, Papa, it is true. Mr. Macaulay is not the heir to a barony. He has no money. Indeed, Charles has said he is in debt."

"What!" cried Mr. Blake. "You mean the man has been misrepresenting himself? He is not the son of Lord Ravenswood?"

Serena shook her head. "There is no such person, Papa."

"Then he is an imposter!"

"You don't understand. It was my idea. I asked Mr. Macaulay to pretend that he was the son of a peer. It is entirely my fault."

"But why ever would you do such a thing?"

Serena looked down at her hands. "I had the idea that if Arabella thought Mr. Macaulay wealthy enough and the son of a peer, she would pursue him, rather than you, Papa. And she did as I expected."

Mr. Blake regarded his younger daughter incredulously. "You devised such a scheme?"

"I am sorry, Papa, but I did not want you to marry Arabella. I thought she would make you miserable. And if I have prevented you from marrying her, I am very glad of it."

Serena's father rose from the sofa. "Serena Blake, I shall never forgive you for such disgraceful conduct. I am ashamed of you."

"Papa!" cried Serena.

"I will not say another word to you." With those words, Serena's father strode out of the room, leaving Serena to regard his retreating form with a stricken look and deeply regret her hasty confession.

A short time later Lucy entered the drawing room to find her sister sitting by herself, staring into the fireplace. "What has happened? Reynolds told me that Papa seemed very upset. I wanted to see him, but Mrs. Bishop said he was resting."

"Oh, Lucy, I have made a great mess of things," said Serena, rising from the sofa to pace across the room. "I told Papa that William was not the heir to Lord Ravenswood, that he was penniless with debts, and that I had invented the story that he was rich in order to make Arabella cease pursuing him."

"Serena! You told him that? Whatever possessed you?"

"It was only that he implied that I might not really love William, that I was just infatuated with him because he was the son of a peer. I could not help myself."

Lucy regarded her sister with a stunned look. "Oh, this is dreadful, Serena. What did he say?"

"He was very angry. He said he would never forgive me just as I expected. Oh, Lucy, everything turned out so dreadfully."

"I must say you are right in saying that," said Lucy. "I imagine Papa will be equally furious with Charles and me when he knows that we conspired with you."

"But it is I he will not forgive," said Serena. "And perhaps he shouldn't. But we did prevent him from marrying Arabella and one day he will realize that we only did what was best for him."

"I do hope so," said Lucy, sinking down upon the sofa.

"I beg your pardon, Miss Lucy and Miss Serena," said the butler, entering the drawing room. "Mr. Osborne and Mr. Bellamy are here to see you."

"We most certainly do not wish to see them, Reynolds," said Serena firmly.

"Mr. Osborne says that it is a matter of some urgency. He asked for the master, but when I informed him that Mr. Blake had retired to bed, he said he wished to speak to you ladies. He was most insistent."

"Damn and blast him," muttered Serena in a most unladylike way. "He must be an idiot if he thinks we will receive him."

"Serena!" cried Lucy. "I do think we should see Freddy. I would like to know why he has come here. Indeed, aren't you the least bit curious?"

Serena shrugged. "I am not at all interested in anything he might say. But if you wish to see him, very well." She looked at the butler. "Show the gentlemen in, Reynolds."

The servant nodded and retreated, returning in a few moments with Osborne and Bellamy. Osborne looked very pleased with himself while Bellamy looked uncharacteristically uneasy.

"Good afternoon, ladies," said Osborne, making polite bows to Lucy and Serena.

"Good afternoon, Freddy," said Lucy. She nodded at Bellamy. "Mr. Bellamy. Please sit down, gentlemen."

They started to take their seats, but seeing that Serena remained standing, Osborne and Bellamy waited politely for her. Frowning, Serena sat down beside her sister on the sofa. The men positioned themselves in chairs across from them. "I am so sorry to hear the Mr. Blake is indisposed," said Osborne.

"It is not serious, I hope," said Bellamy.

"No," replied Lucy. "He has a cold. He is really much better today." She regarded Osborne expectantly. "Our butler said that you have come on a matter of some urgency, Freddy?"

Osborne nodded solemnly. "I had hoped to discuss this with your father, but I feel that I should tell you ladies as well. After all, Macaulay is a friend of Sir Charles's."

"This is about Mr. Macaulay?" said Lucy.

He nodded again. "Indeed, it is. And it is a rather shocking matter. In fact, I hesitate to reveal it to the delicate ears of you ladies."

"Do not be beastly, Freddy," said Serena impatiently. "If you are here to tell us something, I suggest you come to the point. Have no fear for our delicate sensibilities."

"Very well, Serena. This man Macaulay—I hesitate to say gentleman because of his behavior—this man has acted in the most dishonorable fashion in regard to my cousin Arabella.

"Last night we found Macaulay at the Stag's Head. Forgive my bluntness, but he was drunk. Bellamy and I had to help him leave the tavern. Out of Christian charity we took him to my home. It was far too late to go to Mainwaring Hall, you see. We left him on the sofa in the drawing room so that he might recover his senses in the morning.

"I regret to say that he did not remain where we had left him. He awakened a few hours later and made his way to Arabella's room. You are aware that my cousin is very fond of Macaulay. I fear that, like too many of her sex, Arabella is a weak woman. I regret to say that what followed was a most regrettable occurrence."

Serena listened to this tale with increasing dismay. "What do you mean, Freddy? That Mr. Macaulay and Arabella . . . ?"

He nodded. "In the morning I went to Arabella's room. It was far later than her usual time for rising. I knocked at the door and then opened it." He paused for effect. "What I saw shocked me."

"Oh dear," said Lucy, growing pale.

"I don't believe it," said Serena. "You are lying. I suggest you take your leave, sir."

"I am speaking the truth," said Osborne, pleased at her response. "When I opened the door, there was Macaulay with my cousin. Arabella said that he promised to marry her. It appears the poor girl was cruelly deceived for Macaulay denied that he would marry her."

"How dare you come here and tell us this!" said Serena, reddening with anger. "I do not believe a word of it."

"Bellamy was there. Tell her, Bellamy, that what I say is true."

Although Bellamy seemed a bit reluctant to speak, he nodded. "Yes, Miss Serena, I fear it is true. He was there with Mrs. Lindsay."

"And in all decency Macaulay must marry my cousin," continued Osborne. "He has compromised her in such a way that she will never make a respectable marriage. I am certain that Mr. Blake will agree. And Sir Charles as well. He is a true gentleman. I ask you, Lucy, to speak with him. He must tell his friend that he has an obligation to marry Arabella."

Serena rose from the sofa. She controlled her temper with great difficulty. "Freddy, you are to leave Briarly. Go, sir. I do not wish to look at you one second longer."

Osborne got up from his chair. "Very well, Serena. I regret that I upset you. It was not my intention. Good day to you both." They retreated from the room.

"You cannot think there is any truth in what he says?" said Lucy.

"I am sure it is utter poppycock. Lucy, we must go to Mainwaring Hall at once. We must speak to Charles and William."

"Oh, Serena, I do not think that is a good idea. Papa has said you are not to see Mr. Macaulay."

"Papa is resting in his room. You and I will go riding. Who is to know if we go to visit Charles?"

"Serena, I know we should not do so."

"Then I will go by myself," said Serena, walking toward the door. Lucy had no choice but to get up from the sofa and follow her sister.

25

Returning home from Briarly, Freddy Osborne was very pleased with himself. He had thoroughly enjoyed bringing his shocking tale about Arabella and Trenhaven to Serena and Lucy. Seeing Serena's horrified expression as he had told the story had given him a great deal of satisfaction.

Bellamy on the other hand was very much put out with his friend. He had not liked being part of Osborne's plan to force Trenhaven to wed Arabella. He particularly disapproved of Osborne making him corroborate his story with Serena and Lucy. While Bellamy had wanted to voice his disapproval of his friend's behavior, he had refrained. After all, he was dependent upon Osborne's hospitality.

Entering the Osborne residence, Bellamy went to his room where he reflected for some time upon his visit in Whitfield. While he had been enjoying himself a great deal upon first arrival there, Bellamy had lately been finding his time there rather trying.

Going to the window, Bellamy stared out at the village street and considered whether he should leave Whitfield. Of course he had nowhere to go except the home of his aunt in Yorkshire. Although he was not eager to stay with her in her bleak stone house set in the moors, Bellamy glumly reflected that he had best do so. Having made the decision, he set about packing his bag. When he was finished, he made his way to the drawing room to find Osborne.

Arriving at the doorway, Bellamy hesitated at the sound of voices. It appeared Osborne had a visitor. From his vantage point, Bellamy could see a man in a soiled farmer's smock standing in front of Osborne, who was seated on the sofa. Bellamy regarded the scene with interest, thinking it very odd that his friend would have received such a rough-hewn visitor.

Osborne did not seem pleased to have such a guest. "I do wish you had not come here, Griggs," he said impatiently. "I suggest you state your business."

"I shall do so, sir," replied Griggs. "Nay, I'll not trouble you long, Mr. Osborne. But I did not get nearly what I thought I would in selling the dog. You said I'd get nigh on five pounds in Taunton, but the best I could do was fourteen shillings."

"That is ridiculous," said Osborne. "You must have got more than that."

"'Pon my honor, sir, 'twas all I could get. I swear it. I went to my friend Nelson, but he was not in the market for dogs. And he did not seem to think much of Muggins, sir."

"Now, Mr. Osborne, I went to a good bit of trouble on the matter. You know I was going to return the dog to Miss Serena when I found him wandering about. Indeed, I was on my way to do so when you came upon me on the road. You asked if anyone had seen me and when I said no one had, you said I was to take the dog away. And I did so as a favor to you, sir, and at great risk to myself, I might add. Why, should the squire or Miss Serena find out, 'twould not go well for me.

"And there was a reward for the dog, Mr. Osborne. Miss Serena said, 'twas five pounds. I should have done far better if I'd brought Muggins back to Briarly, sir. The least you could do is to pay me for my trouble. I should think four pounds fair."

"That is ridiculous," said Osborne, scowling at Griggs. "I do not see why I should pay you another penny." He shook his head. "Oh, very well, I'll see what I can find. But it will not be four pounds, I'll be bound." He rose from the sofa. "You wait here." Osborne walked out of the room. He did not see Bellamy for that young gentleman was now making his way out of the house with his bag clutched in his hand.

Pulling her horse to a stop in front of the entrance to Mainwaring Hall, Serena dismounted and handed her reins to a servant. Lucy followed suit and the two young ladies entered the great country house.

They were immediately shown to the drawing room by Charles's butler, who was rather surprised to find that his master's fiancée and her sister had arrived on horseback. "I shall inform Sir Charles that you are here."

"Thank you, Davis," said Lucy. When he had gone, she turned to her sister. "I do hope we will be able to find out the truth about this dreadful matter of Mr. Macaulay and Arabella."

"I know that Freddy has concocted this absurd story to spite me. He is the most hateful person imaginable."

Lucy nodded. In a few moments Charles and Trenhaven entered the room. Charles smiled warmly at Lucy. "My dear girl!"

Lucy happily embraced him. Although Trenhaven would have preferred to greet Serena in a similar fashion, he bowed politely and smiled at her. He thought she looked wonderful in her riding habit with her hat at a jaunty angle. "Miss Serena," he said formally.

While she would have liked to run to him and bury her face against his chest, Serena only nodded. "Mr. Macaulay."

"Do sit down, ladies," said Charles, leading Lucy to the sofa. "I have had the most damnable cold, but I am much better. How wonderful to see you. This is an unexpected pleasure."

Lucy placed her hand in his. "Oh, Charles, we have come because Freddy Osborne has been spreading the most horrible calumny about Mr. Macaulay."

Trenhaven looked over at Serena, who frowned and sat down in a chair. "What do you mean, Lucy?" said Charles.

"Oh, I cannot bear to say it," said Lucy. "Serena, you must tell them."

"Freddy Osborne came to Briarly to tell us that Mr. Macaulay has compromised Arabella." She met Trenhaven's gaze. "He said that he found you and her . . . together."

"Damn him," said the marquess hotly. "How dare he come and tell you such a thing? I should like to murder him!"

"Knowing Freddy as I do," said Serena, "I am certain that he is lying. Do tell me he is lying, William. Tell me he did not find you in her bedchamber."

Trenhaven hesitated. "He did find me there."

"What? In her bed?" cried Serena. Lucy gasped and stared at Trenhaven in astonishment.

"But it was not what you would think."

Serena rose from her chair. "Then what was it?" she demanded.

The marquess shook his head. "I don't know, Serena. I was dead drunk. I admit it. I cannot say how I got there. I suspect it was Osborne's doing."

"Then you spent the night in Arabella's bed?" said Serena, her eyes growing wide.

"Perhaps I did, but I was unconscious, I assure you," said Trenhaven.

"This is infamous!" cried Serena. "Oh, William, how could you!"

"You must not let this upset you, Serena," said his lordship.

"Not let this upset me? I cannot imagine how it would not upset me! And you remember nothing of what happened?"

He shook his head. "I am certain that nothing happened."

"How can you be certain?" said Serena. "You said you have no memory of what occurred."

"Don't you see? This is a plot to force me to marry Arabella. She and Osborne thought they could make me believe I dishonored her so that I would agree to marriage."

"And you don't believe you should marry her?"

"Good God, no!" said the marquess. "I am going to marry you, Serena."

"But that is impossible," said Serena.

"Impossible? My dearest Serena, I love you."

"Do not say such things to me, William. Not now. You must know that we can never marry now that this has happened."

"I know nothing of the kind," said the marquess.

"My father said he would never agree to our marriage. When he hears of you and Arabella, he will be even more adamant." She looked over at Lucy. "I think we should be going home, Lucy."

"You cannot go until you promise you will marry me, Serena."

She frowned at him. "I cannot promise that, William. I must go. Come, Lucy."

"But, Serena, you have only just arrived," said Charles. "Stay for tea. We will sort this out. I shall take you home in my carriage."

"No," said Serena firmly. "We will ride back. I do not wish to stay a moment longer."

"Serena," said Trenhaven.

"No!" she said. "Do not say anything more. I will not speak of this any longer." With these words, Serena hurried from the drawing room.

"Serena!" Trenhaven rushed after her, catching up with her in the entry hall. "Wait!" he said, grabbing her arm.

"I must go! Please, William, I must go home!" Pulling away from his grasp, she regarded him imploringly.

"Very well, Serena," he said finally.

"Serena!" cried Lucy, coming up behind Trenhaven with Charles close behind. "Are you all right?"

"I am fine, Lucy. I am eager to return home before Papa wonders where we have gone."

"Yes, we should be going," said Lucy, who was rather reluctant to take her leave of Charles. Planting a quick kiss on the baronet's cheek, Lucy followed her sister to the door. Trenhaven watched them go, a grim expression on his face.

* * *

Bellamy walked along the road carrying his bag. Having walked for a long time, he was exceedingly tired. After a while, he put down his bag and rested.

As he stood there, Bellamy thought of his friend Osborne and the conversation he had overheard with Griggs. A great animal lover who adored dogs, Bellamy had been shocked to discover that Osborne had been involved with Muggins's disappearance.

After having learned the distressing truth, Bellamy had had no wish to speak to Osborne. Having known that he would lose his temper, he had not even bothered to say good-bye to his friend. Instead, he had gone on his way, leaving the Osborne house.

And although it had been Osborne's villainous involvement in Muggins's disappearance that had been the last straw, Bellamy had also been bothered by Osborne's plot to deceive Trenhaven. Since he had always been in awe of persons of rank and title, Bellamy had thought it horrible that Osborne could treat a marquess in such a fashion.

As he stood there resting, Bellamy thought of Trenhaven. The marquess had been so civil to him on the excursion to Glastonbury. Bellamy could not help feeling like a blackguard in aiding with his friend's deception.

Picking up his worn bag, Bellamy started off again. After what seemed like a very long walk, Bellamy turned down the long lane that led to Mainwaring Hall. After considerable deliberation, he had decided to go there, thinking it might be better to face Sir Charles and Trenhaven than Serena. Certainly the baronet and his lordship could do something about Muggins, thought Bellamy.

As he neared the massive country house, Bellamy caught sight of a man walking toward him from the residence. Seeing that it was Trenhaven, Bellamy waved in greeting.

The marquess, who had been very restless since Serena's visit, had gone out for some air. Catching sight of Bellamy, he frowned. Trenhaven had not expected to find Osborne's friend there at Mainwaring Hall and he had no wish to see him. Indeed, the marquess thought it quite remarkable that Bellamy would have the audacity to show himself there.

"Lord Trenhaven!" called Bellamy, waving again.

The marquess eyed Bellamy in surprise. So the fellow knew who he was! "Bellamy?" he said in a calm voice that belied his irritation.

Bellamy hurried forward. Placing his bag down on the gravel, he snatched his hat from his head in a respectful gesture. "My lord, I am glad to find you here," said Bellamy.

"So you know who I am?" said his lordship, regarding Bellamy coolly.

"Indeed so, my lord," replied Bellamy. "I have seen you many times in town. When I first saw you at Freddy Osborne's, I recognized you immediately."

"And you informed your friend and his cousin?"

"Yes, my lord," said Bellamy. "I fear I did so. I now very much regret it. Freddy Osborne is a scoundrel, my lord. I am sorry that I aided him as long as I did. I have come here to tell you this and to apologize."

Trenhaven frowned again as he considered Bellamy's words. So Osborne and Arabella knew who he was. No wonder Arabella was so eager to trap him into marriage. "I assume you can tell me the truth of what happened at Osborne's house?"

Bellamy nodded. "Yes, my lord. Freddy and I took you there and then Arabella had the idea to put you in the bed. She thought that you could be forced to marry her.

"I did not like the idea," continued Bellamy. "Indeed, I am very much ashamed that I allowed myself to be a part of it. And then that is not the worst of it, my lord."

The marquess raised an eyebrow. "It isn't?"

"No. I found out that Freddy had a fellow named Griggs take Miss Serena's dog to Taunton. He sold him to a man called Nelson. Can you imagine that, my lord? What sort of man would do such a thing? I found out just how despicable Freddy could be."

"Good God," said Trenhaven. "You mean that Osborne was responsible for Muggins's disappearance?"

"Yes, my lord," said Bellamy, nodding. "I overheard Freddy talking to this dreadful Griggs person. It seems Griggs found Muggins and would have returned him, but he met Freddy, who convinced him to take the dog to Taunton. I daresay that is where he is. So you and Sir Charles might go and fetch him."

"I am very much obliged to you for this information, Bellamy," said the marquess. "I shall go to Taunton at once to find Muggins. But I fear Sir Charles is not entirely well."

"I could go with you, my lord," said Bellamy eagerly. "I should like to find the dog."

Trenhaven nodded. "Very well, Bellamy. When we have Muggins, we will being him back to Briarly and then you will have the opportunity to tell the Blakes the truth about Osborne. Come, let us go to the stables. There is no time to lose."

Although Bellamy was tired after his long walk from Whitfield, he was more than happy to accompany his lordship to the stables where the grooms hitched Trenhaven's black horses to his phaeton. "Tell Sir Charles that I am going to Taunton," he said, addressing one of the servants. "How far is it?"

"Nigh on eight miles, sir," replied the groom.

The marquess pulled his watch from his pocket. "Tell your master that I will not be back for dinner. Indeed, we may not return until the morning."

Although he thought it very odd that Sir Charles's friend would embark on such a journey that late in the day, the servant could only nod. The marquess and Bellamy climbed into the phaeton and started off.

26

Muggins the dog pulled against the chain with all his might, trying in vain to free himself. Finally, he sat down, panting and surveying his surroundings with a forlorn expression.

There were several other dogs tied outside the rundown cottage. Regarding Muggins as an interloper, the other dogs eyed him warily. Upon his arrival he had tried hard to assert himself, snarling and growling at the others. Now he lay down, trying to get comfortable on the hard ground.

Had Muggins the ability to reflect upon his circumstances, he would have cursed the fates that had brought him to such a place. He was miserably unhappy there, far from his home and beloved mistress. Unable to understand why he found himself in such a situation, Muggins could only close his eyes and try to sleep.

Suddenly a masculine voice made Muggins's eyes open with a start. His tail began to wag as he recognized the sound of a familiar human. The other dogs began to bark loudly as Trenhaven and two other human forms appeared before them. "Here he is! Muggins old boy!"

Muggins leaped to his feet with an ecstatic bark. The marquess knelt down to see the dog. Muggins could not contain his joy. Forgetting his usual good manners, the terrier jumped all over his lordship, covering his face with wet canine kisses. Trenhaven laughed. "Calm down, old boy," he said.

"It appears that is the dog you're looking for, m'lord."

Trenhaven looked up at the rough-looking man who was standing beside Bellamy. "Yes, it is, Nelson," said his lordship, rising to his feet. Pulling a coin from his pocket, he handed it to the man.

"I do thank you, m'lord," said Nelson, looking at the coin and appearing pleased.

"Would you have a lead or a rope, Nelson?"

"Aye, m'lord," said the man, taking a length of rope from his pocket and giving it to the marquess.

Unhooking the chain, Trenhaven tied the rope to Muggins's collar. "Come along, lad, we've got to take you home to your mistress."

Muggins wagged his tail furiously as he followed Trenhaven and Bellamy. "Miss Serena will be very happy to see him," said Bellamy. "And Muggins is obviously a very happy fellow."

The marquess nodded. "That he is. Do not fear, Muggins, we will take you to your mistress as soon as possible." He turned to Bellamy. "I think we had best stay in Taunton tonight. It is too late to start back to Mainwaring Hall. We'll go to the inn."

"Very good, my lord," said Bellamy, exceedingly pleased at finding Muggins. The terrier continued to wag his tail as he was led away.

After breakfast the next morning Charles went to the library where he perused the newspaper for a time. Then putting down the paper, the baronet looked pensive. He wondered where Trenhaven might be. He had been very puzzled on the previous afternoon to receive the message that the marquess had set off for Taunton. The groom who had informed him of this had had no idea why his master's friend had gone off in such haste. He had reported that a young, red-haired gentleman had accompanied him.

Since the only person fitting the groom's description had been Osborne's friend Bellamy, Charles thought it very curious indeed. At first the baronet had been a bit put out at his friend's strange behavior, but now he was only worried.

Glancing up at the mantel clock, Charles frowned. It was nearly eleven. He hoped that Trenhaven would return soon. The baronet picked up his newspaper again.

A short time later, his butler entered the room. Charles noted at once that his servant was unusually agitated. "Sir!" he said.

"Is something wrong, Davis?"

"No, sir, but you have a caller."

"I do not receive callers at this hour," replied the baronet.

"But, sir," said Davis, "it is the Duke of Haverford!"

The newspaper fell to the floor as Charles leaped to his feet. "The duke here? It cannot be!"

"He looks like a duke, sir," said Davis, "and he had a very fine coach. He said he was here to see his son, Lord Trenhaven. I said I did not know Lord Trenhaven and the old gentleman grew quite vexed with me, sir. He is in the drawing room, sir."

"Oh dear," said Charles. "The truth is, Davis, that Mr. Macaulay is actually Lord Trenhaven."

"Indeed, sir!" said the butler.

"Is he alone? Is not the duchess with him?"

"No, sir, he is alone."

"Well, I must go to the duke at once." Charles hastened out, leaving his butler to stand there mulling over the astonishing fact that Mr. Macaulay was the son of a duke.

When Charles entered the drawing room, he found Trenhaven's father seated upon the sofa with a gruff expression on his face. The baronet steeled himself. He was rather afraid of the duke. When he was young, Trenhaven had invited him to London to stay at the ducal residence. His Grace had terrified young Charles, who had been glad to have never received such an invitation again.

"Your Grace," said Charles, coming forward to make a formal bow.

"Mainwaring," said the duke, eyeing him with disfavor, "where is my son?"

"I fear, sir, that Trenhaven is not here. I do expect him to return at any moment."

"Your man did not know who I was talking about," said the duke. "What was wrong with the fellow?"

Charles hesitated. "Nothing is wrong with Davis, Your Grace. You see, sir, your son decided to go by the name Mr. Macaulay when he was here."

"What nonsense is this?" said the duke.

"He did not wish to attract too much attention, sir."

"My son has very odd ideas," said His Grace with a frown. "I have had a very peculiar letter from him. That is why I have come. Now where has he gone?"

"To Taunton."

"Taunton?"

"It is a town, Your Grace."

"I know it is a town," snapped the duke. "Why has he gone there?"

"I do not know, sir," replied Charles, feeling rather hot under the collar under the duke's sour-faced scrutiny. "But, as I have said, sir, I am certain he will be here shortly. I daresay Your Grace must be very tired after your journey from town. Would you like to be shown to your room to rest?"

"Indeed I would not," said the duke. "Now I want you to tell me about this girl my son thinks he will marry. My wife is very upset about the matter. She had found the perfect bride for him, Lady Charlotte Cavendish. Now he writes that he wishes to marry some provincial nobody. Who is she? I daresay she is some fortune huntress."

"But, Your Grace, Serena's family is very wealthy and she will have a very large dowry. And the Blake family is one of the oldest and most respected families in the west country. You must know that I am to marry Serena's sister Lucy."

"I am well aware of that," said the duke ill-temperedly. He rose suddenly to his feet. "I wish to see this girl, Serena Blake, for myself."

"I know you will like her, Your Grace. We can call at Briarly after luncheon. It is not far."

The duke rose to his feet. "After luncheon? Why not now?"

"Now, Your Grace?"

"There is no time like the present I always say," returned the duke.

"Very well, sir," said Charles meekly and he and Trenhaven's father left the drawing room.

Breakfast at Briarly had been a rather strained affair. There had been little conversation and after a quick repast, Mr. Blake had retired to his sitting room, leaving his daughters troubled and miserable.

Later in the morning, however, when he joined Serena and Lucy in the drawing room, Mr. Blake seemed in a much better humor. Lucy appeared encouraged. "I am glad to see that you are feeling so much better," said Lucy. "But you must take care, Papa, that you do not overdo."

"Oh, I shall be fine," said Mr. Blake, taking a seat by the fireplace. "I credit Mrs. Bishop on her excellent nursing care."

"Yes, she is quite wonderful," said Lucy.

Mr. Blake stared thoughtfully into the fire for a time. He then looked over at his daughters. "I have been very angry with you both. And with good reason. I believe I should have remained angry if I had not just now talked over this matter with Mrs. Bishop.

"Mrs. Bishop is a very sensible woman. She made me realize that although you were wrong in what you did, you did it from concern for me. And I must say that if I am to be honest with myself, I must admit that I should not have been happy with Arabella Lindsay. I have been an old fool."

"Oh, no, Papa," cried Serena. "I am so sorry for everything. I am to blame for meddling. You are right to despise me."

A smile appeared on her father's face. "What a silly peagoose you are, Serena. To think that I could despise you. Oh, I was sorely vexed with you, but I should thank you for allowing me to see Arabella's true character."

"Then you can forgive me?" said Serena.

"I suppose I shall," said Mr. Blake.

Serena needed no further encouragement to rise from her seat and go to embrace her father.

When she released him, Mr. Blake looked very happy. Lucy wiped a tear from her eye, relieved that her sister and father had made amends. "There is something I must tell you both. Perhaps I should not mention it now. I know I will shock you. I do not doubt that you will protest the idea."

"Papa," said Serena, "I cannot imagine what you could mean. You must tell us."

He nodded. "Very well. I realize I was foolish with my schoolboy infatuation for Arabella. I have discovered whom I should marry in order to insure my happiness. I only ask that you try to understand. I pray you will not condemn me for my choice." He paused. "It is Mrs. Bishop."

Serena and Lucy exchanged a startled look. Mr. Blake continued. "I knew I would shock you. I am well aware that you will say that she is but the housekeeper and a gentleman cannot think to marry a servant. Yet she is as much a lady as any I have met."

To his surprise, Lucy and Serena burst into laughter. "Oh, Papa," said Lucy, "we were hoping that you would marry Mrs. Bishop."

"What?" said Mr. Blake, quite astonished at his daughter's response.

"Yes," said Serena. "We think she is just the woman to make you happy."

"You cannot mean that you approve?"

"Of course, we approve," said Serena, leaning over to kiss him. "We are so very happy."

"Well, I must say this is quite unexpected," said Mr. Blake, "Of course, I have not yet asked for her hand. She may refuse."

"I do not believe she will," said Serena with a smile. "Lucy and I will convince her to say yes."

"Indeed we will," said Lucy.

Mr. Blake seemed very pleased. "I only wish matters had gone differently for you, Serena," he said. "I know that you are fond of Mr. Macaulay."

"I beg you to speak no more of him, Papa," said Serena. "I think it best that we do not discuss him."

"Yes, perhaps you are right," said her father.

At that moment, the butler appeared before them. "I beg your pardon, Mr. Blake, but there are two gentlemen to see Miss Serena. I have shown them to the library."

"Two gentlemen?" said Mr. Blake in some surprise. "Who are they, Reynolds?"

"Mr. Macaulay and Mr. Bellamy, sir, and they have brought someone else."

"M—Macaulay?" sputtered Mr. Blake. "Have I not said that he was not to be admitted?"

"But he has brought Muggins, sir!" said the butler.

"Muggins!" cried Serena, rising to her feet and rushing from the drawing room. Entering the library, she caught sight of the dog. "Muggins!" The bullterrier ran to Serena, nearly dancing with joy. "Oh, Muggins!" cried Serena, throwing her arms around the dog and hugging him tightly.

Mr. Blake and Lucy had followed Serena. They stood at the doorway watching Serena's reunion with her beloved pet. Despite his anger with Macaulay, Serena's father could not help but be grateful that he had brought Muggins home.

Serena looked up at the marquess. "How did you find him, William?"

"It was Bellamy's doing," said Trenhaven. "He overheard a conversation between Osborne and the fellow Griggs. They were responsible for Muggins's disappearance. It seems Muggins wandered off. Griggs found him and would have returned him, had he not met Osborne on the road. Osborne told him to sell Muggins to a man in Taunton. Bellamy and I went to fetch him last night."

"I don't believe it," said Mr. Blake. "Why would Freddy do such a thing?"

"But it is true, sir," said Bellamy. "I swear to you. He was my friend, but I will have nothing to do with him now that I know what sort of man he is."

"But it makes no sense," said Mr. Blake.

"I suspect that he wished to hurt Serena," said the marquess. "I believe he was sorely disappointed that she showed no interest in him as a suitor."

"I daresay that is right," said Bellamy. "Freddy was very much offended that Miss Serena would not have him."

"This is monstrous," said Mr. Blake. "Well, I shall never allow the young blackguard in this house again. It seems I was very wrong about Freddy as well as his cousin. I am grateful to you, Mr. Macaulay, and to you, Bellamy, for bringing Muggins home."

"Yes, thank you both so very much," said Serena, smiling up at Trenhaven.

He smiled in return. "And Bellamy has something else to tell you, Serena. About what happened at the Osbornes' house."

"At the Osbornes' house?" said Mr. Blake with a puzzled look. "What happened there?"

Ignoring Mr. Blake, Bellamy addressed himself to Serena. "What Freddy told you about Mr. Macaulay and Arabella was not true. Freddy and I took advantage of Mr. Macaulay's condition, placing him in the bed."

"In the bed?" said Mr. Blake. "What is going on? What is this about?"

"I shall tell you all about it, Papa," said Lucy, taking his arm. "But do allow Mr. Bellamy to finish."

"It was Mrs. Lindsay's idea," continued Bellamy. "She thought by making it look as though he compromised her, she might force his lordship into marriage. Oh, I should have said Mr. Macaulay." Bellamy directed a sheepish look at the marquess.

"His lordship?" said Mr. Blake. "What do you mean, Bellamy?"

"I am sorry, my lord," said Bellamy, regarding Trenhaven with a shamefaced expression.

The marquess looked at Serena. "I should have told you earlier. And indeed, I started to tell you more than once."

"Told me what, William?" said Serena.

"That I am not really Mr. Macaulay. You see, I am the Marquess of Trenhaven," he said.

"What?" cried Mr. Blake. "The Marquess of Trenhaven? The son of the Duke of Haverford?"

He nodded. "Yes, it is true."

"But why?" said Serena, having some difficulty digesting this information.

"When I came to stay with Charles I told him that I did not wish anyone to know who I was. In truth, I was sick of people fawning over me and of young ladies throwing themselves in my path." He turned to Lucy. "That is why Charles wrote that letter to you, Lucy, describing me as he did. I asked him to do so."

"Oh, William," said Serena, fastening her hazel eyes upon his gray ones with a questioning look.

Trenhaven smiled. "And I want to marry you, Serena. Do say you will be my wife." He turned to Mr. Blake. "I know how you feel about me, Mr. Blake. But I do love Serena. I will make her happy. I only ask that you do not close your mind, sir."

Mr. Blake appeared thoughtful. "I believe I knew your father," he said.

"Did you, sir?"

"Oh, it was a very long time ago. I daresay he does not remember me, but we were at Eton together. He was called Trenhaven at that time. Oh, yes, your father was a fine young man." Serena's father was suddenly viewing the marquess in a new light. That he was the son of the eminent duke was quite remarkable. Perhaps, reflected Serena's father, he had been wrong about the young man. After all, Arabella and Freddy had been the real culprits. "Perhaps I might have to reconsider my opinion of you, Trenhaven," said Mr. Blake.

The marquess broke into a grin. "Indeed, sir? That would be splendid! Then you might give your permission for me to marry your daughter?"

"I don't know . . ." said Mr. Blake rather uncertainly.

Encouraged by this, Trenhaven turned to Serena. "Will you marry me, Serena?"

"Oh, William," she said, "I wish to marry you with all my heart."

"My dearest Serena!" The marquess could not resist taking her into his embrace.

"Just a moment, young man," said Mr. Blake. "You are a trifle hasty. I shall certainly not give my permission without your discussing this with your father."

"Oh, I shall do so, sir," said Trenhaven, smiling down at Serena.

"Your pardon, Mr. Blake," said Reynolds the butler, stepping into the library once again. "Sir Charles is here with another gentleman. Sir, it is the Duke of Haverford! I have shown them to the drawing room."

"What!" cried Mr. Blake, his eyes widening in astonishment.

"My father is here?" said his lordship, even more startled at the information.

"Well, I daresay you must see them at once," said Serena, taking Trenhaven's arm. "Oh, William, I do wish I had known about you." She looked up at him. "Does this mean that some of the other things Charles said about you were false?"

He smiled. "I am happy to say that the letter was a product of Charles's imagination."

"I am so glad for that," said Serena, "but we must not keep your father waiting."

"Yes," said Mr. Blake, "Come, everyone. We must greet the duke."

When they all entered the drawing room, they found an unsmiling Duke of Haverford sitting in an armchair. Charles was standing beside him, a nervous expression on his face.

Although a trifle unnerved at having such an illustrious visitor, Mr. Blake went forward to greet his guest. "Your Grace," he said with a bow, "it is an unexpected honor. Charles, it is good to see you."

"Indeed, Mr. Blake," said the baronet. He looked down at the duke. "Your Grace, allow me to make the introductions. This is Mr. Blake and his elder daughter Lucy and this is Serena. And this gentleman is Mr. Bellamy."

Ignoring the others, the duke turned his attention to Serena. His eyes went from her head to her toes and back again. Serena did not flinch under this scrutiny. She made a deep curtsy. "Your Grace."

Seeing a very pretty girl who was not cowed by his gaze, the duke seemed slightly less perturbed. He found himself thinking Serena was very presentable. He liked her proud bearing and the faint smile that was on her face. "I do hope that Your Grace was aided by Mrs. Bishop's cure for gout," said Serena.

"Why, I admit that it did have a remarkable effect," said the duke. "I tried the poultice and in but two days, I was much improved. Indeed, I could not have taken this journey if I was not much better."

"That is excellent, Father," said his lordship.

"Oh, yes, Your Grace," said Serena, "I am very glad to hear it."

"I must say I do not care for the vegetable diet overmuch, but I shall endure it if my foot will be improved."

Serena noted that the duke's expression had softened a little. She smiled at him. "My father said that he knew you at Eton, Your Grace."

"Knew me at Eton?" The duke turned to Mr. Blake. "Is that true, sir?"

"Oh, I cannot expect you to remember me, Your Grace. I am Augustus Blake. At that time I was called 'Gussie.' "

Since the fact that their father had had a nickname at school had been unknown to both Serena and Lucy, they viewed their father with interest.

"Gussie Blake?" cried the duke suddenly. "The devil you say! You are Gussie Blake the cricketer!"

"The same," said Serena's father, pleased that the duke remembered him.

"Of course," said His Grace, breaking into a smile. He turned to Trenhaven. "Why, this gentleman was the best cricketer I have ever seen. By God, it is a pleasure to see you again." The duke extended his hand and Mr. Blake shook it heartily.

Trenhaven had the opportunity to exchange a glance with Serena, who raised her eyebrows slightly at him.

Having discovered that Mr. Blake was an old school chum, the duke's demeanor changed miraculously. He bade Mr. Blake sit down and the two gentlemen began to reminisce. The others relaxed for the first time. Charles took Lucy's hands and began to speak to her in a low voice. Bellamy sat down at some distance from the duke where he basked in the reflected glory of such a high-ranking personage.

Trenhaven took Serena's hand and leaned over to her. "Come, Serena, I must talk with you. We will not be missed for a few minutes." She nodded and the two of them slipped from the room into the entry hall where they found Muggins waiting for them. At first opportunity, the marquess took Serena into his arms. "Now, my darling Serena. You did say you would marry me?"

"I don't know, William. I should be very vexed with you for deceiving me in such a fashion."

He grinned. "I suppose you are disappointed that I am not Mr. Macaulay with his debts and his terrible reputation."

She looked down for a moment and then into his eyes. A mischievous smile came to her face. "I was rather fond of Mr. Macaulay, my lord. And now I fear, William, that you are too grand for me. I should make a muddle of being a marchioness. Do you think the duke will approve?"

He laughed. "My dearest Serena, I can tell he approves of you. And that you are the daughter of Gussie the cricketer is the most marvelous piece of luck. He always talked of your father. No, my darling, he will not object and even if he did, I should spirit you off to Gretna Greene."

"Oh, William," she said, looking up at him.

"And you will be a wonderful marchioness. And a wonderful wife. Say you will marry me."

She smiled. "Oh, very well. Yes, I shall marry you, William."

Delighted with this answer, Trenhaven pulled his future bride to him in a passionate embrace and kissed her long and lovingly. Muggins looked up at them both and wagged his tail happily.